EMMA HART

Mixed Up

Copyright © by Emma Hart 2017
First Edition

All rights reserved. No part of this publication may be reproduced, distributed, or transmitted in any form or by any means, including photocopying, recording, or other electronic or mechanical methods, without the prior written permission of the publisher, except in the case of brief quotations embodied in critical reviews and certain other noncommercial uses permitted by copyright law.

Cover Design and Formatting by Emma Hart

Author Note:

Thank you so much for picking up MIXED UP! I hope you enjoy it when you read it.

When I decided to write Mixed Up, I knew I needed to create the cocktails Raven would serve at her bar. You'll find some recipes at the end of the book, so please keep flipping the pages after 'The End!' to get them and hopefully, enjoy them, too!

xoxo, Emma

(Note: These recipes are original cocktails created by me, which means they fall under copyright. Please do not share/publish them. If you would like to use any recipes for a blog/project, permission may be obtained from contacting emma@emmahartauthor.com. Thank you for understanding!)

Mixed Up

1

Life would be so much better if it were acceptable to drink something stronger than a mimosa for breakfast.

Seriously.

That was the only thing that stood any kind of chance at getting me through having a family reunion at the start of summer. There was absolutely nothing good that could come from my crazy, Greek family descending on Whiskey Key in five days' time.

Because why would they go to where my parents actually lived on Key West? No, no. Let's go to *Raven*, they said. Let's take over her corner of the Florida Keys, because it it wouldn't be wild enough *at the start of summer*. It didn't seem to matter to anyone in my family that I was going to be slammed and that closing my cocktail bar for their freaking party wasn't going to happen.

There was no way I was going to be the host for the clusterfuck that would be that reunion. Nothing good happened when the Archers and the Karras' came together. Nothing.

Last time, my uncle on my father's side had his moustache burned off by a firework. Marginally funny for us—not so much for his face. Or the two years he'd spent growing it until he'd gotten it right.

Two years before that, my great-aunt on my mother's side—the wacky Greek side—got arrested. Apparently, carrying baby powder in clear, plastic baggies was grounds for arrest.

In the Whiskey Key PD's defense, they didn't know it was baby powder.

It was easy to see why hosting the family reunion wasn't at the top of my priority list. It was sure to be nothing short of an absolute shitshow, and I had enough of that crap on my hands trying to find a chef for the bar.

The more I thought about it, the more I was coming to realize it was a bad fucking idea. I didn't have much of a choice, though. The kitchen was bought, paid for, and installed. There was no way I was going to lose a few thousand bucks just because the best person I'd interviewed so far was responsible for the burger on the cafe sign downtown.

I called bullshit on that, but I couldn't prove it, so I couldn't do anything except not hire the dude.

Unfortunately for me, chefs were slim pickings in Whiskey Key. It was stupid because we were a tourist hotspot, even if most people did pass through on their way to Key West. We were still enough of a draw to be the final destination for some, and given the success of my bar, Dirty, I didn't think finding anyone to put food out would be hard.

How naive I was. Poor, naive, little Raven.

No. Let me rephrase: I didn't think finding anyone *good enough* to put food out would be hard.

It was the curse of having a brother for a chef—who was refusing to help me.

"Come on, Ryan," I begged, leaning over the bar and

pressing my hands together in a prayer stance. "I'm actually begging you. Help me out, please?"

"I can't, Ray. I told you, I already have a job for the summer." He grimaced, his dark-blue eyes shining with guilt. "I can't back out of it just because you asked me to."

"But it would be so *fun*." I slumped right forward. A thud rang out through the quiet room as my hands hit the solid wood top of the bar. "I would give you so much credit. It would be so cute. Brother and sister running a bar and restaurant together. Come on. Please?"

He held his hands up. The air filled with the cringing sound of wood scraping as he scooted his stool back away from me. "If I could, I would, but I already agreed to help out at Porto's."

"Ugh! That's where you're working? You know they're all assholes, right?"

"Just because Callum dumped you when you were fifteen doesn't make the whole family assholes."

"Sure, it does. Assholes by default." I sniffed and grabbed the cloth I was cleaning the bar down with before he showed up. "You're a traitor."

My brother rolled his eyes. "How do you run a business with those dramatics?"

"Not with the support of my brother, that's for sure."

"Oh, come on. I'll help you, I told you that, but I can't work for you. Not to mention that telling people my baby sister is my boss is fucking ridiculous." He scratched the side of his head. "Let me see your menu."

With a sigh, I reached beneath the counter and handed him the notebook I'd been scribbling on. "Camille and Lani helped me," I said, referring to my best friends.

"Helped you do what?" Ryan asked, his thick, dark eyebrows pulling together into a frown. "Ensure nobody will cook this shit?" He threw the notebook down in front of me with a thwack. "I thought you wanted a restaurant, not a sports bar."

"I don't know what I'm doing! I mix drinks, damn it.

That's what I'm good at."

"Evidently." He stood up and tucked the stool back in. "Ray, this menu isn't right for your bar. Why don't you leave the menu to someone you hire?"

"Because I can't find anyone to hire," I reminded him with another sigh. "That's why I'm begging you."

He grinned. "The last time you begged me was when I had you in an armlock."

"My shoulder still hurts."

"You deserved it. You shouldn't have told Mom you found used condom wrappers in our bathroom."

"You shouldn't have put them there." I poked out my tongue, suddenly fifteen again. "Do you know anyone who can help me?"

His grin went lopsided. "I do, but you'd burn the place down if he set foot in here."

I shook my head so fast that I was surprised it didn't fall right off my neck. "Nope. And if he does set foot in my bar, I'm going to kick his ass right out."

"He's one of the best chefs I know. You should consider it. He's—"

"Yeah, yeah, I know. Mom practically put on a Broadway production with the song and dance she made when she found out." I paused. "I don't care if Parker Hamilton is Michelin-starred or has a fast-track to Heaven. He's not working for me. I'm not that desperate."

And I never would be.

I'd rather lose the money I'd put into the kitchen than hire my brother's asshole best friend.

Ryan held his hands up, a stance he took often with me. There was a chance I was, like the rest of the women on my mother's side, in possession of the stereotypical Mediterranean...flamboyancy.

See: loud, slightly hot temper.

"I'm just saying," he said after a few moments. "I know you don't get along, but the option is there. Isn't hiring Parker better than losing your money?"

"No." I wiped down the handle of the beer tap nearest to me. "I can safely say I would rather gamble my entire life on the entire population of California's porn industry being STD-free."

"That's not a betting tip I would give you."

"It's not one I'd entertain, which tells you how vehemently against hiring him I am."

"Whatever. I don't get it. Think about what I said about that menu, though. Consider asking your interviewees what they'd put on your menu." He rapped his knuckles against the bar. "I've gotta go see Mom. She wants me to put a menu together for the reunion." His eyes sparkled as he said it.

"Sure," I called after him. "You'll help her."

"It's self-preservation!" He threw his hand up over his shoulder in a wave and let himself out of the bar.

I shook my head as I continued cleaning.

I wanted to say that my feelings toward my brother's best friend weren't personal, but they were. I didn't have a reason, I just didn't like him. We'd never, ever gotten along, and there was a reason that every time we were together, we were separated like freaking toddlers.

Sure, I'd once thrown a hunk of pork at him, but that was an accident.

Kind of.

We were opposite people. We made chalk and cheese look like best friends. There wasn't a specific thing I could put my finger on, and whenever either of us were asked why we couldn't be friends, we didn't have an answer. It was just a general kind of mutual hatred.

Funnily enough, the times that everyone accepted we simply despised each other were the times we got along almost like friends.

But, I hadn't seen him for three-and-a-half-years. This was the first time he'd come anywhere near home since he landed a job in some fancy New York City restaurant five years ago. That was where he'd gotten his *three* Michelin stars just before Christmas.

Now, the gossip line—AKA, my mother—said he'd taken "extended leave" for some downtime after achieving his goal at the ripe old age of twenty-eight.

Extended leave my left tit. He'd quit, and that was something I'd put money on.

I had no doubt that despite the time passed, when I eventually saw Parker again, he'd be the same asshole he'd always been to me. I certainly had no plans to be anything but the sassy little shit I'd always been to him.

In fact, sassy little shit was my default personality. This mouth was made for sassin'.

A huff escaped me as I finish cleaning the taps. I would take my brother's advice on the menu, but I wasn't going to hire Parker Hamilton to work in my kitchen.

There were few things I really loved about my life. The freedom with my business, the fact I lived right on top of my business, and my friends were the top three.

On the other hand, there were also things I really didn't love about my life. Like last-minute corralling into dinner because my grandfather arrived a few days early and my dad wanted a nice peaceful dinner before the Karras tornado lands. All fifteen of them.

The last-minute dinner meant I had to leave the bar in the hands of my very capable bartender, Sienna. I didn't like doing it, but I was learning to trust her. She could mix almost as well as I could, save for a few drinks she couldn't get quite right. Luckily, they were the ones not usually ordered on a Monday evening.

Still, I would have rather been there than here at my parents' in Key West. Not that their beachfront home wasn't gorgeous bliss, but because the Hamiltons lived right next door. My conversation with my brother had been playing in my mind all day, and the last thing I wanted to do was accidentally run into him.

Or walk into my parents' house and find that they'd been invited to dinner, too. That was the problem of having your mom be best friends with your mortal enemy's mom.

Alright, mortal enemy is an exaggeration, but what's life without a little extra oomph?

Probably a damn lot more peaceful.

My palms got sweaty when I turned onto my parents' street. The sleepy, idyllic street was days away from being turned into a big, fat, Greek street party, and I couldn't help but feel a twinge of sympathy for the neighbors who'd have to put up with it. All things considered, it was preferable to a wedding. That was when shit really went down.

If I didn't know it was tradition, I'd tell you that my grandmother had a real thing for smashing plates.

Actually, she probably did. She was a little too passionate—if we got through this reunion without smashing anything, I'd call it a win.

Until then, I was destined to live in a state of temporary fear for the coming disaster and the fact that there was an extra car parked up in the Hamilton's driveway.

I pulled up behind my Dad's Chevy truck and waited before I shut off the engine. I still had time to—nope, I didn't have time to run. Mom already had the front door open and was standing there with an expectant look on her face.

Awesome.

"I have work to be doing, you know," I told her, getting out of the car. "I have a stack of paperwork as high as my butt in my office, and I need to get this week's order in."

"Then you should have done that earlier, shouldn't you?" she shot back, raising one perfectly plucked eyebrow.

"I don't pencil in surprise dinners, believe it or not."

"Start." She kissed my cheek and nudged me through the door. "We have guests."

"What guests?" I stopped, making sure my voice was

13

low.

Slowly, her lips curved up, making her dark eyes sparkle. "I thought you'd want to catch up with our resident celebrity."

My nostrils flared as I took a deep breath in. No—she'd given up on that Cupid plan when I was sixteen, hadn't she? "Mom—"

"Relax. I'm messing with you, Raven. But, you're not getting out of dinner. He's your brother's best friend. You're mature enough now to tolerate him for two hours."

That's what she thought. "I'll do my best. Although, disclaimer—if you find his body and I'm missing, I'm in Cuba, and I didn't do it."

"Understood." Mom winked. "I'll give you five minutes. Your father is grilling on the back porch."

I ran through that freaking house like my ass was on fire. Any break she was willing to give me, I was going to snatch with two hands and run with.

"Hey, pumpkin," Dad said without turning around. "Your mom told you?"

I mumbled a disgruntled sound and sat on the chair close to the grill. "Is that why you're grilling steaks?"

"Because I'm outside and her wonderful best friend is inside? Happy coincidence." The flash of amusement that altered his expression for a brief second gave away his lie.

"Sure. It's just coincidence I'm outside, too."

My father and I had always had the same feelings for one member of the Hamiltons. He got on just fine with Craig, Parker's dad, and he loved Parker like a second son, but he despised Ilsa, Parker's mom. Whereas my mom couldn't understand why I couldn't get along with Parker, Dad understood perfectly. He always said that he'd inherited his mom's best qualities.

By best, he meant worst. I was hard-pressed to disagree with him. Ilsa Hamilton was stubborn and hardheaded, and so was Parker. Both had the inability to accept being wrong. Ilsa I could understand—I mean, hello, she's a woman—but Parker? No.

"Where's Grandpa?" I asked Dad, pulling off my sandals.

"Bathroom." He paused and looked at me, his bright, blue eyes blinking at me. "Someone should probably go check on him. He's been up there for thirty minutes."

"He is old."

"He's probably asleep on the toilet."

"Why don't I keep an eye on the steaks and you go check on Grandpa?" I jumped up and held out my hand for the flipper-thing.

I loved my grandpa, but I wasn't going to visit him in the bathroom. No way.

Dad chuckled and handed the utensil to me. "Try not to burn them."

"I can cook, you know." Mostly Greek food, but that was neither here nor there. Steak I could manage.

Dad patted my shoulder and left me to it.

I rolled my shoulders and cast my gaze down to the steaks. They were cooking slowly, and from where I was standing, I could hear my mom laughing in the kitchen with Ilsa. They were giggling like a couple of sixteen-year-olds, and I smiled, shaking my head.

I really needed to organize a girls' night. I had the feeling I'd need it soon enough.

"Well, look who showed up."

I'd know that voice anywhere.

Parker Hamilton.

"Trust me, if I knew you'd be here, I'd have set off for a colder climate. Like Alaska," I replied without turning around.

"Damn, and here I was thinking that your lack of clothing was for my benefit." Laughter twisted his words.

I knew he was doing it to get a rise out of me, and I was determined not to give him what he wanted.

The time that had passed hadn't changed a thing--it was the same old game with him. Rile up Raven. I used to fall for it, but not anymore.

"I'd rather be hit on by a drunken frat boy than do anything for your benefit, Parker."

"Then go put some clothes on, because I'm feeling pretty benefited right now."

2
Parker

My words had the desired effect on Raven Archer.

The steak she'd been holding in her hand clattered off the grill and to the wooden floor of the porch when she dropped it. Her dark hair swung around her shoulders with her smooth turn to face me.

Annoyance immediately flashed in her bright, blue eyes as they fixated on me. Nothing had changed—she still had that quick, fiery temper that was oddly attractive on her, and she was still unable to control it, if the pursing of her bright, red lips was anything to go by.

"Wonderful," she said slowly, keeping her gaze trained on my face. "You're not just an asshole anymore. You're a pervy asshole."

My lips quirked to one side. "I've been called worse."

She rolled her eyes and spun back around. She grabbed the cooking tongs from the hook and moved for the first steak.

"You're flipping it wrong," I told her for no other reason than to annoy the shit out of her. There was no wrong way as long as it didn't break.

"Oh, I'm sorry, do you do it differently in New York?" she fired back at me, flipping the second steak exactly the way she did the first. "Because let me tell you all the ways I give a fuck."

She didn't continue talking.

"Is that because you don't give a fuck or are you trying to put your words together?"

"I actually have the perfect words put together for you: Fuck off."

I grinned. "Do you want your gold star now?"

"Is it hard enough to shove up your ass? If so, hand it over."

"Oh god," Ryan groaned as he walked outside. "You're fucking adults. Can't you be nice?"

"No." Raven put the tongs down and turned to face him. "Not when you leave him unsupervised. You know he needs minding or he misbehaves."

I snorted. "You're the one barely dressed."

"I'm an adult. I can wear what I want."

"He has a point," Ryan agreed warily. "There isn't much fabric on that dress."

Raven hit him with a look so piercing *I* felt it. "Compared to the things your ex-girlfriend wore, I'm practically dressed for Church."

"It'd go up in flames if you walked in there," I said, perching against the end of the table and stuffing my hands into my pockets. "Demons can't enter holy buildings."

That sharp gaze snapped from Ryan to me. She held it with an unwavering intensity.

I was almost impressed.

"Ryan, control your pet."

She couldn't have injected anymore snark into that line if she'd tried. I don't know if it was meant to annoy me, but all it did was make me laugh. Her attempts to bite back to my uncontrollable need to annoy her were more cute than they were offensive.

"Can't you two just be nice?" Alexandra Archer asked, stepping onto the porch with a bowl of salad in her hands.

"No," Raven snapped to her mom. "Not as long as he opens his mouth."

Behind Alexandra, my mom rolled her eyes. "Parker, you're twenty-eight. Control yourself, please."

I held up my hands and stepped back. "Don't blame me if she takes something the wrong way. I was paying her compliment."

"In what state is "I thought you were wearing that for my benefit" a compliment?" Raven slammed the tongs down on the grill. Once again, her hair swung as she spun to face me, and she had to free a few strands from her lips.

"That's clearly me telling you that you look nice."

Her jaw drops. "That's not even close to that. Next time, I'd advise using "You look nice," you moron."

Both our moms rubbed their foreheads.

"I get it." Ryan shrugged, and I nodded to him.

"Whose side are you on?" Raven demanded. "I'm your sister."

"Oh no, Parker, don't be a dick to my sister," he replied flatly.

I coughed to hide my laugh.

"Ryan," Alexandra said sharply. "Sit down."

I dipped my head so I didn't laugh when he did it.

"Gee, Parker." Raven tilted her pretty head to the side, a dirty smirk teasing her full lips. "Do you think your mom would like the fact you're laughing right now?"

My amusement vanished in an instant. I glared at her, and as her smile widened, I knew exactly what was about to happen.

The sharp sting of my mom's hand clipping me around the back of the head radiated across my scalp.

"Sit down, Parker," she said, just as sharply. "Show

some restraint. I raised you to be a gentleman, not an uncouth horror."

Raven grinned. She was obviously trying not to laugh because that smile was a little too wide.

"Fuck you," I mouthed to her before I turned and sat down at the table.

She didn't respond. She'd won the first round, and she damn well knew it. My mom would always side with her, mostly because she knew that if I pushed her too far she'd probably lose control of that hot little temper of hers and do some damage.

We all remembered the summer of two-thousand-and-seven. She was seventeen and just caught her boyfriend making out with the head cheerleader.

Long story short, it took her six months to earn enough money to pay her parents back for the windshield they had to replace.

The brick she'd used was still in the front yard, used as part of the decoration. Nobody else would think anything of it, but I chuckled whenever I saw it.

Mostly because as Ryan had reasoned after: "Nobody needs to worry that I'll break their face—now they'll be worried Raven will do it instead."

The only reason she'd never smashed my windows was probably because it'd have been too obvious.

I was still amazed she never had—and waiting for the day she did.

It was probably going to be soon.

"How did your interview go this afternoon?" Alexandra asked her, taking the cooking tongs.

"Don't," she muttered, stepping away from the grill. "His resume said he was twenty-five and competent enough to be an assistant in the kitchen, so I brought him in for a shortlist if I ever happen to find a head chef. He strolls into the freaking bar and I swear, I got an arrest warrant signed just for him walking in. He wasn't even legal. I asked him to prove his age and he's freaking twenty. He's still in college

Mixed Up

and thought it was a summer job and that nobody would need proof of his age."

"Where are you advertising?"

"Everywhere except my naked body," she replied, sitting down at the table opposite Ryan. "Lani's even taken pity on me and is giving me free full-page ads at this point."

"Who's Lani?" I asked.

"One of my closest friends. She runs the Whiskey Key paper."

"Are you just advertising in Whiskey Key?" I raised my eyebrows. "Why don't you do it here, too?"

"I'm advertising everywhere in South Florida," she shot back. "It's not as easy as you'd think it is."

"That's because you've had a shitty menu," Ryan said with a snort. "Maybe you should call back some of the better guys you interviewed and offer them to submit you a menu."

"What was your menu?" I asked her. "Didn't you ask Ryan to help you?"

"When has my sister ever asked for my help? Except earlier, of course, when she begged me to work for her."

"I did not beg you." Raven bristled. "Well, maybe a little. You know I need the kitchen open before everyone comes for vacation."

"Then sort out your menu," he shot back.

"Kids," Alexandra interrupted, putting the plate of steaks in the middle of the table. "Eat. Ilsa, can you see where Danny is when you get Craig?"

"Of course." Mom set the bottle of wine she was holding down in front of Alexandra and turned back to the house.

"What is your menu?" I steered the conversation back to Raven.

"Awful," she responded. "I think I'll make some calls."

"Why don't you just serve Greek food?"

Her fork clattered to the table.

"It's a good idea," Alexandra picked up where I'd left

21

off...Just like I knew she would. "You are half-Greek, it's good food, and there isn't a place for Greek food on the Keys. Plus, your grandmother would be very happy."

Raven pressed three fingers to her temple and glared at me through her eyelashes. "Have you considered there isn't a Greek restaurant because nobody wants Greek food, Mom? Not to mention I'm not sure that gyros or moussaka would fit too well with my cocktail menu."

"I still don't understand why you have those vulgar cocktail names."

I raised my eyebrow. I knew her bar was called Dirty, but I thought that was just because she could make a mean martini.

Her cheeks flushed light pink. It was barely noticeable through her tanned skin. "Because it's different," she replied. "It gets people talking, and that brings business. Not to mention that three-quarters of my menu is original, and people love that."

"Yes, but what's that new one you just added?"

Ryan grinned. "The Slutwhisperer."

I smirked. I couldn't fucking help it.

"It's a horrible word," Alexandra sniffed.

"I'd like a slutwhisperer." Raven and Ryan's grandfather shuffled out onto the porch. "Do you think it would spice up my life?"

"Maybe," Raven answered. "But I'd wait until the reunion is over. You know Great-Aunt Maria gets rowdy after a drink or two. It's probably best not to give her an opening, Grandpa."

He grumbled something as he settled into his chair. Something that sounded an awful lot like "Fuck that shit," and made Raven choke on her laughter.

"You have a cocktail called The Slutwhisperer?" I asked her, hiding my smile behind my glass of water. "Where did you come up with that?"

She tapped her finger against her temple and reached for her own water. "That's probably one of the best names.

Although, some of the others are pretty epic."

"Now, I feel the need to come and find them out."

"Imagine my bar is a church and you're a demon," she said. "I'll be holding the matches."

"She isn't kidding," Ryan muttered.

"Do you still do that screwdriver twist one?" Their grandpa asked.

"Reg," Alexandra groaned.

"You know the one," he continued, oblivious to her discomfort. "With the orange juice."

Raven cleared her throat and looked down at the table. "You mean the Dirty Screw, Grandpa."

"Yes!" He thumped the table with his fist. "I'm coming for breakfast. I need a Dirty Screw."

"What the hell is a Dirty Screw?" I looked at Raven.

She glanced over at her mom, biting the inside of her cheek and fighting a smile. "Exactly what it sounds like."

"If I order one, how happy will it make me?"

"Not very. I'll probably throw it over you."

"I'll take my chances."

"Fool."

I knew I was making a mistake. After what Raven said last night at dinner, I had the strongest urge to find out what her cocktail menu was. With names like Dirty Screw and The Slutwhisperer, what other gems did she have hidden on there?

Shit, what gems were hidden inside her apparently filthy mind?

I had no place to be thinking that. She was Ryan's sister and the bane of my goddamn existence. I didn't give a shit what was inside her head or how she came up with a filthy cocktail menu.

I was going to believe that she'd spent stupid

amounts of time on the Internet coming up with those kinds of names. Seeing her in that damn short dress yesterday had already affected me enough—not to mention the fact that she'd changed since I last saw her.

I didn't know people could change so much in only three years, but Raven Archer had. She was no longer post-grad, trying to seriously figure out what she wanted to do with her life, uncertain and serving burgers to people to make money.

She was grown-up, in more ways than just her age. She was even hotter-headed than she was back then. She seemed stronger and more stubborn, and her tongue was so sharp I probably had scars from how quickly she cut me with her words.

She was taller and fucking curvier, too.

Her lips were fuller. Her eyes were brighter. And the general air that hung about her, that hint of sass and sexiness, the very same thing that made me insult her whenever I opened my mouth almost made me want her, too.

And that was exactly why I couldn't sit and think about what went on in her mind—filthy or otherwise.

No matter what she looked like or how fucking hot she was, she was my best friend's sister. Nobody was more off-limits than she was. That wasn't a new development. It had always been that way.

Thank fucking god I was only here for the summer, and only because my mother had guilted me into it.

As soon as the summer was over, I'd go for my next challenge.

I could get through a few weeks of being in the same town or two as Raven—because after today, avoidance was at the top of my life.

Otherwise, I'd go fucking insane.

Dirty was right on the seafront, only meters away from a small, sandy bay. It'd only taken me a few minutes to walk here from where I'd parked downtown, and despite the music coming from inside the bar, I could still hear the gentle crashing of the waves as they crawled up the sand. The water was right out, and I stared out at the water as I headed up the hill to the bar.

Fairy lights twinkled along the underside of the roof that jutted out over the sidewalk. It was like a goddamn princess castle from the outside, but the beachy vibe was evident. Different sized and colored shells covered the pillars that held up the balcony that jutted out over the front doors.

I pushed open the door. Cold air blasted into me, and so did the heavy bass beat of the music that blared out from the speakers just above my head. There were more fairy lights inside, but they were strung all beneath the bar, across the beams on the ceiling, and over the back wall where the spirits were on the wall. There wasn't much else in the way of lighting, but what there was was effective enough in holding the entire space into a balance between bright and dusky.

The inside of Raven's bar was like being outside at the moment the sun set.

I cast my gaze over the rest of the bar. The solid, wood tables and stools that lined the walls and filled the space to my left all had tiny vases of fresh flowers in. Even those were surrounded by fairy lights.

Fucking hell, did she let a class of little girls in here to decorate?

No matter what I felt about the fairy lights, it looked good. Damn good.

I stepped up to the bar and leaned forward on it. Raven was at the other end of the bar, wearing jeans and a tight tank top that tucked beneath the waistband. Strappy, silver heels on her feet glinted off the under-bar lighting, and it was all too easy for me to drop my eyes there then slowly drag my gaze up the length of her entire body.

Light bounced off the chrome cocktail shaker in her hand as she shook it. She popped off the top with one flick of her thumb, and without spilling a drop, poured the pink-red liquid into two martini-style glasses. With her other hand, she reached back to the register and jabbed at it.

Seconds later, she was handing them back their change. It all happened in a flash.

How did such she go from lost to...this...so quick?

"Raven!" A dark-haired woman sitting a few stools away from me with her friend yelled. "There's a hot guy staring at you!"

I laughed loudly as Raven jerked around. Her gaze landed on me with what felt like a snap, and I swore she mouthed, "Motherfucker," before she stalked to this end of the bar.

Her hands slapped on the bar in front of me. "What are you doing here?"

"I told you I was coming to check out your menu."

"He was checking out more than the menu," the woman's friend giggled.

Raven held her finger up to them, and with her other hand, slapped a smooth, laminated menu in front of me. "Did you drive?"

"No, I walked all the way from Key West." I picked up the menu. "Of course I drove."

"Pick one," she said, moving away. "I'm not serving you any more than that. Make it a good choice. What can I get for you?" she asked someone else, cutting me off before I could say a word.

I raised my eyebrows.

"She runs a tight ship," the first woman said. "Three days ago, there was a guy in here spiking drinks. She caught him and bashed him in the balls with her cocktail shaker so he couldn't run from the security guard."

Could my eyebrows go up any higher? "That doesn't surprise me in the slightest. I've seen her do worse."

The second woman's eyes narrowed. "You have? You know her?"

The first woman rolled her eyes. "Of course he does, Cam. When have you seen her react to a customer like that? He obviously pissed her off in a past life or something."

"I should be so lucky." I smirked. "More like all in

this life."

"Her brother's friend, right?" She tilted her head to the side. "Yeah, she mentioned she hated you."

She'd talked about me?

"She didn't say you were hot, though," the second woman said.

"Camille!"

Ahhh.

The best friends.

"What?" Camille said. "I'm just saying."

"No more Slutwhisperers for you," the other woman—the one I presumed to be Lani—said, reaching for her glass.

Camille leaned over and slurped the last of the drink through the straw.

That explained the name of the cocktail.

"What are you doing?" Raven asked, stopping in front of them. "Cam? Your glass is empty. Let me refill that for you." She winked to the other girl as she turned around.

What was she doing?

She put her back to her friends and grabbed the tequila bottle. She tipped it over a cocktail shaker without actually pouring anything into it. My lips quirked up as she put together what was some pink juice or something and blended it with raspberries.

She poured the mixture into a glass with some vigor in front of Camille.

She'd made her a placebo.

"Made your choice?" Raven turned to me, holding onto the shaker.

"No." I spun the menu to face her. "What do you think I should have?"

Completely straight-faced, she said, "The Blue Balls."

3

Raven

Parker blinked his dark, brown eyes at me. I thought my suggestion was valid, but whatever.

Out of the corner of my eye, I saw Lani smile around her straw. Sure—I'd told them that my brother was in town with his best friend and that me and his best friend didn't get along, but there were a lot of things that I didn't mention about Parker.

Mostly that he was unfairly handsome these days, because I didn't know that myself until he walked out onto my parents' porch yesterday. I didn't know that his voice was deeper and sent a shiver down my spine. I didn't know that his strong jaw was now dotted with a five o'clock shadow that only drew attention to his annoyingly pink lips. I didn't know that he now spiked his thick, dark hair at the top and left the rest to sit normally.

I didn't know that I would be marginally attracted to him...Or that I'd have to lie about how attracted to him I was.

I didn't want to be attracted to him. The only thing I had going for me right now was that my dislike for him was still overwhelmingly stronger than that tiny speck of attraction that was tickling in my tummy.

"Well?" I asked him in my most innocent voice.

"I never thought I'd say this," he said slowly in that low voice of his. "But I'll have the Blue Balls."

"Coming right up."

A smile twisted across my face so quickly I couldn't hide it in the slightest. Judging by the giggles from my friends, they couldn't control themselves either.

It wasn't often a guy asked for blue balls, after all.

I switched out cocktail shakers with one hand and measured out one and half shots of coconut rum with the other. My eyes scanned the side for the blue Curacao as I poured it in, and I hadn't even finished the pouring when I grabbed the tell-tale bright, blue bottle. One shot of that and one shot of blue raspberry sours, and the sapphire-blue liquid reflected off the sides of the shiny shaker until I dulled it with lemonade.

I added more of the lemonade than usual, since I knew he had a good forty-minute drive to get back to his parents' place. I didn't want him to be halfway home and suddenly lose concentration—like its namesake, the Blue Balls tended to hit you when you least expected it.

"Eight dollars, please." I put the glass down in front of Parker.

He slid a ten across the bar until the note tickled my fingers. "Keep the change."

"Thank you." I smiled and went to the register. That was about as polite as I could be where he was concerned. But hey, he'd been nice, too. "What do you think?" I grabbed two empty glasses from the bar.

"This is good. Is it one of yours?"

I nodded as I put them in the glass washer. "All mine."

"Has your grandmother seen this menu?"

I bit back a laugh.

"You know her grandmother?" Lani asked. "How? Wait—never mind."

"By the time their reunion is over, the entire state will know her grandmother."

I turned in enough time to catch his smirk. "No, Yia-Yia hasn't seen my menu, and you're not wrong."

"What the hell is a Yia-Yia?" Camille asked, frowning. "Is that a rash or something?"

I laughed and leaned against the bar. "No. It's a rough translation of the Greek word for grandmother. She won't be called anything else."

"You're Greek?"

"Half."

"Why the fuck didn't we know that?" Cam turned to Lani. "Did you know that?"

"I don't exactly advertise it on a billboard, yano." I picked up their empty glasses with one hand and looked at Parker. "You see the kind of thing you've started now?"

He held up his hands, his eyes sparkling. "It's not my fault if you don't tell your friends about your crazy family."

"Why are you here again?"

"I'm waiting to see if you'll burn down the bar."

"I'm seriously contemplating it. I do have matchbooks behind the register."

"Do you want me to start it for you?"

"Only if you'll trap me in here so I don't have to speak to you ever again."

"Damn," Lani breathed. "That's some real hatred right there. Hey, Raven, remember when I hated Brett?"

Cam giggled.

"Brett?" Parker glanced at her.

Her lips twisted to the side. "My boyfriend."

I stared at Lani. "Don't you have work to do or something?"

Her smile grew when she met my eyes. "Point taken. I'll call you tomorrow."

"No, you won't."

"Yeah, I will." She laughed as she stood with Camille. "Early. Make sure you're awake."

I rolled my eyes. She knew I was always up at six. I had to be if I wanted to open by midday. This bar didn't organize itself, and I had an interview at nine-thirty tomorrow.

I hoped like hell it'd be better than the one I'd had this afternoon. The poor girl thought I meant a bar position, not a chef. And she was twenty.

I was attracting all the underage people, it seemed.

"How did your interview go this afternoon?" Parker asked when I got done serving a couple.

I sighed heavily and leaned against the bar again. "It was a mess. At this point, I'm hoping tomorrow's will be better."

"Did you take Ryan's suggestion?"

"No, I ignored him, obviously."

"You just breathe sarcasm, don't you?"

"What can I say? You bring out the worst in me." I shot him a smile before taking two more glasses from the bar. "Thank you!" I called after the pair of girls who left the bar. They smiled and waved before leaving.

I paused after putting the dirty glasses in the washer. The only people who were here now were the couple in the corner. Otherwise it was just me and Parker. I let out a long breath—that couple would be the last customers of the night, so I picked up the controller for the music and turned it down a little so it wasn't so deafening.

"What are you going to do if tomorrow's interview isn't better?" Parker asked when I got closer to him.

All I could do was shrug. That was my last interview that was lined up. I had no idea what I was going to do, if I was honest. Abandoning it was the best option I had at this point.

He finished the last of his drink and put his empty glass down in front of me. His dark gaze captured mine as he said only a few words.

"If it fucks up, call me."

Then, he left, leaving me taking a deep breath in and staring at him.

No way.

No way in hell.

The guy looked promising. He at least seemed to match the age on the resume he'd sent in. From the moment he'd stepped through the door, he'd been looking around the bar as if he was taking it in. He'd even asked to see the kitchen and seemed suitably impressed with the setup I had.

He should have been impressed. My brother was responsible for the kitchen because apparently, he didn't trust me to buy a toaster.

"So, Alex," I said, tapping my pen once against my notepad. "How many years have you been in a kitchen?"

"Only two," he answered, flicking his dark hair from his eyes. "I was a late starter, but I've had a few months experience at a restaurant in Miami."

"Are you still there?"

"No...I didn't get along well with my boss."

Awesome.

I pulled out his resume and scanned it. "And that's The Red Snapper?"

He nodded.

"Will they give you a reference if I call them?"

"They should." Alex clasped his hands in front of him on the table. "It was a...personal disagreement."

"A personal disagreement," I said flatly, sliding the paper back beneath my notepad. "Is that something I should be worried about?"

"Do you have a daughter old enough to date?"

"How old do you think I am?"

He grimaced. "That came out wrong."

"Why don't we move on?" *This guy is thicker than two girthy cocks put together.* "Here's the menu my friends drew up. How would you change this to be more unique and appealing for my customers?" I pushed the laminated sheet across to him.

He picked it up. His brows drew together as he read it, and only a minute later, he set it back down and met my gaze. "I'd add some seafood, but other than that, I don't see many other changes. How fancy does a cocktail bar food need to be?"

Given that I was as qualified as a mixologist at my age could be, it needed to be goddamn fancy.

"Well, that is the question." I did my best to keep my dryness out of my tone. "Thanks, Alex. I think that's everything I need from you right now. I have your number, so I'll be in touch." I closed my notebook and scooted my chair back so he got the message.

"Thanks, Ms. Archer. Or can I call you Raven?" he asked, as he stood up.

Oh, poor, sweet Alex.

If he weren't applying for a job, he could call me whatever the hell he wanted.

"Why don't we stick to Ms. Archer for now?" I smiled and walked to the door of the bar. "Thanks, Alex."

The second he stepped outside, I shut the door. I barely waited ten seconds before I twisted the lock and turned away.

God, that was so promising.

I was going to blame Ryan and Parker. There was no way I would be feeling like this if they hadn't trashed my menu. Expanding into food was a bad idea. I could feel it now. The knowledge was burying itself into my bones with my doubts laughing at me the whole time.

I collapsed onto the bar and grabbed my phone.

Me: *I hate you.*

My brother replied almost instantly.

Ryan: *Bad interview?*
Me: *Went well until he told me to just add seafood to the menu.*
Ryan: *Why is that my fault?*
Me: *You told me it was shit and now it's all shit.*
Ryan: *It is shit. You're better than that stuff. Your food needs to reflect you and your ability to mix drinks.*
Me: *Not helping.*
Ryan: *Just ask Parker.*

I blew out a long breath. I didn't like the idea. In fact, I loathed it, but he had offered.

The problem was that hiring Parker Hamilton was so far down my to-do list, I'd rather be fucked up the ass by Satan.

Ironically, hiring him and having Satan fuck me up the ass would probably be equally uncomfortable.

Me: *Mmph.*

That was the best answer he was going to get from me. It translated roughly to 'I'll think about it, but I'll do it with a huff.'

Ryan: *Did Mom call you?*
Me: *No. Why?*

That one question was sure to set alarm bells ringing in my mind. My mom never called—she avoided talking on the phone as much as possible.

Ryan: *Uncle Deion got earlier flights. They'll be here three days early.*

Oh no. No, no, no.

Me: *They'll be here in two days instead?!?!?!?!*

Ryan: *Happy Wednesday, sis. Yia-Yia's gonna flip when she finds out you don't have a chef yet.*

Oh god, he was right. I didn't always speak to my family in Greece, but when I did, it was always my grandmother, and she always wanted to know what I was doing with the bar. I'd left a lot out—like the dirty names of the drinks I mixed—but she was so excited to have her granddaughter open a restaurant and eat there.

It didn't matter that Dirty was a cocktail bar first. She was thrilled at the idea. The last time we'd spoken, she told me she wanted to eat here straight away.

She was already going to smash a plate or ten when she found out I wasn't serving Greek food.

I couldn't break her heart twice, as crazy as she was.

I was going to have to bite the bullet.

Me: *You win. I need Parker's number.*

My brother's next message was his number followed by a stream of 'haha' over and over again. I knew he was delighting in this a little too much, but I wasn't going to give him the satisfaction of knowing he'd essentially won.

He was almost thirty, for the love of god. He really needed to grow up.

I literally had to bite my tongue as I tapped out a message to Parker asking if he was free tonight. I didn't send it until I'd walked into the kitchen. I actually hit the button by accident, but that was a good thing. I knew I'd chicken out otherwise.

The kitchen was a mass of gleaming stainless-steel. Every inch of it was clean, as nobody was allowed in here except the chefs I'd interviewed, and even then, I'd politely asked that they didn't touch anything.

What? Stainless-steel was a royal bitch to clean. I wanted to wait until I had someone else I could make clean it before anyone got to touch.

My phone dinged in my hand.

Parker: Yep.

Just that. Nice.

Me: *Do you think you can come to the bar?*
Parker: ...Sure?
Me: *Is that a yes or a no? You sound confused.*
Parker: Yes. Is 6:30 good?
Me: *Can you make it 7? We get a rush around 6.*
Parker: No problem. See you then.

I hated myself.

That was the only explanation I had for what I was doing. Twenty-four hours ago, I was resolute in the fact that I would not offer Parker Hamilton and his handsome face a job. Not even when he offered himself was it something I allowed myself to consider. It was a ridiculous idea that would ultimately go up in flames, but I'd spent the entire day reasoning with myself.

Mixed Up

It buys me time. My family will be here for two whole weeks, during which, I can get interviews done for someone to replace him. It also means I can open for food every afternoon the way I want to during my busiest period. Spring Break clued me in to how much money I could make if I offered food, and the math worked out after.

Of course, that depended on whether or not I could afford Parker Hamilton.

He was one of the best chefs on the east coast. People would kill to have him in their kitchen for just one week. Could I really afford to pay him the kind of wage he'd demand?

I didn't think I could. I wasn't a big shot restaurant with reservations six months out, as his New York City spot was rumored to be.

I was a beachfront cocktail bar with a dream.

At least I served damn good cocktails. I knew I could mix as well as he could cook. I'd perfected my skill the way he had.

"Look," Sienna, my bar girl said to me as she served up two dirty martinis. "Think of it this way—the summer is the important part of this, right? So, hire him for the summer and then you have until Spring Break to find another chef. It doesn't have to be a year-round thing right now."

I knew what she was saying, but I wanted it permanent. There was enough local business to warrant it. "If that's what I have to do, that's what I'll do. The problem is my lack of wanting to hire him at all."

"Fifteen dollars please." Sienna took the card from the girl in front of her and turned to the register. "I know that," she said to me. "But, it could be a good thing. Think of the business his name would bring in."

She had a point.

"Thank you." She handed back the card and turned to me, her hand on her hip. "You're his best friend's sister. He's not going to ask you for your firstborn. Hell, what guys like him make, he probably doesn't even need any money."

"I don't want him doing me a favor. I don't want to owe him anything."

"You'll figure it out." She peered toward the door. "Holy shit, who is that?"

I took a deep breath. I already knew. Still, I glanced in his direction anyway.

Yep. Wearing a white polo shirt that hugged his apparently muscular body and dark blue, jean shorts, Parker Hamilton entered the building and commanded the attention of everything with a set of ovaries in the immediate area.

"That'll be Parker," I said reluctantly.

"How the hell do you hate him?" Sienna breathed. "I think I'm pregnant from just being in the same building."

"He hasn't opened his mouth yet."

"He doesn't need to."

"Sienna." I snapped my fingers in front of her face, drawing her attention back to me. "Focus. Do you think you can calm your tits enough for me to be able to speak to him?"

She blinked rapidly. "Got it. Focus."

I nodded behind her at a waiting customer.

"Got it," she repeated, stealing once more glance at Parker.

I will not shake my head. I will not shake my head. I will not shake my head.

I motioned for him to follow me with a wave of my hand and stepped out from behind the bar. He followed me out to the back where my office was, and I opened the door and walked in without saying a word.

I had no idea how to start this. Judging by the way he shut the door and settled into the chair on the other side of my desk, Parker wasn't going to give me an inch in it.

"I spoke to Ryan earlier," I started. "Apparently the Karras Circus is descending on the Keys three days early."

"I did hear your mom's panic at seven a.m. when I got back from a run. It was followed by your dad leaving with his gun case in his hand." He smirked. "Some things don't change."

No. He was right. Usually the closer we got to a reunion, the stronger Dad's need to shoot something got.

"Well, I didn't know that." I grabbed my water bottle from earlier. "But Yia-Yia is expecting me to serve food. I'm pretty sure it'd break her heart and then she'd be going home in a box."

"Because she's old or because she'd give herself a coronary with her dramatics?"

"Both," I hedged. "But that's why you're here."

He folded his arms across his chest, the barest hint of a smile playing on his lips.

I was going to throw up.

"I would like to talk about your offer to work here."

4

Parker

Her jaw clamped shut the moment she stopped talking. God, she hated every second of that, and I fucking loved it.

I studied her a moment before talking. Her hair was tied back into a ponytail high on her head, and her bangs swept smoothly across her forehead, just touching her eyebrows. Her bright-red lips were pursed in annoyance--at herself--and her white knuckles gave away how tight she was holding her water bottle.

"Then start talking," I told her, sitting back in the chair and getting comfortable.

If she wanted to be awkward and not spit it right out, I'd play her game. I didn't particularly want to work for her. It would be hell on fucking Earth to take orders from her. I have no idea why I told her to call me if her interview went wrong, but I'd been regretting it all day long. I was only here because I knew Ryan was feeling guilty that he hadn't thought to call Raven before getting his summer job.

I was here as a favor to him, not her.

We'd be lucky if we got through the summer without killing each other.

"It would be on a super temporary basis," Raven started, releasing the water bottle and resting one hand over the other on the desk. Her bright blue eyes locked onto mine. "I'll continue searching for kitchen staff while you're working here until I find someone suitable. If, at the end of the summer, I haven't found anyone, we'll close the kitchen until Spring Break next year."

She didn't look particularly happy about that, either. That same, pursed-lip expression was still on her face. She looked a lot like she was sucking on a sour gummy treat that never stopped.

"Menu control?" I questioned.

"Final approval is mine," she replied. "Otherwise, control is yours."

"Work hours?"

"Full-time? Two through nine, Wednesday through Sunday."

"Twelve through nine-thirty, Tuesday through Sunday," I countered. "Seven days until the other staff are comfortable with my menu."

Raven swallowed. "Okay, but how much is that going to cost me?"

I hadn't thought about that side of it. "How much were you offering in your advert?"

"Um." A light flush raised up her cheeks. "It was negotiable by experience. Most of the people who applied at first didn't have much experience and I realized pretty quick I couldn't pay them the going rate if they didn't really know what they were doing."

She was smart. Smarter than I'd given her credit for.

I took the small pad of paper from next to the keyboard and took a pen from the mug that said, "This is probably vodka." My lips twitched into a smile as I read it, and I caught Raven's tiny smile as I clicked the pen and wrote down a figure.

Sliding her the paper, I said, "That's my figure."

Her throat bobbed, and she cast her eyes down to the sheet I'd put in front of her. "I can't pay you that."

"Sure, you can."

"That's not enough for what you can do." She pushed it back to me. "I'd be taking advantage of your skills. You might piss me off at every turn, but I'm not going to do that."

"Raven, listen to me." I put the pen down and leaned forward. "I don't need or want your money. I could not work for five years living here. You wouldn't be paying Ryan if he were here, and the only reason I've put fucking anything on that paper is because I know your pride won't accept paying me nothing."

Her hard blink told me I'd hit the nail on the head.

"I won't take any more money than the number that's written on that bit of paper. So, do yourself a favor, and accept my offer. Use your money to find decent sous chefs who won't take forever to pick up what I'm going to need to teach them."

"There are probably a couple who weren't suitable for the executive job," she admitted, toying with the paper. She curled the end of it right up. "I still don't feel comfortable with this."

"Four thousand a month is hardly a small amount of money."

"It's a tenth of what you could earn if you went to Miami."

"I don't care about that. I just told you—that's my number. Take it or leave it."

Her entire body heaved and then sagged as she exhaled. "Fine. But I want it on record that I was forced into this arrangement at your insistence."

"Absolutely not. I don't have to force anyone into anything, much less of the opposite gender."

"Then you know delusional women." Raven wheeled back to a filing cabinet.

Mixed Up

I winced as the squeaking of a drawer opened bounced off the walls. "Usually, they're more intelligent than delusional."

"Of course, they are. That's why you're single now." She offered me a thin-lipped smile and slid back over on her chair. "Here's the contract my legal team drew up. Obviously, the times need changing, but I have the files to edit it. Read those tonight and call me if you have any questions. I'll print out some new ones for you to sign in the morning. How long will it take you to get a menu together?"

"Tomorrow morning." I took the contract from her. "Is there a clause in here about not murdering your boss?"

"Of course. I chose to leave out the employee one, though."

Of course, she did.

"All right, hotshot," I said to her. "Call those guys you think are good enough and have them in here at eight-thirty tomorrow."

"Morning?" Her eyebrows shot up.

I stood up and looked down at her. "No, evening. I plan to interview them into the small hours of the morning."

She flipped me the bird. "Until you sign a contract, I can't do that."

I swallowed a laugh. This was going to fuck up so damn bad. "Bring those guys in so I can interview them in the kitchen. Be ready to accept my menu, too. I'll be placing an order before I get here in the morning."

Raven stood up and hit me with a hard gaze. "That's not how this works, Parker. You don't demand shit of me. Make sure you're here at seven with your menu and your order ready to go. You make your order when *I* say so." She picked up her phone and glanced pointedly toward the door. "I'll make sure you have interviews tomorrow. Show up ready to sign a contract or I'll shove it up your ass and face some Mediterranean wrath instead."

Smirking, I walked back toward the door with a salute. "Yes, ma'am."

Her angry stare didn't diminish in the slightest. Two thoughts followed me out of the building. She was goddamn hot when she took the reins. This was going to be an issue.

"These guys." I slapped two resumes onto the desk in front of Raven.

It was eleven a.m. She'd managed to schedule me all her second choices, and while they weren't bad, they weren't earth-shattering either. I chose to focus on the fact they weren't total fucking disasters.

Silver linings and all that shit.

Slowly, Raven slid her blue gaze from the resumes to my face. "So, call them."

That was an order, not an idea.

"You're the boss," I replied.

"Your kitchen," she said simply, looking back down at her computer screen. "Your staff. I don't know who's a good fit for you, Parker. Bring them back for a double interview today."

"And if they can't?"

"Call someone else." Her tone was flat and emotionless. "It's not my problem. The fact that some crazy Greeks are about to descend onto my relatively quiet little Key are. Staff your kitchen. You signed the contract."

Shit, flat and emotionless was an understatement. Her response was robotic.

But, she was right. I'd signed her contract. It stated that the kitchen staff were ultimately my responsibility. In all honesty, I'd already decided that the two I'd put in front of her were right. I only did it out of courtesy.

"Then pass me the fucking phone, because I have two calls to make."

"Settle down, Gordan Ramsay. This isn't Hell's

Kitchen." She plucked the main phone from its dock and handed it to me anyway. "And wash your mouth out with soap before you speak to me again."

I raised an eyebrow, but I backed out of the office before saying anything else. I still had yet to show her the menu, and I knew she was going to hate every second of it. The only reason I hadn't shown her it yet was because she hadn't asked—and I wanted her to have as little time as possible to rebuke my suggestions.

She was gonna make me pay for the Greek and seafood menu, but the annoyance she'd feel would be worth every second of paying for it.

I sat up at the bar and dialed the first number. He didn't answer, so I left him a message asking if he could come back at one o'clock. The second call was much more successful, and he agreed to come back.

Raven was so damn last minute it was ridiculous. I didn't know why she didn't just tell her grandmother she wasn't open yet. Granted, I knew her grandmother and that she was crazier than a room full of cats on catnip with a ping pong ball, but still. It was the easy selection.

I still didn't know why I'd fucking offered to work for her. It was going to be nothing short of pure hell for as long as I was here.

It was a damn good thing I wasn't so good at relaxing.

"Did you do it?" Raven walked into the bar carrying a crate full of beer bottles. "They coming back?"

"One is. One I'm waiting to hear back from. You need a hand?" I nodded toward the crate in her arms.

She set it down on the end of the bar. "Not as heavy as it looks. There are two more in the cellar if you want to be useful, though."

She was a fucking delight.

"Where's the cellar?"

"Out the back, take a left at my office, past the bathrooms and into the door marked staff only. The doors open." She pulled the crate down to the floor and knelt in front of the fridge.

I saluted her—only because she wasn't looking—and headed down to the cellar. The door was propped open using a rubber doorstop, and the two, black crates were stacked on top of each other just a few feet away.

I picked them both up and carried them out to the bar. Raven glanced up and rolled her eyes the moment she saw I had both crates.

How was that for appreciation?

This was going to be worse than a nightmare.

"Anything else you need doing?" I asked, smirking as I set the crates down.

"Yep. I need to see your menu." Glass bottles clinked in her grip. "Read it to me while I restock."

I'd barely gotten through the first two appetizers when she stopped me.

She slammed the fridge door shut. Her foot slammed into the side of the crate, kicking it with such force that it skidded across the floor and bounced off the corner of the bar into the wall. "Give me that goddamn menu." Her nimble fingers snatched it from my hand with a flash of scarlet red nail polish.

I leaned against the edge of the bar and folded my arms. A light pink flushed up her neck and crept onto her face, moving a little further up each time her eyes flicked across the page. Slowly, her expression became pinched, from the hard purse of her lips to the quick drawing together of her curved eyebrows.

If there were any doubt left in my mind that Raven Archer was pissed off, the cutting glare of her bright blue eyes as her gaze slammed into mine was the final nail in the coffin.

"This is Greek food." Each word was perfectly formed and articulated in a voice so sharp diamond would shatter if it came into contact with it. "One thing, Parker. I wanted one thing."

"Listen to me—"

"One. Thing." She slapped the paper down onto the top of the bar and pinched her nose.

"Why won't you just embrace your fucking heritage?" The words snapped out of me before I could stop them. "Jesus, Raven, it's like you're ashamed of who you are."

"The last two Greek restaurants on the Key went out of business." Her voice was softer than a moment ago and punctuated with a sigh, but the edge of annoyance was still present. "One lasted six months and the other even less than that. Greek food is simple, but not easy to get right. It's not a matter of being ashamed of my heritage—it's a matter of respecting it and not wanting to screw it up."

Well, fucking hell. Why didn't she just say that in the first damn place?

"Do you trust me?" I asked her after a moment.

She tucked her dark hair behind her ear and looked at me. "I'd rather trust a crab to flick my clit."

Jesus.

"There's an image I never thought I'd have in my mind." Coughing into my hand, I shook my head. "Raven, your mom taught me and Ryan to cook. I can do anything on this menu to perfection or I wouldn't have given it to you. You might be a pain my damn ass, but I don't want to be the person who ruins your business."

Her throat bobbed as she swallowed, and her tongue flicked out across her red lower lip. "I have control issues, all right?"

"You don't say."

"You're not doing good in convincing me to let you cook this." She paused. "And it's not about trusting you to cook it. But, when this menu is out, it has to stay pretty much this menu even when you leave. It's being able to find someone else who can cook this food to a good enough standard, because Ryan isn't exactly going to come and work for me, is he?"

No. And I was starting to understand why he wouldn't.

"You know I'm on extended leave—"

"You mean you quit."

"—From my job," I continued, twitching at her word 'quit.' How the hell did she figure it out? "So, if you need me to, I'll train whoever you hire for real. I won't leave until they know how to cook this stuff as well as me."

She arched one eyebrow in a silent, "Really?"

All right, so that wasn't gonna happen, but still. "As well as they can," I amended.

"Do you swear?"

"On my life."

"That means that if you bail, I get to kill you. Slowly and painfully."

It took everything I had to fight the grin that was creeping onto my face. "Understood."

"But, before I agree," Raven went on, sliding the menu back to her. Her gaze briefly dropped to it. "I want you to cook me some of this stuff. I want to know if you're as good as you say you are."

"Tonight?"

"No, next week." With a snort, she continued, "Yes, tonight. For me, Lani, Camille, and Ryan."

"No pressure, then."

"I'll let you place your order." An evil glint flickered in her eyes. "You either cook for me, or you cook for Yia-Yia and her opinion."

Hell fucking no. Cooking for Aleta Karras' opinion was like standing in front of a firing squad at your own execution and asking them not to shoot. I'd made the mistake of that once before, when I was fourteen. I was still fucking scarred from her verbal beat down.

I also had to remember to thank her. Without her fifteen-minute tirade of how I'd never cook more than a bowl of cereal, I probably wouldn't be where I was.

"All right, hotshot. I'll cook for you tonight." I snatched up the menu and folded it in two. "You make the drinks and I'll make the food."

"Aw, cute. Our first dinner party." She paused. "Don't wear white. I'm prone to throwing drinks at assholes."

I looked her up and down. "How aren't you permanently covered in your own drinks?"

"Get the hell out of here before I spray you with soda." Her hand inched closer to the soda tap. "Seven-thirty. I want food in that kitchen, or I'm feeding you to Yia-Yia."

I'd never left a bar so fucking fast in my life—and I doubted I ever would again.

5

Raven

Every single conversation I had with Parker only reinforced to me that I was making mistake after mistake.

The first mistake was going to my parents.'

The second was not biting the bullet and canceling the food for the summer until I actually had my shit together.

The third was hiring him.

The fourth was letting him cook for me.

I didn't want to not serve Greek food at Dirty because I was ashamed of my heritage. I wasn't lying when I told him that—In fact, I was more than proud of it. I loved every bit of who I was and who my family was.

Most days.

I was scared. For whatever reason, Whiskey Key had never been able to hold down a Greek restaurant. I didn't know why—I'd never been to the others simply because I knew my mother could cook better than they could. Hell, I could cook good Greek food. I'd been raised on it, and if I couldn't cook Greek, my mom insisted she wouldn't teach me to cook at all.

Which is great...Unless you want to live with your parents forever.

I was lucky. I had the cocktail side to fall back on, and that was always the plan. If it all went ass up, I knew I could rip out the kitchen and use that area for more seating or something. Sure, it would be a cash drain, but there were always options.

I wanted the food to succeed, though. Badly. I wanted to have something fun and unique that made people want to come back.

Now, I had more fear. What if Parker was so good that nobody would ever come close to his standard? Of course, that was a slightly irrational thought, but from what I could remember, the man could cook his way out of a death sentence. A sharp decline in quality when he eventually left would be more than I could handle.

I was a control freak with my business. I knew it. Telling Parker to get his own damn kitchen staff was a battle in itself—I wanted to vet and interrogate the people he was calling, but I couldn't. The kitchen was his domain, and the people hired to help him had to be his choice. It's like having a mini-manager.

The only reason I was okay with leaving the bar completely in Sienna's hands was because I knew I wouldn't be leaving the building and because, well, I wouldn't be leaving the building. I was there if an issue arose and I could deal with it.

I had issues.

Dirty was my baby, and also my—not crazy—grandmother's legacy. There was a reason she'd left me money when she'd died. The reason was this bar and her love of a good cocktail.

I didn't want anything destroying that.

Even hiring Parker was a leap of faith. Maybe telling him that I'd rather have a crab flick my clit than trust him was a step too far. The guy wasn't going to poison me. He wouldn't want my family's wrath. Not even he hated me enough to risk it.

The big problem that kept smacking me in the face was the fact I did trust Parker...With food.

Nothing else.

I didn't even trust him to flip me off correctly.

I also didn't trust myself. He was the ultimate thorn in my side, the biggest pain in the ass I'd ever have. He was more annoying than stepping on a Lego. Stubbing my toe paled in comparison to the frustration of being around him on a regular basis.

But, dear god, I was attracted to him.

I was attracted to him and his dark hair, his full, smirking lips, and his deep, cocky voice.

I didn't know how to stop it, and it only made me hate him more. How dare he be so hot? What right did he have to be so goddamn handsome? His looks didn't match his personality—not to me, anyway.

There was nothing I wanted more than to punch that attraction out of myself, fire him, and pretend I was still in a Parker Hamilton drought. One I'd very much enjoyed for the past few years.

Yes, that was it.

The Parker Hamilton drought had been so enjoyable that, now, I was Parker Hamilton drunk. And not the good drunk—the wheezing, sobbing, over-apologizing for breathing kind of drunk.

There was simply too much of him in too little time.

That wasn't going to get any better, given that he was now my employee. A fact we both loathed. It was evident when he spoke to me this morning. He liked it no more than I did.

I didn't have to be a genius to figure out that he was only working for me out of pity for my brother. I wanted to know how much Ryan was paying him to work for me. He was either paying him or he had dirt on him. Dirt that, if it existed, I wished I could know.

There wasn't dirt. Parker wasn't that kind of guy. He never had been, and I don't think he had that kind of bone in his body. He was the kind of guy who would rather chew his own foot than cheat on a girl. He'd never dream of not holding a door open for a woman, and he would always pay for dinner.

He just wasn't that kind of person to me.

Then again, I was hardly that kind of person to him.

I didn't know how we'd get through however long we had to work together, but I knew it wouldn't be pretty.

"If you don't want him," Camille whispered, leaning in toward me, her eyes on Parker, "Can I have him?"

I side-eyed her. "What is he? A kitten I picked out of the parking lot?"

"No, but I kinda wanna pet him like he is."

I jerked my elbow into her side so she sat up straight. "Cut that shit out," I told her. "I'm not listening to you fawn over him like a newborn baby."

"Are his toes that cute?"

Lani leaned forward and looked at Cam. "You're seeing Xavier, remember?"

Cam rocked her head side to side. "So are two other girls, so I'm not thinking we're on the serious side of the line."

I rolled my eyes.

She knew better than to get involved with Xavier Ryan. He went through women the way a public bathroom went through water. I had my money on the fact she was only sleeping with him to piss off her brother, Brett.

"Gee, you think?" Lani drawled. "I thought he was proposing anytime."

Camille punched her.

I took a sip of my drink. "I don't know why you're seeing him."

"He has an eight-inch dick," she responded without missing a beat.

"You can find them on the Internet without baggage," I reminded her.

My brother blinked at me. "I joined this conversation at the wrong time."

I grinned. "Serves you right for eavesdropping. Did he kick you out of his kitchen?"

Ryan's eye twitched. "He's a little uptight in the kitchen. I retreated before we reached rabid, hungry tiger level."

I dropped my eyes and put my straw in my mouth to hide my smile. Dear god, if Parker really was that bad, this entire thing was going to go up in flames.

"At least he's passionate," Lani reasoned.

"So are hungry tigers," Camille added.

"I can hear you, you know," Parker yelled from the kitchen over the sound of things frying and sizzling and cooking. "Shut up!"

Ryan had a point. He even glanced at me with raised eyebrows and a small smile.

I shifted forward in my seat. "What is he doing in there?"

"Cooking," my brother answered. "It's somewhat stressful, you know."

"I'm going in there."

"No, you're not."

"I'm sorry, do you own that kitchen?"

He didn't answer.

I mimed zipping my lips with a smile, much to the amused giggles of my friends, and got up. We were sitting in the back, outdoor area of the bar. I'd closed it off to the public tonight, leaving the side area for anyone who wanted to venture outside or needed to smoke. It was quieter at the back, the only real sound the low hum of the music from the main bar area. It was occasionally broken by the crashing of the waves if they were a little rough, but otherwise, the only hint that we were by the ocean was the gentle breeze that wafted over every now and the light scent of salty sea water it brought with it.

That was a stark contrast to the kitchen. The moment I stepped through the back door into the kitchen, I was hit with the thick heat that even a Floridian summer could only wish to emulate. It was almost as if I'd stepped into one of the deepest levels of hell.

The sound of cooking was stronger here. The sizzles and frying and sssh-zz-whrr-ing noises that made up a busy kitchen buzzed all around the air, bouncing off the plain, white walls until they vibrated across the stainless-steel surfaces.

And in the middle of it was Parker Hamilton. His t-shirt was almost slicked entirely to his body thanks to the heat, and it held firm to his strong back where the fabric flattened against his spine before it bunched right above his waistband. The tiny gap between the cotton and jean hinted at his tanned skin. I had to physically drag my gaze from that strip of skin.

I needed food before I had another cocktail…And I'd only had one.

"What do you want?" Parker asked without looking at me.

"I'm being nosy." I clasped my hands in front of me and peered around. "It's pretty hot in here."

"I didn't notice." His tone was dry. "Why are you here?"

"You can't throw me off that easily."

"I was hoping that was code for, "Five minutes, go away.""

"No chance."

"Raven? Go sit down and send Ry in here. I'm almost done."

"What did you make?" I asked, reaching up onto my

toes. I never asked him to make anything specifically, and all he'd told me was that he was essentially cooking a buffet of things from the menu. I had no idea what to expect, and that was why I was peering at all the things beneath the hot light thingy on the other side of the kitchen.

"I need Ryan's help," he repeated, cutting through my nosing. "Five minutes."

One look at the concentrated furrow of his brow had me backing away. This was serious for him, and his passion somehow shone through in every word. If he needed my brother's help, I'd give it to him—begrudgingly, but still.

"Ry, he wants you," I said as soon as I stepped back outside. The jugs of the Pussy Pounder I'd made earlier were still holding strong on the table, although one round of drinks would kill the first jug.

Camille grabbed the jug before I'd taken my seat. She poured the red drink into all our glasses with such *elegance* that the orange slices I'd chopped up and added for extra flavor all plopped into our glasses, splashing the liquid everywhere. Red droplets splattered across the black, glass surfaces of my outdoor tables, and I wiped them up with a napkin.

Lani smirked.

"Make room!" Ryan said, carrying out a giant tray from the kitchen. He had to turn sideways to get out of the back door.

That drew a tiny wince from me. The idea was to have food served out here, too. It wasn't always a day from weather hell, after all...

Ryan put one tray on the table behind Camille. Parker brought up the rear with another tray that he set on the table behind me. The warm, homely smell of the Greek seasoning filtered through the air. Instantly, that deep part of me that always roused with the scent of what I counted to be home sprung to life.

My eyes flitted across the dishes of hummus and calamari until they landed on the gyros plate. The kebab-like meat took up half the plate, just dipping into the glob of tzatziki sauce on the side of the plate. Pita bread that was obviously warm from the soothing scent of it was on the other side of the plate.

"I'll just take that..." I reached over and picked up the plate.

Both my brother and Parker hid a smirk.

Gyros was my weakness. Hell, if he had this done good, the rest of the menu could be screwed.

Wait, no. That was my stomach speaking.

I didn't pay much attention to the distribution of the other dishes across two tables as I tucked some meat and sauce inside a pita bread. The bread was so soft and fluffy, and there was no doubt that Parker had baked this earlier today. It just had that...light feeling that fresh bread had.

He watched me with amusement glinting in his eyes as I bit into the pita bread.

The classic, simple taste of Greece exploded in my mouth. Literally exploded. I was smack-bang in the middle of a freaking foodgasm, and if I were alone, I'd be moaning my way through it. It was so damn good.

"Good?" Parker asked, his amusement giving way to a hint of smugness.

I swallowed and dabbed the corner of my mouth with a napkin. "It's not bad," I answered.

Yes, it was good, but I wasn't going to give him the satisfaction of finding that out just yet.

It didn't matter much, though. The upturn of his lips said it was good and he knew it.

The slight arch of his eyebrows told me he'd play this game if I wanted to.

"I think I just came," Camille muttered, holding a skewer with what looked like pork souvlaki on it. "Why haven't I eaten this before?"

"At least someone appreciates my skills." Parker glanced at her before sitting down between Lani and Ryan.

I flipped him the bird when Camille winked.

"Two dinners in one week," Ryan said, mostly to his

plate. "What was I thinking?"

"This is your penance for not working for me." I nudged him with my elbow. "You're being judged and this is your payback."

"Shit. Do you think they'll know if I pretend to be religious for the next two weeks?" He turned to meet my eyes. "Yia-Yia will have my ass for breakfast if she thinks I don't practice anymore."

"You don't," Parker pointed out. "You go at Christmas because she calls you every year on Christmas Eve and you feel guilty."

She did that to me, too.

She also liked to drink and believed I was doing Christ's work by feeding people cocktails and that he would forgive me for skipping church during such a stressful period.

I was going to take it. Take it, record it, and run with it.

I also suspected she liked me more.

Yia-Yia was a strange woman.

"This is really good," Lani said, steering the conversation back to the here and now. "I'm kind of annoyed Raven's been hiding you. Can you cook for me every day?"

Great. He'd even charmed the reporter.

"I haven't been hiding him," I told her, grabbing some calamari. "Avoiding him, yes, but not hiding. Besides, he's been in New York for years."

"Almost four years isn't years," Parker retaliated.

"Is it more than a year?"

"Well, yeah..."

"Then, it's years." I grabbed my glass and met his gaze. "And not nearly long enough."

His response was a smirk followed by a bite into a ring of calamari. He held my gaze just long enough for Lani to cough and draw my attention.

She raised her eyebrows quickly in a silent question.

I shoved the rest of the calamari into my mouth.

Whatever.

Mom: *Flight lands at 9pm. Me and Dad are driving up to get everyone. Breakfast tomorrow.*
Me: *Let me know when, I'm up until close.*

I tucked my phone back into the drawer beneath the register and took a deep breath. As glad I was that my family wasn't landing until late, giving me an extra twenty-four hours of peace and Parker an extra day in my kitchen, it didn't seem like long enough.

I'd made the decision to open for food tonight. Only for three hours, but it was important that we had some kind of flow going before my family came here to eat every night. After all, over the next week, more and more of my family would arrive.

I was still not happy about being the central point for the reunion. I didn't even know why we needed a reunion. It wasn't like it had been ten years since we'd all been together. The kids wouldn't even remember us, they were that young.

Yeah. I wasn't exactly thrilled at the prospect of having kids in my bar either. Dirty simply wasn't made or designed for functions. It was enough hard work to make it right to serve food.

I picked up the stack of menus Brett and Camille had arranged to be printed overnight.

"They're good, right?" Brett asked, wiping his hands on his jeans.

I nodded. "Thank you for getting them done quickly. I feel so unprepared."

"Do you want me to come serve food?"

My eyebrows shot up as I looked at him. "I want people coming in here to eat food, not to want to eat you, Brett."

He grinned. "Six months ago, I would have been all

over that offer."

"I know. I still pinch myself just to make sure I'm not dreaming and that Lani has actually tamed you."

"I didn't say she'd tamed me. She gets all my wild."

"That's way too much info." I laughed anyway. "Are you busy or can you take the board out to the front for me?"

"I'll take it out. Where is it?"

"In my office. Thanks." I walked across the bar and put the menus by the door. Sienna had already agreed to be my front-of-house girl until we hired another member for waitstaff. I kept a few menus back for the bar in case people wanted to eat there and almost collided with Brett on my way back.

"What's this made of? Rock?" he huffed, righting it in his grip.

"Oh, come on. I move that twice a day without complaining. You could put someone's eye out with your arms—stop whining." I slipped the menus in the upright file holder next to the register and turned back. He was bumping his way out of the door, and it wasn't until a familiar figure showed up and grabbed the door and held it open that Brett successfully got the board outside.

"What's with the torture?" Parker asked, gesturing to Brett.

"Torture my ass," I replied. "He's just being a wimp."

"Hey," Brett said, coming back inside. "Just because you're stressed doesn't mean you get to be a shit to me."

"The fact the first words you said to me two years ago were 'Nice ass, how does it look in the air?' does."

Parker's lips twitched. "I don't know if that's awful or brilliant. Slightly inclined to lean toward brilliant."

"Brett Walker." Brett stuck out his hand.

"Lani's boyfriend, right? Parker Hamilton."

They shook.

"He's my kitchen bitch," I told Brett before he could speak.

6
Parker

Kitchen bitch?

That was a new one.

"I don't know how to respond to that," I admitted. "That's the first time anyone has ever called me their bitch, much less their kitchen bitch."

"Then you've been hanging around the wrong people." Raven's tone was matter-of-fact.

Wrong people? That depended how quickly or easily I wanted my dick sucked, I guessed.

Like, right now? Raven was the wrong people.

Not that I'd trust her mouth anywhere my dick. She'd probably use her teeth a little too enthusiastically.

Raven grabbed a cloth and wrapped her hand around one of the taps. "Don't either of you have something to do?"

I blinked and dragged my eyes away from her hand. That was the wrong thing for her to do when I'd just been thinking about my cock. "Did my delivery get here?"

"Five minutes ago. I was going to call you to see

where you were. Wes got here just before the delivery and I told him to make sure all the dishes from last night were put away correctly."

I gave her a thumbs up and headed back to the kitchen. After greeting Wes, the twenty-one-year-old recent graduate we'd selected as the best prospect to be the third chef, I headed for the walk-in fridge where he said he'd put the order.

Two hours later, we were done and I sent Wes for his lunch. The dark-haired kid who was all limbs ambled out of the kitchen, inadvertently knocking over a pot of pens on the side table by the door. The sharp clatters of them as they hit the floor reverberated around the kitchen, bouncing off each shiny surface until I winced.

"Sorry, Chef," he muttered, picking them up and putting them back where they belonged. He disappeared before I could reassure him that it was okay, but I couldn't lie—if he couldn't even leave the kitchen without messing something up, would he be able to handle it when it got busy?

It was too late to have those doubts. I had to take a chance on the kid now. With any luck, he'd be one of those guys who was a fucking mess generally, but a whiz when he needed to be.

I retrieved the ingredients for hummus and brought them over to the main counter. My phone was plugged into an outlet on the shelf above my head, and I started my most recent Spotify playlist to counteract the quiet of the kitchen. It only needed the slightest bit of volume since it was so empty.

"Hey." Raven's voice came just as the door opened.

I glanced over my shoulder. "What's up?"

"You sent Wes for lunch?" She cocked her thumb over her shoulder, and I nodded. "You're not stopping?"

I grabbed the chickpeas. "Nope. Hummus."

"Yum." She paused, her tongue flicking across her lips. "When will you be stopping?"

"When I have a chance."

Mixed Up

"Which is…"

"Raven? I'm busy."

She tutted so loud any disapproving aunt would be impressed. Then, she left. The door slammed behind her, and I shook my head as I threw a few other ingredients in with the chickpeas. The sound of the blending whirring to life with my push of the button drowned out any lingering echo from her annoyed tut.

The last time I'd heard a tut like that was when my grandmother discovered I was going into cooking instead of pursuing what she insisted was a promising football career.

I didn't count having a two-hundred-and-seventy-pound man ram into you several times a week a "promising career." A painful one, but not promising.

I killed the blender and, slowly, separated the hummus into tubs and dated each one. I didn't expect to need a lot, so I hadn't made a lot, but just in case there was some left over, it would be good tomorrow, too.

I didn't know what time Raven thought I had. Granted, in almost every restaurant I'd been in, I'd always been told that I worked hours ahead of where I needed to be. I didn't know how that was such a bad thing—it was how I was so efficient. If I needed something, I knew it would be ready for me, with the exceptions of things like steak that were cooked to order.

I turned my attention to seasoning. Greek food always tasted better when it was seasoned a couple of hours in advance, at least in my opinion. Plus, it was one less thing I'd need to fuck about with later.

Raven walked back in right as I was cutting the pork into chunks. She came up beside me and looked at my board. "Souvlaki?"

"Prep," I answered simply, cutting the pork. "What are you doing back out here?"

She put a pre-packed sandwich on the counter just out of my reach. "I went to grab lunch. You need to eat. There's a cafe just down the road that makes these fresh. I took a punt on chicken." She paused. "Unless you'd rather have beef?"

Any other day, I would have said beef just to piss her off. But, this was unusually thoughtful for her, and I didn't actually care either way.

"Chicken is great. Thank you." I shot her a smile as I cut some more pork.

"You're welcome." She stepped back. "Do you need anything else?"

"Yeah, can we get some water in the fridge? I asked Wes to come and get you an hour ago but you were...screaming at somebody." I glanced at her in time to see her cheeks flush.

"Some suppliers are assholes," is all she said. "I'll be right back."

She scuttled out of the kitchen. The second the door closed behind her, I chuckled to myself. Some suppliers were indeed assholes, but did she unleash her temper on them unnecessarily, or did they have it coming to them?

Either way, I made a mental note to use her for any asshole suppliers around here.

I threw the chopped pork chunks into a bowl and washed my hands. The seasoning I needed was sitting on the shelf above me, so I grabbed it, uncapped it, and sprinkled it onto the meat. With one hand, I stuck in and started mixing it all up. I added more seasoning as and when I needed it until I heard the door open again.

"Ugh," Raven said. "I don't usually want to eat raw pork, but that smells pretty good."

I laughed and washed my hands again. "I'd advise against it."

"Is this enough water?"

I looked over my shoulder. It was a package of twenty bottles, and she was holding it like it was nothing. I expect it would be if you carried that shit every day. "More than. Thanks. Just dump it on the side and I'll have Wes put it in when he gets back."

Mixed Up

"Nah, I got it." She opened the smaller fridge a few feet away from me. "How does he seem?"

"Wes?"

She nodded.

"Dunno. I'd have him do some prep when he gets back. I need some fries cutting."

Raven paused by the fridge door, three bottles in each hand. "Really? You're gonna make him cut fries?"

"Executive chef privileges." I grinned and put some clear wrap over the pork to keep it fresh. Carrying it over to the fridge, I said, "Nah, I do it with all new hires, especially if they're young. I cut one or two potatoes exactly how the fries need to be cut, and how well he copies me is an indication of his ability in general."

"His ability to what? Slice a fucking potato?"

"Primarily." I set the bowl on the bottom shelf. "But also to listen to instructions. If I want chunky fries half an inch thick, that's what I want. Not a quarter-inch or three-quarter-inch. Half an inch. If I want skinny fries two-tenths of an inch, that's what I want."

"That's kind of picky."

"Picky got me Michelin stars."

"I don't know how to argue that point." She shrugged and finally slipped the bottles into a shelf in the door. "All right, but remember that half-decent kitchen staff are slim pickings around here. If he gives you one three-quarter-inch fry in a batch of half-inch fries, it's not his fault."

"Sure it is. He put it in there. He cut it. I didn't."

She hits me with a withering look that draws a tiny smile from me. "And men are prone to exaggeration, so your half-inch thick fries are probably not even a quarter."

"God, I've never heard that before."

"It's nice to be original." She grabbed more water bottles.

"I had a woman work for me last year at the restaurant. She constantly told me I got my sizes wrong." I ran the tap and put the chopping board in the sink. "I put up with it until I told her I had a firm eight inches of my own, so I was pretty sure I was accurate."

Raven met my eyes with a raise of her eyebrows. "Classic overcompensation."

"I'd prove you wrong if I didn't think you'd slice it clean off."

"It's always nice to have a healthy dose of fear in my employees."

"I'm not afraid of you, Raven. I'm afraid of what you could do to my cock. There's a very big difference." I shut off the tap and grabbed a towel to dry the board.

"Sorry, I don't sleep with the staff. They get crazy when you do that." She paused. "Not that I've ever done that."

"You've done that, haven't you?"

"Accidentally. Honestly, you sleep with a guy once and he thinks you're in love. I had to fire him because, no matter how pretty he was, he couldn't make a Screwdriver...And he was a little crazy."

"You are the authority on crazy." I flashed her a grin.

"Keep talking, Parker Hamilton."

"That's Chef when you're in my kitchen, thank you."

"Let me show you all the fucks I give." Her intense gaze never wavered. "Oh look, I ran out."

My lips pulled to the side. Fucking hell, she was sass central, wasn't she? "They must have disappeared to where mine have. Now, thank you for lunch and the water, but get out of my kitchen."

In a great show of defiance, she opened the fridge and yanked out a bottle of water. It was so petty and childish that laughter bubbled up deep inside me. Both the fridge door and the kitchen door slammed in her wake, because she left in a flash of dark hair, leaving behind such a silence that my music seemed to boom.

I'd forgotten it was on.

I shook my head, ridding it of thoughts of that crazy, sassy woman I worked for, and got back to work.

Much to my surprise, Wes was the whizkid I'd dismissed when in the kitchen. He chopped everything to perfection, and his batter for the calamari was pretty damn good. By the time we'd finished serving food, he was practically floating out of the kitchen, and I'd permanently delegated batter-mixing to him.

That was the best thing about being in control.

You got to delegate the shit you hated to others.

I shut off the lights for the kitchen after one last look around and stepped out into the bar. Raven and Sienna were both slammed behind the bar. The girl—I'd already forgotten her name and she'd told me five times—they'd hired to run the food had finished her shift when the kitchen closed forty-five minutes ago, and they were clearly alone.

I took some empty glasses from the table nearest to me and set them on the end of the bar.

"Thank you!" Sienna yelled over the music.

I hadn't realized it was so loud in the kitchen. Looking around, I saw why. Some of the tables had been cleared and there was now a dance floor at the opposite end of the bar. It was darker than it was the night I came in here, and now I understood why she had fairy lights. The bright-white bulbs she had in place emitted a light pretty close to daylight, and it was just bright enough that the bar was completely illuminated.

It looked even better like this.

"Do you need some help?" I offered.

"No," Raven shouted just as Sienna shouted, "Yes!"

Both women stopped and looked at each other.

Raven's eyes seemed bluer in the light as she flitted her gaze between me and Sienna. She held up one finger and then smoothly poured a yellow liquid from the cocktail shaker in her hand into two glasses, filling them halfway up.

Seemingly without blinking, she pulled cranberry juice from the fridge and poured, topping them up. The vibrant, red liquid mixed with the sunshiney yellow until the middle strip of the cocktail was a bright orange.

I would never understand how people made those layered cocktails.

It was some mad fucking skill.

She ran the order then, holding two fingers up to her next customer, she slinked past Sienna in the bar and leaned over the edge of it to me. She grabbed my shirt and pulled me into her, putting her mouth right next to my ear. "One of my girls is on vacation in Jamaica and the other called in sick. I'm trying, but we're running out of glasses. Can you grab all the empty ones and run them through the washer in the kitchen? We have both running and they're taking forever. I just need them clean."

"Sure."

She released me the second the word left my lips, and her hair tickled across my cheek when she turned and called, "Sorry about that! What can I get you, sir?"

She stepped from mild panic into a smooth, calm bartender in a heartbeat.

"Motherfu—"

My hand shot out and grabbed the falling glass before it could drop too far. I winked at Sienna as I handed her the glass. She dipped her head, blushing, and put the glass down to reach for a clean one.

"Thanks!" she called as I put my things just inside the bar.

I smiled and caught Raven's eye.

Her expression was flat—hard. She dropped her gaze to the back of Sienna's head before turning away and dropping two shots of spirits into a shaker. I hesitated for a moment, but Sienna hadn't noticed, and now Raven was busy with the cocktail.

I shook that off like I had so many things Raven and focused on getting the empty glasses. The second time I returned to the bar, Raven whipped a black, circular tray out from the depths of the bar and handed it to me over Sienna's head. She had a shaker in the other hand and was talking to a customer getting his order as she did it.

Her efficiency was something else. There she was, making one customer's drink, taking another's, and making my job a little easier.

Fuck. How did she remember and notice all those things? I was glad I had tickets for customer orders, because my memory was so fucking shit a goldfish could remember stuff better than I could.

Slowly, after weaving my way through bodies and tons of people, I managed to get through to collect all the empty glasses. I took that tray right out to the kitchen dishwasher to put on a quick cycle. Raven's words about them just needing to be clean ran through my mind, so I ran a sink full of hot water to hand wash some.

I had no fucking idea what I was washing. They were all different shapes and sizes, fucking big, small, round, triangle—you name it, I had it in front of me to wash. I scrubbed each one and drained them until I was done and could hand-dry them. Then, after a wipe of the tray, I took them all right back out to the bar.

"Raven." I stopped at the door to the bar when I saw she was close to me. "Here."

She poured tequila into a metal shot measurer and glanced at the tray. "You run out of room?"

"No. They're clean."

"How?"

"I used this wonderful creation called my hands."

"You're so cocky. Thanks. Two seconds." She poured some blue and then some yellow liquid into a shaker and then put on the cap. "I need a few of these done. Could you...?"

"You owe me breakfast," I warned her.

"Fine—whatever." She shook the shaker with some serious vigor before pouring the now-green liquid into two martini glasses. She garnished each sugar-rimmed glass with a slice of lime. Then, she turned to two girls just feet from me. "Two Panty-Melters for you, ladies. Sixteen dollars, please."

The blond one handed her a twenty with a wave. "Keep the change. That's on my boyfriend."

Raven half-grinned. "Tell him I said thank you and that he's welcome."

The girls both giggled as they turned away. I watched them with a slight smile of my own.

"Panty-Melter, huh?" I asked, one eyebrow arched.

"Does what it says on the box," she defended, holding up her hands. "Two of those suckers and there are some happy boyfriends."

"Is that the strongest one you have?"

She pulled four martini glasses from the tray and set them on the shelf. "No. The strongest one I have isn't on the menu. Mostly because the name isn't exactly...printable."

I was intrigued. No lie, no way around it, no denial. How could I not be? A name so bad she couldn't print it? What the hell was she putting in it?

"How do people order it?" I asked, handing her two wine glasses.

"They just...do."

"So, you're kind of drug dealing?"

"Not at all. What can I get for you?" she asked a guy who caught her attention with a wave of two fingers.

"Can I get a Makers on the rocks?"

"You sure can." She whipped a small, square glass from the shelf. "Single?"

"Make it a double."

She scooped a few ice cubes into the glass and held it up the optic for two shots. "Ten-seventy-five, please."

The second she had the glass on the bar, his money was in her hand.

"Rest is yours, darlin'."

"Thank you." She smiled and ran it through the till, glancing at me. "It's not on the menu because of its name, but also because it started out as a joke. When I was in school, one of the assignments was to create our own drink. I did it with some friends, and accidentally, the name slipped out of me. They all insisted I submitted that for my drink, but I changed the name and watered it down slightly. Now, if my friends are ever in Florida, they come down just to get that drink. It's very slowly started to be known amongst the locals here, but many don't ask for it. The last person to ask was Camille and she passed out ten minutes after she finished her drink."

My eyebrows shot up. "It's that strong?"

"Cam isn't exactly the poster child for holding her liquor. Hold on."

I waited while she served another three customers.

"Keep it to yourself," she said out the corner of her mouth, pouring vodka freehand into a glass. "Ryan doesn't know I have a cocktail so dirty it's not on my list, and the last thing I want is Yia-Yia asking me what it is."

But the problem was now, I wanted her grandmother to ask her.

I also wanted to know what it was.

Badly.

7

Raven

I slid the bolt across the front door and sagged against it with a sigh. Rosanne calling in sick at the very last minute had really fucked us over. It was Friday night, it was the start of summer, and the first night of food.

If she'd called me this morning, I could have had Vicky, the waitress, stay on for an extra hour or two to help us manage the crowd outside of the bar. Instead, I ended up having Parker stay for longer.

Worse: I opened my mouth about my deadly cocktail. The one I rarely made because of its potency, and the one I never freaking named because, well, it wasn't the kind of thing you yelled about unless you were starring in a fucking porn movie.

Now, he knew about it, and the way he'd looked at me every time since that conversation made me realize that he isn't going to stop unless he knows its name, too. I didn't know if it was the way he side-eyed me or that amused yet determined glint that flashed every time I caught him blinking.

Right now, I was choosing to focus on the miracle that we hadn't killed each other.

And a miracle it was. We'd successfully gotten through twenty-four hours of a legit work day and neither of us had hurt or maimed or even attempted to kill the other. Sure, it'd probably be a different story if we were working in the same room, but we kinda had been. As it was, it was just past midnight and although we'd shut down before I'd anticipated, it was still late.

After all, I'd been on my feet since seven this morning.

And I'd finally been able to check my phone and see that Yia-Yia and Company had touched down in the sunshine state and were now safely tucked into my parents' spare bedrooms.

There was also a message from my brother asking if he could steal my spare room above the bar.

That was a big, fat no.

Penance for not working for your sister. I warned him, it was real. I just didn't tell him I'd be the primary deliverer of it. Sibling prerogative, I figured. He deserved it. He knew I was looking for a chef before he got his job in Key West so his excuses were worthless.

As it was, I'd ended up with Parker, and as much as I might have hated that fact, I couldn't deny the endless stream of compliments I'd gotten on the food tonight. Everyone who'd ordered had loved every mouthful they'd had, and I was equal parts happy and still terrified.

Happy because I knew that meant I was set for a while. Terrified because he'd still leave one day and then...Well.

"Tired?" Parker asked me, perched on a bar stool with a finger of whiskey in front of him.

I nodded twice and pushed off from the door. "I

have to count the tips. Hold on." I retrieved the mason jars with our names on from beneath the bar and set them on top of it.

"Want help?" Parker motioned to Sienna's jar.

I nodded again. "Take twenty percent when you're done. That's for Vicky."

"Vicky?"

Oh dear god. "The waitress. The person whose face you've seen fifty thousand times tonight."

"Oh." He took hold of the mason jar and tipped it upside down, scattering notes and coins across his immediate area of the bar. "I forgot her name. She became Food Girl after a while to us."

It took every ounce of my strength not to roll my eyes. Fucking Food Girl was the most ridiculous thing I'd heard in ages. "How did Wes do? I didn't get a chance to ask you earlier." I stacked twenty dollars in ones to the side.

"He did good. I'm surprised, not gonna lie. I thought he'd be a fucking mess, but he did great. No complaints, no issues, nothing."

"Good. Did he actually cook at all or did you monopolize that?"

"He took control of the calamari toward the end," he said, pushing some ones to the side. "Something little, but he's basically still in his workplace diapers. He took to it well. He makes a pretty mean batter."

"I've made a mean batter since I was fifteen. What's your point?"

"You were taught to cook by the same person I was. That's my point."

It was a relatively strong one, too. My mom was, hands down, the best cook in the world. She could cook any cuisine to perfection, and it wasn't that she'd been trained, because she hadn't. She'd recently discovered the brilliance of YouTube, and apparently, that was encouraging her to broaden her horizons.

I didn't know how much further hers could broaden

given that she was proficient in Greek, Mexican, Italian, French, and German cuisine, but whatever. It was her spare time, and as long as she still made me gyros when I asked for it, I was good with that.

"Fair enough, but Mom is crazy good in the kitchen. You can't hold everyone to her standard," I reasoned.

Parker caught my eye and said, "If she hadn't held me to her standard of cooking when I was a teenager, I'd be flipping burgers in a taco truck."

"Taco trucks don't flip burgers. And they make mean tacos, so watch your mouth."

"Isn't that cultural cheating?"

"Do you want me to throw this quarter in your mouth and choke you?"

He burst out laughing. "I think I'll pass, thanks. Here." He slid me a pile of notes and change. "That's twenty-percent of what Sienna took tonight."

I hesitated. It wasn't that I didn't trust him, but... "Are you sure?"

One by one, Parker counted out the notes from Sienna's pile, followed by the ones from Vicky's percentage. He nailed it, as close as he could get, and I tucked that money into an envelope along with the money from my tips to give to her tomorrow.

"Thank you." I sealed the envelope with a lick and scrawled her name on it. It went inside the register to keep it safe until I headed upstairs—then it'd come with me. I hated leaving any kind of money in the bar. Only one lock separated my apartment from the bar, but that one lock was just a little more safety in the path of anyone trying to do bad.

"Done." Sienna bounded back into the bar, her reddy-brown hair bouncing around her shoulders since she'd freed it from her braid. "Is there anything else that needs doing, or am I good to head home?"

"You're good to go. Thanks, See. Can you cover for Rosanne tomorrow? I'm gonna call her in the morning," I added before she could answer. "She's due to start at eight."

I declined to mention that my family would be here.

"I can. Just let me know by twelve, okay? I have my niece until six, so I need to make sure my sister or my mom can get her on time."

"No problem. I'll call her at nine and give you plenty of time." I smiled.

She returned it and glanced at Parker. She was almost shy as she tucked her hair behind her ear. "Are you leaving now?"

I leaned a little further forward and hit him with my gaze, too.

Yes, was he?

Was he leaving at the same time as Sienna?

Motherfucker—why did I even care? Aside from the fact I didn't like workplace relationships, it was none of my business what he did in his spare time as long as he didn't bring it into work.

But she was work.

Double motherfucker.

Parker held up his basically-untouched drink. "Soon as I'm done with this. You need me to walk you to your car?"

Sienna glanced at me. "It's pretty dark out."

No darker than fucking usual, is it?

I busied myself cleaning a glass and turned away. Not my circus or my monkeys or my elephants or my clowns. I didn't care what happened there and nor should I. As long as it didn't affect their work in any way, I couldn't care any less if they dated.

But...Could I stop them? I mean, this was my business. Technically, I probably could.

Damn it, I still didn't care. Why did I have even the barest reason to care? I loved Sienna and I loathed Parker.

Even if he was kinda really hot now.

Fuck it.

The door opened and closed and a stool scraped. "You've been cleaning that glass for five minutes."

I jerked back to attention at the sound of Parker's

voice. "It was really dirty," I said, barely glancing in his direction. "Awkward smudge."

"Right. Your bargirl just asked me out."

My throat burned with the harshness of my swallow. "Mhmm."

"Well, she didn't ask me out, per se." He paused.

I gave in.

I turned around and met his dark gaze.

"She asked me what I thought you'd think about her asking me out," he said slowly.

"Is this you asking me what I think about it?" I shot back, finally putting the glass down. "Because while, personally, I think she'd be better off dating a bag of rocks, professionally, I think it's an even worse idea."

Parker's deep chuckled elicited goosebumps across my skin. "I'm not gonna go out with her, Raven. I don't have to be Einstein to see how you feel about workplace relationships."

I snapped my gaze to his. "Sienna doesn't have relationships. She has short-term meetings."

"In that case..."

I felt my gaze darken before I could stop it.

He laughed again. "Calm down, hotshot. I met enough of her in New York. I'm not looking for that while I'm here."

"You weren't looking for this job, either," I pointed out.

"True." He sipped his Makers. The glass clinked against the wooden bar when he set it down.

I swept it up and slipped a paper coaster with the logo on beneath it. His amusement was evident in the upturn of his lips, but he didn't say anything as I wiped up the water mark from his glass.

"I don't think you can compare a job and...something personal. This job pretty much fell into my lap."

I raised my eyebrow at him. "I know Sienna, and if she falls in your lap, I hope your pants are on or that

77

someone can perform the Heimlich on the girl."

"That sounds like a back-handed compliment on the size of my dick."

Of course it was. That's exactly what he heard. Why wouldn't it have been?

"Yes, that's exactly what I meant to say." I rolled my eyes and opened the glass washer door before its beeping drove me crazy. Given my current tired mood, it wasn't going to be hard to annoy me.

Ignoring that I was already marginally annoyed for the dumbest reason—which just annoyed me further.

I was a mess.

"Still not interested in meaningless hook-ups." Parker finished the whiskey and slid the glass across the bar to me, making sure it was on the coaster.

I snatched it up. "I don't really care what you do. Where you put your cock is none of my business." Yanking the tray out of the washer, I stared at him out of the corner of my eye. "As long as it doesn't interfere with your job, shove it wherever you like."

His lips tugged up, a hint of smugness breaking through the genuine half-smile. "Was that an offer?"

"So help me, Parker, get your ass the hell out of my bar before I hit you."

He grabbed his stuff, laughing, and headed for the door. "See you tomorrow."

"Unfortunately." I yelled the word after him, and the second the door clicked shut, I scrambled from behind the bar to lock it.

One look around the quiet, empty bar, and I made an executive decision to grab the register and do the money upstairs tonight. It was late, I was tired, and as much as I didn't want to admit it, my stomach had twisted every single time Parker had mentioned his penis.

I wanted to throw up at the thought of him and Sienna together.

And I didn't want to think about the ramifications of

that at all.

Waking up after a dream about walking in on your gorgeous employee having sex with your brother's best friend wasn't something I'd advise.

Actually, I advise not having such a dream at all. It was disturbing and uncomfortable, and I didn't want to address the hard-hitting anger I'd felt when I'd woken up from it.

Even now, an hour later, I was still annoyed. I didn't know if it was a warning from my subconscious or some screwed-up dream designed to torture me and admit that I maybe had the slightest crush on Parker Hamilton.

As long as he kept his mouth shut and had a paper bag over his head.

It was unfair. My entire life I'd gotten by happily hating him, him happily hating me, and both of us co-existing in a state of basic avoidance, not even trying to ignore each other when forced together.

I liked that. It was easy. It had always been the status quo of our relationship—mainly, there wasn't one.

Then, this curveball happened. Now, I'm forced into spending more time with him than I'm truly comfortable with, and every time he switches that dumb little smile onto me, I'm not gonna lie, I get...tingly.

I'm a woman. I have needs. I also have feels, and these feels are fucked up.

Add in Sienna's obvious crush on the guy... I was between a rock and a hard place. Sadly, the rock wasn't a wall and the hard place wasn't Parker.

Wait.

What?

No. That's not what I meant. I meant a guy. Any guy. Any guy except him.

Dear god, I had to get out more. Or I just needed a break. A day off, even.

Something had to give if I was thinking about that.

My phone rang on the bar. Mom's name flashed on the screen, and my stomach sunk right through my feet and disappeared into the ground. It was earlier than I'd expected her to call.

"Hello?" I answered warily.

"Yia-Yia has decided she's cooking breakfast at the bar," came her response.

I choked on thin air. "She's doing what?"

"She's making everyone omelets at the bar."

She was doing what? "Why can't she do that in your kitchen? It's huge. Tell her to leave mine alone."

"No idea."

"Have you even attempted to talk her out of this?"

There was a rambling in Greek in the background, and Mom's next words were in Greek, too.

"Oh no," I said, instantly understanding. "You did not just tell her that I'd love to have her here?"

"The Karras' are in town. Every woman for herself." She hung up.

I pinched the bridge of my nose before dialing back. She answered on the first ring, and before she could say a word, I said, "It's not my kitchen! Technically, it's Parker's, and he's not here for another hour, so she's gonna have to wait."

Mom coughed, but its suddenness hinted that she was hiding a laugh. "You know if I tell her that she's going to march right next door, don't you?"

"Yes," I answered. "Like you said, it's every woman for herself."

It was my turn to hang up.

I was probably going to pay for that later, but there was nothing Parker could do or say to me that outweighed the potential backlash from Yia-Yia if she thought I didn't want her cooking omelets in my kitchen.

I didn't want her cooking omelets in my kitchen, but that wasn't the point. The woman was old, but that didn't mean she'd slowed down any. She was like a tiny, five-foot-three hurricane that would take down a building if you didn't give her what she wanted. Hence my mom's placation and my diversion.

I wrote down what needed to be filled in the fridges and went to the cellar. By the time I'd picked the stock and carried it back through, my phone was flashing with a notification. One peek at it showed three missed calls from Parker and one text message.

Damn. My grandma was on fire.

I set the crate on the floor and picked up the phone to read his message.

Parker: *I thought I hated you before, but this is a whole new level.*

I bit the inside of my cheek as I replied.

Me: *Good morning, sunshine.*

He was going to kill me.

My phone rang again. This time, it was his name on the screen, and it took me two rings to debate on whether or not to answer it.

I had to, so I tucked my lady balls in and swiped toward the green circle. "Good morning," I trilled.

"Good morning? What's fucking good about this?" His voice was low...husky...sleepy. Sexy. *Damn it.* "Your grandmother just woke me up with fifteen fucking rings of the goddamn doorbell. I barely had time to throw on sweats before she thumped on the damn door and then, when I finally got my half-asleep ass down there to answer it, she stared at me for a full sixty seconds before launching into a tirade in Greek."

"Was my mom there to translate?"

"No, she was not there to translate, and she didn't need to be." Something slammed. "When she was done in Greek, she started in English about how she didn't care if I was your chef because she was going to cook her omelets in that kitchen whether I liked it or not. Then, she kissed me on the damn cheek, said it was good to see me, and hobbled off back to your mom's!"

"At least she was nice at the end."

"Omelets? I have no idea what she's fucking talking about, Raven!"

"Ah, well, yes." I paused. "She wants to cook omelets in the kitchen."

"Pretty fucking clear on that part. Why did I need to know?"

"I might have informed my mother that it was technically your kitchen and that's why I couldn't give her permission."

He didn't reply.

"Parker?"

"Of course." More silence for a second. "You threw me under the big fat Greek bus, didn't you?"

"Survival of the fittest and all that." A nervous giggle escaped me.

"When I get there, I'm going to tell her what you did."

"And I'm going to tell her you're lying because I'd never do that to her."

"You don't want her cooking at the bar."

I fake-gasped. "How dare you suggest that?"

I was a dreadful person.

Parker chuckled, his ire seemingly relenting. "Ray, I can smell your bullshit from here. I'll be there in half an hour to supervise her, okay?"

A very undignified snort escaped me. "You want to supervise my grandmother? Do you like your life?"

Nobody shadowed Yia-Yia in the kitchen unless you

were under her instruction.

She was kind of a difficult person.

"Fine," he continued. "I'll hover."

"You hover and she's gonna remove your manhood," I warned him. "You know what she's like. Just get here before she does and make sure it's clean before she loses her ever-loving mind. I'll put the spare key under the mat outside the door so you can get in."

"Why? Where are you going? Don't fucking leave me with your batshit family."

"To shower," I said flatly. "I don't feel like running naked through the bar to let you in in case you get here before I'm done."

"I would be totally okay with that."

"Parker. Fuck off."

On that note, I hung up.

8

Parker

I was still chuckling to myself as I pulled up outside Dirty.

There were worse things in life you could see than Raven Archer naked. Not that I'd ever seen it—and I never would. As Ryan's sister, she always had been and always would be firmly off-limits.

Maybe if I kept telling myself that, I'd stop imagining her naked.

But messing with her was too damn fun. Last night, when she'd said about me sticking my cock anywhere I wanted, and I'd asked her if it was an offer, she'd blushed as she'd told me to get out.

She was too hot for her own fucking good, that woman. I wasn't going to beat around the damn bush. When she got pissed off, she was even hotter. It was the way her cheeks flushed and she pouted her full lips. The way her eyes, brighter than they had any right to be, glared at me with an ire that stoked the fire that burned only to annoy the shit out of her.

It was a disease, I'd swear.

But I'd found the line, and I wanted to toe it as much as possible. I wanted to see how much shit she'd take before she finally snapped and really lost it with me.

Maybe it was because I wanted her to break her own line—to go past the point of annoyance where she tells me to go away and tries to make me.

Maybe it was because ever since I'd come back and laid eyes on her, I'd been unable to shake her. I wanted to know how much it would take for my lips to wipe that glossy, red lipstick off hers. I wanted to know how hard I'd have to kiss her before she'd be whimpering in my mouth.

And that was a problem. I had no idea how to handle it. All I could do was chant "off-limits" inside my head before I did something stupid. I needed to remember that. She was the one person I couldn't have.

It made me want her more.

I had no place wanting her. She was so many different kinds of forbidden it wasn't even close to funny. My best friend's sister, my boss, the person I'd hated my whole life.

The only thing that would hold me back was the knowledge she hated me more than I did her.

If I kissed her, she'd probably remove my cock with her bare hands and then hit me with it.

That was just the kind of person she was.

I was a little scared of her, if I was honest. Even if I knew she had a softer, rarely-seen side, the fact remained that Raven Archer was a brutal, sharp-tongued vixen capable of building you up and tearing you down in the same sentence.

I got out of my car and headed for the bar. From what Alexandra had told me, they wouldn't be far behind me, and although I'd left the kitchen clean, I was smart enough to know that my kind of clean wasn't Aleta Karras' type of clean.

I retrieved the key from beneath the mat in front of

the door and let myself in. The lights were all on, and the door echoed around the open space when I closed it behind me. It was completely silent with Raven nowhere in sight, so I tucked the key into my pocket for safe keeping and headed for the kitchen.

It was just as silent in here. Checking the dishwasher was my first job, as well as glancing around the place just in case there was something I'd missed last night.

There was always something I'd missed.

"Shit fuck shit!" Raven burst through the doors, her wet hair bundled into a mess on top of her head.

"Good morning." I smirked over my shoulder as I opened the dishwasher.

"Ten minutes!" She tucked a wet bit of hair behind her ear. "Ten freaking minutes. Not to mention I have to call my supplier again because my invoice is wrong yet again which always takes half an hour and we don't even have the ingredients for omelets at least not the kind my grandmother makes and she's not coming alone they're all damn well coming except Ryan who managed to get out of this so why does it always fall to me?"

I blinked at her. "Now, take a deep breath, and start again."

Raven curled her fingers into a handgun motion and poked herself in her temple with her middle finger. "Boom," she muttered. "Gotta call the shitty supplier. No ingredients. Ryan got out of this."

"That's stressful. Yet, I notice you had time to do your make-up."

Those bright blue eyes of hers pierced into me. "Don't fuck with me today."

"Fucking hell, Raven. The second your family walk through the door, your grandmother will take over and nobody will notice if you go make a damn phone call. Your mom said they were getting ingredients on the way, and there's a meat and fish delivery coming in forty-five minutes."

She threw her arms up in the air and turned away.

"Of course there is! Let's add one more thing to the list!"

I got up and followed her out of the kitchen, stopping her by grabbing her shoulders from behind. "Did you have coffee yet?"

She took a deep breath. Her shoulders sagged on its release. "When do you think I've had time to have coffee?"

Slowly, I steered her toward the nearest seat and sat her down. "Let me make you coffee."

"I don't have—"

"Sit!"

She lowered herself back down into the chair at my sharp look. She wasn't the only one who could stop somebody in their tracks with one glance. I already knew that having her family in town was enough of a clusterfuck without Raven being out of control.

I smiled to myself as I turned on the coffee machine behind the bar. She was the quintessential control freak—everything had a plan, and every plan had its own time and place to be enacted. But, sometimes, just sometimes, that control flew out of the window when she reached a point that she no longer had fingers on which to count the things she *couldn't* control.

I'd almost forgotten that little gem.

While I wasn't entirely sure that giving her coffee was the best idea in this instance, I didn't have anything else to give her. Water wasn't going to do anything and it was too early for alcohol.

"Do you know how to make a mimosa?" Raven asked as if she were reading my mind.

"It's just champagne and orange juice," I replied slowly, tightening my grip on the coffee mug. "A child could make that."

A slow smile spread across her face. "So, make one."

"Are you sure that's a good idea?"

"No. I'm one hundred percent certain it's a dreadful idea, so that's exactly why it should happen. Good things come from bad decisions."

She was philosophical this morning.

"Uh...Okay." I, however, was a fucking idiot. "Where is the champagne and the orange juice?"

"Champagnes in the middle fridge, orange the furthest to the left."

I had to bend right down to get a good look in the fridges. Thankfully, I found both items without toppling over or causing myself some serious damage, so I was counting that as a win by the time I stood up, carton and bottle in hand.

"Champagne glasses above your head," she instructed, pointing to the wine and champagne glass rack above the bar.

I pulled down two glasses, then another two, and then more.

"Why so many?"

I swung my gaze from the glasses to her face. "Let's call it a lucky guess."

Her bright, red lips pursed before curling to one side. "In that case, you're gonna need a jug."

I laughed and grabbed one from beneath the bar. She joined me and reached for the champagne, prompting me to ask, "I thought I was doing it?"

She waved a hand as she peeled off the foil from around the cork. "You'll probably take a window out. I've seen your dad attempt to pop these things. He almost blinded the neighbor's dog once."

"The nearest dog is three houses down."

She briefly cut her gaze to me. "Exactly."

"Come on, I got this. I'm not an idiot. My dad is challenged." I took the bottle from her and positioned it to uncork it.

Her eyebrows shot up beneath her now-dry bangs, but she didn't say a word.

I slid my finger and thumb up the neck of the bottle to where the roughness of the cork was and pressed. It didn't budge, so I pressed down a little harder. Still, nothing happened.

A little harder again, and nothing.

Annoyance sparked within me. Why was it so fucking hard to pop a cork?

"You're holding it wrong." Raven folded her arms.

All that did was make her tits pop.

And all her tits popping did was make me look there.

Which was when my hand slipped, shoving the cork. It burst from the bottle with the force of a bullet, slammed into the wall an inch above the window, and bounced right back.

Raven moved quicker than I ever thought anyone could. She literally dodged the flying cork by all of an inch as it came firing back into the bar and bounced onto the floor.

For a moment, neither of us moved.

Then, she flew to the bar and kneeled down, pressing her hand against the wood.

"Goddamn it, Parker, you are so damn lucky that cork didn't break a window or dent the wood." She stood back up and took the bottle from me. "You open champagne like a savage."

"You wanted a mimosa when I was happy to make you coffee," I reminded her.

"I need the straight champagne to cope with this." She tilted the jug to a 45-degree angle and poured the champagne in it.

"Why don't you just tip it straight in?"

The withering look she gave me shrunk my balls. No fucking joke.

"The bubbles," she answered as if it were the simplest thing in the world. "Stops it fizzing over."

Right.

That was why *she* mixed the drinks and *I* cooked the food.

She emptied the last of the champagne into the glass and motioned for the orange juice. I didn't want to risk her wrath, and since we were already crunching time, I didn't want to be the one who was responsible for giving her mimosas, either.

I was already taking the wrap for the kitchen. She could take the wrap for the nine-a.m. alcohol.

No sooner had she emptied the juice into the jug and stirred it with a bright green, plastic cocktail stirrer than she was filling one glass with the mixture.

I stared as she lifted that glass to her lips, pursed them around the clear rim, and downed the thing in one.

My eyebrows shot up, but she didn't stop—and nor did her lipstick come off. She put her glass down perfectly clear and, with one hand firmly around the stem of it, poured out mimosas for every glass I'd set on the bar.

She did it much more smoothly than I ever could.

I was pretty sure not even condensation dripped onto the bar.

The second she put the jug down, like it was synced, the doors opened. Her mom lead the way, but her grandmother's turquoise maxi dress was the showstopper. I couldn't look away from the luminescent garment. It hung and flowed like it was the gown of a Greek Goddess herself.

Aleta Karras stepped into the bar with one smooth movement. She was barely across the threshold when I heard Raven's deep inhale. Dark eyes canvassed the entire space, lingering on me for the slightest moment, before sweeping across the rest of the room and ultimately onto Raven.

Her knuckles whitened with her grip on her glass.

I waited for the moment the stem snapped.

"Raven!" Aleta threw up her arms and hobbled across the bar toward her.

I was barely able to swipe the glass from Raven's hand before she was swept into a giant hug by her tiny grandmother. It was quite a sight to see, given that Raven had a good foot on her grandmother. The top of Aleta's head barely came to her shoulders, and if if weren't for Raven bending down just in time, it would have been a pretty uncomfortable situation to be in.

Alexandra headed straight for me and pointed to Raven's mimosa. "Please tell me that's got alcohol in it," she whispered.

I nodded and handed her a new glass from the bar.

Like Raven just did, she downed it in one. Then, she handed me the empty glass and picked up a new one.

"I feel better already." She blinked and smiled.

I glanced at where Raven was trying and failing to extract herself from her grandmother's grip. My lips pulled to the side at the sight of her unable to pull her away. Mostly because now, the rest of the Karras' had surrounded her, and it was the biggest group hug I'd ever seen. There were literally eleven people all surrounding her. The only part of her visible was her head because she got her height from her dad, so her mom's family were all shorter than her.

I set down Raven's glass and escaped to the kitchen before she was released. I knew that the moment she was, she'd be on my back, using me as a shield just to annoy me. I was getting the heck out of dodge before shit got crazy.

"I cannot believe you left me out there!" Raven hissed, slamming the kitchen door behind her. "Two hours, Parker! How could you leave me for two hours?"

I sealed the tub of hummus I was holding. "Your family. Your circus. Your monkeys."

"Damn it. I knew I should have put some small print in your contract."

Laughter escaped me as I put the hummus in the fridge. "They haven't been that bad."

Annoyance sparked in her eyes. "Haven't been that bad? Are you freaking kidding me? Are you high? They've been insufferable. My twenty-three-year-old cousin is married with a baby on the way in four months and asked me when I'm getting married because I'm so old now. I'm twenty-six!"

"It's a different culture," I said slowly, grabbing the things for a salad. "You know that."

"That doesn't mean it's okay for her to say that."

"When did she get married?"

"Three weeks ago."

"So, is she married despite being pregnant or because she's pregnant?"

Raven's jaw dropped, and it took her a moment to pick it back up. "I didn't even think of that. I'm so using that next time one of them ribs on me about being single."

I shook my head and chopped the lettuce. "They can't all be on your back about your life."

"Well, they don't have to be. Yia-Yia asked me for a Dirty Screw, my Uncle Christian asked me the potency of the Blue Balls, and Aunt Alexa asked me if the hot guy who had the mimosas would serve her a Pussy Pounder."

"That depends on your aunt."

She rolled her eyes. "She's fifty-two and once put her back out hanging up laundry. Calm your cock."

Again, I laughed at her. "I was just saying. I'll have to pass."

"Why? Are you discriminating against the older generation?"

"I didn't see her asking you if a gentleman of the older generation was dishing out Pussy Pounders."

"Touché," she muttered, pushing off the door. "I'm in hell fresher than a field full of spring flowers here. I can't handle this for two weeks. There's just no way. I'm over it already."

I felt like it was my turn to roll my eyes.

"First you, and now this. I'm ready to go for a swim with the sharks."

"That's mildly dramatic," I said, throwing diced tomatoes into a bowl. "Besides, last I heard, sharks don't eat bitch."

"I really hate you."

"I know. It makes my life much more amusing." I

flashed her a grin over my shoulder. "If you didn't hate me, you'd probably be fucking me."

"With a machete," she snapped. "I don't know what's worse. Being in here with your ego or out there with that crazy."

I'd found her new line.

"Be honest, Raven." I put down my knife and walked to her. "Are you telling me we wouldn't be fucking if we actually liked each other?"

Her eyes pierced mine, but the lightest flush crept up her cheeks. "I'd rather have sex with Satan than with you. Oh—wait. If I slept with you, I would be sleeping with Satan."

"That sounds like you're saying you'll fuck me anyway."

"Go outside, Parker. The heat in the kitchen is getting to you. I have better things to do than waste my time on a hate-fuck with someone like you."

I didn't know why, but I stepped closer to her.

I stepped right into her personal space, still holding eye contact, and ran my thumb down the sleek curve of her jaw. Her lips parted as she drew in a deep breath, and she raised her hand to where I was touching her.

Before she could pull my thumb away from her, I clasped her fingers in mine and murmured, "I'd hate-fuck the hell out of you on this counter, right here, right now, if I didn't think you'd alarm everyone with your screaming."

"Because you'd be coming onto me?" She batted my hand away and took a step back.

"No. Because I'd be fucking you and you'd know about it." I smirked and turned back to the salad.

Raven darted in front of me and jabbed her finger into my chest. "Talk to me like that again, and you're gonna find your balls inside that blender on the highest setting before I drown you in your own cock. I'm still your fucking boss. Are we clear, Parker Hamilton?"

I curled my hand around hers and dropped it. "As

clear as the fact you're wearing a white shirt and no bra. I'd go put one on before you head back out to your family."

She looked down at her chest and let out a whispered curse before turning away and slamming through the back kitchen door. The door bounced on the hinges a few times before finally settling against the frame. No sooner had it done that than Raven had shoved it back open, gripping it tightly, and met my eyes.

"You could have told me that three hours ago!" she snapped.

"Wasn't looking then!" I yelled as she spun and left again. Her frustrated scream reached me right before the door closed once and for all and cut it off.

I slammed the knife onto the board, just narrowly missing my finger.

What the fuck was I doing?

9

Raven

C razy grandmother.
Randy aunt.
Inquisitive uncle.
Sexy Parker.
No fucking bra.
Check, check, check, check, motherfucking *check*.

I was so over today. It had to have been the worst day of my entire goddamn life. Well, that was probably an exaggeration, but it was pretty close.

The worst part was when I'd gotten dressed this morning, I hadn't even *thought* about putting a bra on. There wasn't one on my bed when I'd gone back upstairs to put it on after Parker had pointed it out.

I couldn't believe I'd forgotten to put a bra on and nobody had told me. What the hell was wrong with the people in my life? Not that I was complaining, exactly. It was a Saturday morning, after all, but Parker had been all up in my business with some dirty words.

Dirty words and braless weren't exactly the dream team combination when you didn't want the speaker of said dirty words to know you thought he was hot or that you were affected by him in any kind of way. Any other time, perfect. They would have been besties. But not today. Not in my life. Not in the slightest.

I adjusted my now-present bra and headed to unlock the bar door. I'd seen people hanging around by the beach before I'd come downstairs, so although it was a little early, I wanted to put the sign outside and hopefully bring some customers in.

Thank god Wes was here. He'd saved me from having to have any more conversations with Parker. I didn't know what I was supposed to say to him after this morning. He'd actually told me he'd hate-fuck me on the kitchen counter right before stepping away like he'd asked me how my freaking day was going.

What did you say to someone after that?

Did I demand an apology? Maybe I should have—maybe I *should*. He was my employee and he had no right talking to me like that. But he was also my brother's best friend and, well, it was the closest thing I'd had to a decent offer in a while.

By a-while, I meant six months.

My sex life was so dry it made the Sahara look like a freaking ocean.

That didn't mean what he'd said to me was okay. Never mind that the prospect of it flashed through my mind for a moment. Clearly not wearing a bra had been impairing my judgment this morning.

Right now, I was just thankful I'd managed to convince my family to go somewhere else until dinner rolled around. I'm pretty sure Yia-Yia had said something about a nap on her way out, but I'd seen that woman nap, and if riding a horse bareback was the only place she could sleep, she'd do it. God only knew where they were or what hell they were unleashing upon Whiskey Key, but I didn't much care as long as they weren't unleashing it in Dirty.

I pushed open the door to the bar and reached back for the sign. The wooden feet dragging against the bar floor screeched like nails on a chalkboard, making me wince as the sharp sound danced across my skin. I shook it off as I grabbed the chalk pens and a damp cloth.

It was Saturday, and I felt like doing a special to counteract the hellish day I'd been having. It took me only minutes to decorate the board, complete with a drawing of a cocktail.

The door opened behind me.

"*"Buy one Dirty Screw, get one half-price!*"" Parker read over the top of my head. "Is this a bar or a brothel?"

"A murder site," I muttered, capping the orange pen and standing up. "It's quirky. That's the whole point. It makes you stop."

He pouted out his bottom lip before tilting his head to the side. "If I had to buy sex, I'd definitely be stopping to check out this offer."

I rolled my eyes. "Now you're just being annoying. Don't you have anything better to do? Like your job?"

"I can't think of anything better to do than piss you off, hotshot."

I looked at the board. I was going to ignore him. "Damn it, I should have said buy a Filthy Hooker and get a Dirty Screw for half-price."

Parker choked on a laugh. "What the fuck is a Filthy Hooker?"

"Jack Daniels, tequila, and coke."

"Do you put tequila in everything?"

"A good three-quarters of my drinks. I like tequila. It's kind of my thing."

"Your thing? Is that like big hair was an eighties thing and pot was a sixties thing?"

I raised an eyebrow. "Pretty sure pot is just a 'thing.' It didn't exactly go out of fashion the way neon leg warmers and over-crimped hair did."

"Fair point." He shoved his hands in his pockets and looked out over at the beach. "Is tonight going to be as wild as last night?"

I shook my head and gripped hold of the pens tightly. "No, we have the right number of staff tonight. Don't worry. You won't be dragged into being my bar bitch tonight."

He laughed. "It was pretty fun. I didn't know you could mix drinks that fast."

"Ah." I smiled and backed up to the door. "That's why I use tequila in everything."

"Lazy bartending."

"Do you want a Filthy Hooker?"

"Will I get the Dirty Screw?"

"No. The Dirty Screw offer is for Dirty Screws. You have to buy one of those first, but it'll cost you."

"How much."

"Like eight bucks. They're cheap."

His laughter followed me into the bar. I walked around the back as he pulled out a stool and spun it between his legs.

"All right," he said. "Get me a Filthy Hooker."

I reached for the cocktail shaker, then paused. "Do you want a Wet Filthy Hooker, or just a Filthy Hooker?"

His eyes flashed with amusement as those goddamn full lips tugged to one side in a smirk. "What's the difference?"

I held out my hands and waited.

"I might regret this. A Wet Filthy Hooker."

I grabbed a shot glass with one hand, lifting it to the optical on the Jack Daniels bottle, and picked up the tequila bottle with the other. I topped the JD with the tequila, added a dash of lemon juice and coke, and set the double-measure shot on the bar in front of him.

Parker picked up the glass with his finger and thumb. "Am I allowed to drink this on the job?"

"Can you handle your liquor?"

"Not as good as I can handle a woman, but well enough."

He was so fucking cock-sure of himself, it was almost too much. "Yeah, well down that and see if you can handle a Wet Filthy Hooker."

He met my eyes and held my gaze as he lifted the glass to his unfairly pink lips and threw back the shot. He'd barely swallowed it when he shuddered, and I grinned, sweeping the glass up.

"Motherfucker," he whispered, banging his chest. "That's strong."

"That's why she's a wet one." I couldn't wipe the smile off my face as Sienna walked in.

She glanced at us. "What did you give him?"

My smile widened.

"A Wet Filthy Hooker?" She shook her head. "How's he going to cook tonight?"

I held up my hands. "He insisted he could handle it. If he can't, Wes is up for a promotion."

"Shut up and get me water," Parker demanded. "You're not giving the kid my job, and you know it."

I pulled a glass off the shelf behind me. "You're the one who's drinking on the job."

"Doesn't count when your boss gives you the alcohol."

"Are you at work?"

"I'm on a break. Double doesn't count."

Setting the glass of water in front of him on the bar, I raised my eyebrows. "Someone could have a gun to your head and you'd talk your way out of them shooting you, wouldn't you?"

He flashed me a half-smile, picking up the water. "That's the closest thing to a compliment you've ever given me."

"Don't get used to it," Sienna said, smiling in Parker's direction in a way that was a little too friendly. Her gaze lingered a little too long even though he didn't turn to look at her.

"Si, I didn't get a chance to sort the delivery since my family showed up for breakfast this morning and it took forever to get rid of them." I gripped the edge of the bar and leaned into it. "Could you go out to the cellar and get it sorted for me?"

"Sure." She shrugged off her light cardigan, finally dragging her gaze away from Parker. "Do you need anything out here?"

A glance at the fridge told me I did. "Orange juice. Dirty Screws are on special so make sure it's easy to grab. When Katie gets here, she'll have to keep an eye on it."

She gave me a thumb up before she disappeared back to the cellar.

Seconds after she disappeared, Parker said, "You're pretty obvious, you know that?"

I swung my attention from the hall Sienna just walked down to him. "That doe-eyes at work aren't acceptable? I don't pay her to ogle you, Parker. I pay her to get shit done."

His lips twitched up to the side once again, and the stool scraped against the floor when he got up and kicked it back under the lip of the bar. "That may be so, but that's not what's obvious."

I gave him an "Oh, really?" look. "Then enlighten me as to what is."

He opened his mouth right as the bar door opened to a group of five women and two guys. "Breaks over." He smirked and pushed back into the kitchen.

I glared after him for a second before turning to my customers.

I'd be annoyed with him later.

For now, I had to work.

"Katie, I need shot glasses!" Sienna yelled a few feet

Mixed Up

away from me.

I didn't know when it'd gotten so busy, but it was only eight and the bar was packed. Granted, fifteen or so of those people were related to me, but I didn't know how they could stand it. I'd had to turn up the music when people started coming in and gravitating toward the dance floor. Hell, I'd had to have Wes come out since the kitchen was quieter just to move tables to free up the dance floor.

As Katie waved in acknowledgment while running another food order out to the kitchen, I wondered if I'd bitten off more than I could chew. The bar, the weekend club atmosphere, and now food. Was I doing too much? Dirty was a big bar, but was I trying to cram too much into it?

Or did I just need another member of staff? Katie was good. She was barely twenty-one, but she'd never missed a shift in the six months she'd been working with me. Since she had no qualifications as a mixologist, only Sienna and I really worked the bar, but that didn't mean she couldn't be taught. She'd shown interest.

I poured a jug of Dirty Screw and threw some extra orange slices into it.

Maybe I should give Katie more hours. There was no doubt how helpful it would be to have one more person around.

I'd also get a little time off.

"Your grandmother wants a Slick Lovestick."

I blinked and looked at my dad. "I'm starting to rethink the names of my cocktails."

His grimace said it all.

And there I was, thinking the names would have been too much for Yia-Yia. Apparently, she was embracing my list. She'd already had herself a Ball Buster and a Tit Toppler.

I didn't know she could hold her liquor as well as she could.

"What does she think of the food?" I asked Dad as I reached for the Chardonnay bottle.

"She thinks it's pretty damn good, not that she plans

on telling Parker that anytime soon."

I hid my smile. Yep. That sounded like Yia-Yia. She'd spend the next few days telling him how to make his food better, make him recook her the exact same dishes, then tell him they were just fine the first time—but who wants just fine?

I wanted to bet that he knew exactly what she was going to do and was going to humor her, but she didn't know that.

It was always fun to watch her torture someone other than me.

I topped the Slick Lovestick—named after a dare—with lemonade and handed my dad the glass. "Do you need anything?"

"A ride home." He took the glass and disappeared.

I laughed. I knew he was going to say that.

The next two hours passed in a blur of drinks, food, and orders on top of orders. There wasn't much to do except run back and forth constantly, including fulfilling my family's orders for what I was starting to think of as my inappropriately named cocktails.

Nobody wanted their slightly tipsy, fifty-something aunt asking for a pounding for her pussy. No matter how many times my uncle told her it was a Pussy Pounder and she had one, she insisted it was a pounding for her pussy.

She wasn't wrong. She just rearranged the words.

Aunt Alexa came to the bar, her arm through my mom's. "Thank you for pussy pounding," she slurred, grinning wildly. "You must share recipe."

"You got it, Aunt Alexa. I'll write it down for you."

"Now!" She threw her arm in the air, almost punching the guy next to her in the face. "Oh!" She turned and cupped his face and apologized in Greek.

My mom managed to pull her away in a flurry of apologies and a high-pitched scream that she planned to call me.

Oh, joy.

I, meanwhile, turned to the guy my aunt almost punched. "I'm so sorry. My aunt just got in from Greece yesterday, and I don't think jet lag and cocktails mix," I said, leaning forward slightly.

He laughed. "Don't worry about it. Can I get a Slutwhisperer for my friend's girlfriend?"

"Sure. Normal or sexy?"

"I'm sorry?"

I bit the inside of my cheek. "A Sexy Slutwhisperer has vodka as well."

"Oh." He looked over his shoulder but apparently not finding his friend, shrugged. "Make it a sexy one. I'm sure my friend won't complain."

"Sure." I grabbed a shaker.

"Are you still serving food?"

"Sorry, the kitchen closed an hour ago. There are some great little places around here, though." I talked through mixing.

"It's all good. I heard you were looking for kitchen staff. Is the owner around?"

"You're speaking to her." I flashed a small over my shoulder.

He laughed. "Well, that was easier than I thought. Are you still hiring?"

I held up two fingers as I blended the raspberries and threw in the other ingredients. I grabbed a tall glass and scooped ice into it before answering. "I think we're actually good right now, but I know the two guys my chef hired are on a trial, so there's always a chance. Twelve-fifty, please."

He handed over fifteen dollars. "Keep the rest. Can I leave my name and number with you in case a position opens up? I'm staying in Key West with family, so I'll be around all summer."

"You can leave it with me." Parker stepped up beside me and held his hand out to the guy. "Parker Hamilton, executive chef. Raven, do you have a pen and paper?"

I hit the button on the register for some plain receipt

paper and handed it to him with a pen. "There you go."

"Thanks." He winked at me and put the stuff down in front of the unnamed—yet cute—guy. "Write down your details and I'll get in touch."

I side-eyed him. Why would he be in touch? Was there a problem with one of the guys in the kitchen?

Parker and the guy exchanged a few more words before the guy grabbed the drink he'd ordered and held a hand up to me in goodbye. I smiled and returned the gesture, then immediately gave Parker my attention.

"Don't go anywhere," I told him. I walked down the bar and grabbed Sienna. "Are you good for five minutes?"

She nodded, a shaker in each hand. "It's quieter. Everything all right?"

"Fine and fucking dandy," I answered, leaving her staring after me with her eyebrows shooting up. "You," I said to Parker. "With me." I didn't wait before I stormed into the kitchen and caught a shocked Wes's eye. "You're good to go, Wes, thanks."

He nodded and headed out to the bar. He'd changed and had his stuff nearby, so he met Parker on the way through.

"What," I said the moment the door shut, "Was that?"

He folded his arms across his chest. "That was me taking details for a section I hire."

"And he couldn't give me his details because?"

"Because he was making an obvious play to give you his number."

My eyebrows shot up. "And you know this how?"

"Because it's the oldest trick in the fucking book. Give your number to the hot girl behind the bar and hope she calls it and invites you for a job interview," he said, his tone flat. "Pretty sure I made that up before I'd even fucking graduated."

"Why does it matter to you if he gives me his number? Did you consider I might have wanted it?"

He stops with his mouth open. If he had a response, he changed his mind about saying it. Instead, he stared me down. He locked his gaze onto mine and holds it, the intensity of his dark eyes too much to keep looking at, yet too compelling to turn away from.

We stayed like this, a silent battle of wills, for a good minute. Neither of us moved or spoke, almost as if time had frozen, suspending us in it. There were plenty of places to move to, but no room to go. I was locked entirely on him, held in his space by nothing more than one stare I couldn't help meeting.

"You want his number?" Parker's voice was low, yet it sliced through the silence as if it were a scream. "Here."

My heart skipped as he closed the distance between us in a few long strides. He stopped only inches away from me and held the small, torn-off sheet out for me.

I didn't want the guy's number.

But I took it anyway. Just to make a point.

His eyes searched mine with the closer distance, and I couldn't help but notice the amber flecks that speckled the dark brown of his irises. They glinted gold when the light caught them right, and momentarily, I was struck by how handsome he actually was. Not only was the color of his eyes mesmerizing, they were surrounded by thick, dark eyelashes I'd give my left ovary for. Even the mole just below his right eye, in the corner, added to the perfection when it had no right to.

My heart didn't just skip. It sprinted, beating wildly against my ribs, trying to outrun itself even though there was nowhere to go.

I wanted Parker Hamilton.

I wanted him to kiss me just so I could see if his lips were as soft as they looked.

I wanted him to fist the back of my hair just to know if his grip on it would be as firm as it was when he held a knife.

I wanted him to sit me on the edge of the goddamn

counter to see if he'd keep his word.

And it was wrong. It was so, so wrong.

"I can tell you all about him," Parker said, his voice still low. "Call him, Raven."

I hated the way my name rolled off his tongue.

"He'll fuck you to get a job. Then he'll tell you he doesn't mix work with pleasure."

I hated the way he said pleasure, with a low inflection at the end.

"And when he's bored, he'll move on until something challenges him."

I hated the smugness that tinted every word he said.

"The woman or the kitchen—it doesn't matter. He's not a career chef. If he were, he wouldn't be buying drinks for his girlfriend and chatting you up at the same time."

"His friend's girlfriend," I finally said, clearing my throat.

"I watched him walk to the bar. He was alone at a table with a girl who, seconds before, had kissed him."

Shit. He had me there.

His lips curved into a smug little smirk I wanted to pluck right off his face.

"Don't ever undermine my authority again," I said, my voice matching his. "You won't like what happens when you do."

Parker took my chin in his hand, his thumb brushing the underside of my lower lip. "The next time I undermine your authority, you'll be on your goddamn knees in front of me with my hand print on your ass."

"Over my dead body."

"That can be arranged."

I smacked his hand away from me and forced myself not to look at his mouth. I couldn't—I wouldn't. "Get yourself the fuck out of here before I listen to the voice telling me to fire your ass for overstepping the line again."

His hand fell to his side, and I didn't know what I expected, but it wasn't what he said next. "If I didn't respect your brother so much, you'd have a fucking good reason to fire me."

"What the hell does that mean?"

"It means that your brother is the only reason you're not against that wall with your legs wrapped around my fucking waist."

The words were a warning.

A threat.

Maybe even a promise.

"Try it," I bluffed despite the shiver that tickled my spine. "See what happens if you do."

He grabbed my wrist and pushed me to the wall right next to us. One hand fisted as he rested his knuckles on the wall near my hip, and the other flattened just above my head. He wasn't touching me, but his breath fanned across my lips, making it seem as if he was.

I held his gaze. I wanted to look away, to stop this from happening, but I couldn't. I refused to back down from whatever the hell this was. I didn't know if his heart was beating anywhere near as fast as mine or if his stomach was flipping the same way mine was, but I could see what I wanted to see in the twitch of his jaw.

He was barely holding onto his self-control.

It was hanging by a thread, and one more word would snap it.

One more word, and it wouldn't matter how much he respected my brother.

He'd kiss me anyway.

I didn't give him the word.

He didn't say it either.

He pushed off the wall, away from me, and stormed away without another word.

Heaviness lingered as I watched him go. A heaviness I didn't want to feel. One I had no right to feel.

It was because of the situation. That was what I was going to tell myself. It wasn't because his mouth had been inches from mine. No way.

I took a deep breath and headed back for the bar. Getting out there was the only thing I could do. It was busy enough that it would keep my mind off whatever the hell had just happened.

The noise and busyness of the bar hit me like a freight train. It was almost as if being inside the kitchen had been like another world. An alternate universe, actually.

"Raven?" Sienna asked, catching my eye. "You good?"

With a firm nod, I headed back to work.

10
Parker

The morning came like the bright, cheery bitch that summer in Florida was. Not that summer in New York wasn't great, but Florida had it beat. Except the afternoon storms, which were ironically more welcome than a nuisance. If you were unlucky enough to be out in the humidity all day long, that was.

I'd barely been back here for a week, yet so much had happened.

Loss of my sanity had happened. Inability to think rationally had happened.

Raven Archer had happened.

And she had me fucked up.

She wasn't what I'd expected when I'd come home. I knew that now more than ever. She was so much stronger and controlled than I remembered, and the girl I was once able to walk over, I could barely push back a step. She had a bite that matched her bark. Maybe it even surpassed it. I wasn't sure I'd felt the full force of what she had to give just yet. Whether she was saving it for a rainy day or I hadn't pushed her to that yet, I didn't know.

But, I'd seen it in her eyes when I'd pinned her to the wall. I'd seen the fire that burned in their depths, and I could still feel its heat.

When Raven Archer snapped, she was going to burn the world down with her. And it would be all my fault.

I needed to stop. I'd already gone too far. I'd already gone beyond my own line of what was right.

If I was honest, none of it was fucking right. It was childish, especially for a man who was almost thirty. There was something about her, though, and now, I knew was it was.

Temptation.

I couldn't have her, so I wanted her more. More than I'd ever wanted anyone. It was clichéd to fuck, but I didn't care. Something about the way she looked at me when she got annoyed sparked something deep inside me.

The fuckboy's number from the bar? Bullshit. I made it all up—except the girlfriend part. He had a girlfriend alright, and while I didn't believe for a second Raven wanted his number for anything more than business purposes, I didn't want her having his number at all.

Of course, it'd backfired.

She'd called me on it, and I'd had no choice but to hand it over.

I didn't know why that pissed me off so much. I had no claim to her, no matter how tempted I was. I could tell myself it was because she was Ryan's sister, but there was only so long I could use that excuse. There was only so long I could tell myself that before I wasted my own damn time.

It was because I wanted her.

I wanted her.

I couldn't have her.

Problem was, I didn't want anyone else to have her, either.

I was selfish, and I didn't give a fuck. The more time I spent with her, the stronger I felt about her. I still didn't even fucking like her. I tolerated her at best, but now, disliking her was less about her being *her*, and more about myself.

I disliked her because resisting her was impossible. Because I was getting weaker. Because I was so fucking close to giving in and tasting her.

I couldn't.

But soon, I would. I knew I would.

And there wouldn't be a damn thing I could do to stop myself.

I blinked at the sight before me. "What are you doing?"

Raven dragged her eyes from the instructions she was holding and met my gaze. "Building."

"What is it?" I scanned the pieces that were strewn across the back area. "And why are you doing it yourself?"

"A pool table. Uff!" She pulled something that resembled a leg and looked like it weighed a ton toward her. "And I'm doing it myself because I'm an independent woman."

I folded my arms and leaned against the wall. "Your dad is busy and Ryan wouldn't help."

A heavy sigh escaped her red lips. Did she ever take that lipstick off?

"My dad is fishing and my brother is an asshole," she said after a moment. "This thing is really heavy, but I have to build it, because I don't have anywhere to store it."

"How long have you been sitting here?"

She clicked her tongue, followed by a shrug.

"Raven."

"Two hours," she muttered, picking up the tiny bag with some screws in.

"Two hours?" Laughter bubbled inside me. "You've been sitting in the middle of this for two hours?"

"Not right here." Her gaze flitted to two other spots where, amongst the crazy, the floor was suspiciously empty. "I also had to go fix my nails, because I broke one."

I glanced at the hand she held up. I had no idea what her nails were supposed to look like, so I had no comment. "Why didn't you call for help?"

"Because I try to spend as little time with you as possible."

"And you were too proud."

"That may have been a contributing factor."

I shook my head and pushed off the wall. "So, this was your answer? Sit on the floor for two hours staring aimlessly at an unbuilt pool table? Wow, I hope you've had fun."

She flicked her eyes up to mine sharply. "Don't mess with me. My ass is sore."

"Good. Serves you right for sitting here like an idiot all day." I joined her on the floor and whipped the instructions off her lap. The tiny, bright orange shorts she was wearing were just that—tiny. Which meant I could see the lacy edge of her underwear. "Shut your legs."

Raven looked down at herself and, with a squeak, uncross her legs. She leaned to the side and tucked her feet beneath her ass, dropping the screws in the process. "This is awkward."

"Speak for yourself." Getting a glimpse of her bright, red panties wasn't exactly the way I wanted to start today's work day. I had to hold the instructions in such a way that she couldn't see my cock hardening in my pants.

My cock was such a fucking traitor.

"The hardest thing about this is how heavy it is," I told her, looking intently at the instructions. "How did you expect to lift this table when you were by yourself?"

"I was going to make it on its side. Then it'd be halfway there."

Mixed Up

I looked at her before I could stop myself. "You'd probably break your back."

"Why? I'm quite strong."

"I'm not saying you're not." I'd seen her lift some pretty heavy crates full of bottles without breaking a sweat, after all. "But this is a two-man job, Raven. Like it says on the top of the instructions."

She squinted, leaning forward. "That'll be why I struggled to put a leg on the top, then."

"You think?" I asked dryly. "Do you want my help?"

"Are you gonna go all "Me man, me strong" on me?"

"Depends how "me woman, me weak" you go on me."

"Well played." She tucked her hair behind her ear. "Fine."

"I didn't hear you ask."

"Now who's ridiculous?"

I raised my eyebrows. "Ask me nicely and I'll help you."

She narrowed her eyes at me. "I'd rather break my back right now."

"All right, then." I dropped the instructions and stood up. "I'm sure your customers looking for a nice Sunday cocktail will enjoy seeing this mess when you open in six hours."

She bit down on the inside of her cheek. "You offered your help. Why do I have to ask?"

My lips quirked up to one side. "Because I'm going to enjoy your discomfort more than you know."

She blinked at me for a second. Then, she swung her legs around and crossed them.

I didn't mean to look, but my eyes had other ideas.

Once again, the soft fabric of her shorts meant her underwear was on show. Something about the bright red lace that seemed to match her lips and nails perfectly set me on edge, and it took only seconds for the stirring of desire to come to life. My blood rushed to my cock, and before I could turn to adjust my pants, Raven glanced at my rapidly-hardening cock.

The tiniest of smirks curled her lips, and when her eyes met mine, there was nothing but smug satisfaction glinting back at me.

Discomfort.

She was playing me at my own fucking game. Because now, even if she changed, every time I looked at her today, I'd be thinking about her underwear. And something told me she damn well knew it.

Shit, she wasn't playing me at my own game. She was playing me by her own damn rules.

Raven Archer would be the death of me.

"Shut your legs, or the next time you open them, you won't be wearing a goddamn thing." My voice was steady but low, and there was no threat in it. It was a promise, pure and simple.

I could play by her rules, too. If it was good enough for her, it was good enough for me. Except I would follow through on my words.

She waited a moment, clearly in defiance, before she closed her legs. "Now you're in discomfort," she said through her smile, "Will you please help me build the pool table?"

"Can I bend you over it after?"

"Only if you want to be punched in the face."

"We'll see." I sat back down. Fuck, it was uncomfortable. My cock pushed right against my zipper, and a grimace crossed my face as I not-so-discreetly tried to push it out of the way of the zipper.

Raven glanced down—three times—before looking away quite obviously. If I was bad at hiding my erection, she was bad at ignoring it.

That didn't make it any damn easier.

"Let's get this shit over with," I muttered, holding my hand out for the screws.

***

"Wait, wait, wait!" Raven flapped her hands. "I can set them up!"

"I've been waiting for five minutes." I rubbed my fingertips across my forehead. "Just use the fucking picture, would you? I still have prep to do."

"I know, I know." She picked up the ball nearest to her with her finger and thumb. "I told you, we'd have a quick game. I'm pretty bad at this, so you'll beat me in minutes."

"Assuming you ever get the balls in the triangle to actually pot anything."

She slammed her hands against the side of the table and glared at me. "If you'd be quiet, I'd be able to concentrate."

"And if you used the picture, you'd be done already."

She dropped her head back with a groan. "Fine, give me the damn picture."

I slapped it down in front of her and walked to the other end of the table. She'd gotten changed from what she'd called her "slob" clothes into something more appropriate for work.

Appropriate was a relative term. Truly a matter of opinion. I didn't believe the skin-tight, scarlet skirt she was wearing was at all appropriate. Not because it was only a few inches long, but because it hugged her ass so unfairly well that I was glad the pool table hid my boner.

For the most part, at least.

Untucking my shirt was doing the rest of the work—except I was damn hot. The table had weighed a ton, and Raven hadn't really been much help at all. She guided it more than she lifted it.

Just like she'd supervised as I'd built it.

"There." She whipped the triangle off the table with a flourish. As she bent to put it inside the little hole in the table, her white blouse gaped, offering me a generous view of her cleavage.

I rubbed my hand down my face.

Was this my punishment for ignoring my mother's attempts to drag me to church this morning? Because it sure as fuck felt like it.

Raven's hand curled around the top of the cue. She used a chalk cube on the tip of it as she asked, "Am I breaking?"

"The pool balls or my balls?"

"The pool balls. I don't care about yours."

I did. Unfortunately. "Yes. You're breaking."

"The pool balls or your balls?" She smirked as she came up next to me, the white ball in the palm of her hand.

I swallowed and looked down at her. Her eyelashes were darkened with a coat of mascara, and that only made the blueness of her irises seem as though they were ten times brighter.

"Both," I answered, my throat dry.

"Excellent." The happy inflection as well as the way she slid her hands down the pool cue simultaneously pissed me off and made my cock twitch.

She bent forward, getting into position to break. Stepping back, I realized instantly that it was a mistake. The hem of her skirt was now perilously close to the curve of her ass cheeks, and it was only thanks to the shadow that fell across her skin that I couldn't see if she was still wearing those goddamn red, lacy panties.

I was fucking imagining it though, wasn't I? It didn't help that I could see a thick string raising the fabric of her skirt. Or maybe the fabric of her skirt was pressing down on her underwear. All I knew was that red panties or no, if her skirt rode up anymore, I'd be seeing more than just her underwear.

The small pop of the cue knocking into the white ball was overshadowed the moment the white hit the pack. That click was loud, filling the air as balls bounced off each other into the cushions at the sides.

Each time the balls hit each other, it sounded exactly the same as a smacked ass.

I had issues. Major issues.

Raven straightened. "Huh. That was better than I thought."

I blinked, dragging my eyes from her ass to the table. "Yeah. It was good."

"Are you gonna take your shot?"

Cum shot?

Fuuuuck. Why was everything dirty to me today?

Oh yeah. I'd seen goddamn lacy panties and she was wearing a skirt that should be rolled up over her hips so she could get a good fucking.

"I have a shit ton of work to do," I said slowly, putting the cue down on the table. "And you should really be encouraging that."

And if I have to stay here, I'm gonna stare at her ass, and I'm gonna do something to get myself fired.

Plus: Ryan. Ryan's sister. Ryan's *little* sister.

Raven sighed like me wanting to do my job was a hardship for her. "Fine. But I was looking forward to this, so now you owe me a game."

"Yeah, yeah." I turned and walked in the direction of the kitchen. "Wear fucking sweatpants next time, wouldja?"

Her laughter followed me even after I'd yanked the door shut behind me.

I knew better than anyone she'd had fantasies about torturing me—except those were violent ones.

Right now, the violent methods were definitely preferable to the literal case of blue balls I was developing.

11

"I'm telling you," Camille said, perching on the edge of the pool table to take her shot. "The guy wants to fuck you."

I put my hand on my hip and rolled my eyes. "He's a guy and I happen to be wearing a tight skirt. It's just a...thing. We spent half the afternoon fighting."

"Sounds like he spent half the afternoon fighting with whether or not he should do the dirty with you," Lani put in, typing on her laptop. She didn't even look up from the screen. "And it sounds like you spent the other half perving on his cock."

"I couldn't not!" I covered my hand with my mouth at the admission. Damn it. I wasn't going to say that out loud.

Why did it have to be quiet? And why did I call them to come hang out because Sienna had the bar covered?

Camille grinned. "Spill it."

I pursed my lips as I took my shot. My ball bounced

off the corner into the pocket. "Why do you care about it?"

"Because if you still don't want him, I'm still up for taking him off your hands."

"Xavier," Lani reminded her. "*Xavier.*"

She waved her hand in response. "He sleeps with other people, so can I."

"You're not going to take him off my hands," I said, hitting my ball. "He's not on my hands in the first place."

"Doesn't sound as though he'd complain too much about being *in* your hands." Lani smirked, still not looking up from her screen.

"Lani Montana, I will beat you unconscious with this pool cue if you don't stop that."

"No, you won't. Then you won't get to read what I'm writing about your bar."

"You're not supposed to be working!" Camille tapped the side of Lani's leg with the edge of her pool cue. "Raven's in a crisis!"

Shit me, she was a walking soap opera. "I'm not in a crisis!"

"Methinks the lady doth protest too much."

"Methinks the lady wants to be beaten to her death."

"Methinks the lady loves the other lady too much to do such a thing."

If only she were wrong.

"Do you think he's your person?" Lani finally peered up at me.

"The person to put me in a jail cell for murder? Probably." I picked up my drink. "I've come close a few times in the last week. Tomorrow he might push me over the edge."

The edge of what, I wasn't sure. Anger? Annoyance? Sexual frustration? Temptation? It was all relative at this point. Either one of them could be the first to go if he pushed the right button...Or the wrong one.

I wanted to punch him as much as I wanted to kiss him. I just didn't know which one would be more satisfying.

"You need to be pushed over the edge," Lani said, her attention back on the laptop screen.

"Of an orgasm." Camille snorted and filled up our glasses from the jug on the side. "What you need, my friend, is a break."

I wished. "Where do you expect I get myself one of those? The closest thing I've had to a break in three months is a Kit-Kat."

"Have one right now." Lani closed the computer and set it down next to her. "Why not? It's quiet and Sienna can handle it. Why don't we get Parker to make us some food to go and we go eat down at the beach?"

That did sound good. And they were right—I did need a break. The last week had been crazy on top of crazy, and I really needed to get out of the bar for a while. Not to mention a breather before Yia-Yia showed up tomorrow to finalize her menu for this goddamn reunion...

"Fine. He has to-go boxes. I'm gonna go make us all a Dirty Screw each, so tell him I want a gyros with extra gyros meat and tzatziki sauce." I put all the balls back into the pockets and grabbed the cue from Camille.

"Thank god," she muttered. "I'm shit at that."

No kidding. She hadn't potted a thing except the white. She was very good at potting the white.

I headed out to the bar while they got their things together and poked their heads in the kitchen. There was barely anyone in the bar, which wasn't a surprise for a Sunday, even in the summer. Mostly everyone was recovering from the night before and doing family stuff. I told Sienna where I was going and reminded her to call if it got busier. By the time I was done mixing our drinks, the girls emerged from the kitchen with some take-out boxes, so I put our drinks into some tumblers with the bar's logo with "This is definitely vodka" written on them.

That drew some chuckles. There was definitely vodka inside those tumblers. That was why I liked them.

I waved goodbye to Sienna and we made our way

down to the beach.

The soft sand shifted as I sunk my toes into it. It was mostly golden, but tiny flecks of both darker and lighter grains reflected through it, stealing my attention as they all flowed together, moving to make way for my feet.

Our finished take-out containers were dumped in a pile to our side, and Lani had been keeping an eye on a seagull that ventured too close, clapping her hands and screeching at it every now and then.

This was a 'now.'

"You know that egg in *Harry Potter*? The one with the clue?" I said, staring at her. "You sound like that when it's opened outside of water."

She turned her head around and met my eyes. "It's keeping the seagull away."

"Or you could get the boxes and put them in the trash," Camille drawled.

She was right. We were only feet away from the sidewalk, which meant in less than two minutes, we'd be able to get rid of the trash and sit back down.

"Give them here." I stood and held out my hands.

Lani passed them up to me, and I tucked them against my body with a careful glance in the direction of the seagull. I wasn't interested in losing my hand to a seagull just because it decided it was hungry.

Thankfully, I managed to get rid of the boxes without any harm coming to me from the seagull, although he did turn his attention to the trashcan as I joined the girls again.

"So," Lani started. "Parker."

I blinked and looked out at the Dalmatian playing in the water.

"Yes. Parker," Camille continued.

The Dalmatian jumped to avoid some light spray

from a wave.

"Oh, good, she's ignoring us."

The echoes of a few barks traveled up the sea breeze to where we were sitting.

"You'd think she'd know better by now," Lani mused.

"We're like dogs with a bone," Camille agreed.

"What are you doing?" Brett's—strangely welcome—voice carried over their going on. "Who's ignoring who?"

"Raven's ignoring us because we want to know about Parker," Lani explained.

He snorted. "Smart chick."

I smirked as I glanced his way.

"Watch it," Lani warned him.

"But of course she should listen to you, kitten," he said, surprisingly without an inch of sarcasm. He sat next to her and draped his arm over her shoulder. "You speak total sense all the time."

Lani cleared her throat. She wasn't buying it.

I leaned forward with a grimace. "You almost had it believable. You should have stopped before you sat down."

"Damn it. Overcompensation," he muttered, shaking his head. "Do I get points for trying?"

I nodded while Lani and Camille shook their heads.

Outnumbered. He was always outnumbered with these two.

"Really," he drawled. "This from the two bugging her about something she clearly doesn't want to talk about?"

"Suck up," Camille said under her breath.

He flipped his twin sister the bird.

"It's been ever since they got here," I told him. "Yet if I bring up Xavier or you and they don't want to talk about it, crickets would probably lay eggs in my pillowcase and chirp all damn night."

"That's because he and I are assholes," Brett answered.

"You assume Parker isn't."

"Assume Parker isn't what?"

I turned and looked back as the voice of the subject of far too many of my thoughts and conversations traveled through the air. He'd changed out of what he'd been wearing all day into some brown chino shorts and a white polo shirt that fit his muscular upper body a little too comfortably. Forcing myself to look away from his arms and up to his face, I wrinkled my nose and said, "An asshole. Brett's assuming you're not an asshole. Incorrectly, I might add."

"Dunno," Lani said. "Brett is the authority on assholes."

"On being an asshole," he quickly corrected her. "Not assholes in general."

I bit the inside of my cheek to stop a giggle escaping. Of course, he'd notice her wording on that.

Parker held up his hands which did absolutely nothing to distract me from the vein that curved down the inside of his left bicep, disappearing briefly before snaking down his inner forearm. "I'm only an asshole to people who make a point of being an asshole to me." His dark gaze landed on me as a flash of amusement crossed his expression.

"Yeah, right, I started it," I snapped back at it. "Who pulled the head off my favorite Barbie and flushed it when I was three?"

"You're the one who kicked a ball into my guinea pig."

"*Accidentally*. I was aiming for your fat head."

"You had a shit aim."

"Yeah, well, your ego was a lot smaller than it is now."

"You're right." He grinned. "Now, it'd probably bounce right off it without touching me. You'd need someone to hit you in the ass for you not to feel anything."

"I wish someone would hit you in the ass. With a bullet." I turned around, sticking my middle finger up over my shoulder.

Annoyance tickled down my spine. I didn't give a shit

that he'd basically called my ass fat—he'd been saying that since I hit puberty. I was annoyed because once again, I'd fully risen to the bait and given him the satisfaction of knowing he'd pushed my buttons.

"See?" Lani whispered not-so-quietly to Brett. "Real hatred or sexual tension hatred? We can't decide."

"The most sexual thing about our relationship is the pleasure I'll get when someone finally rams their fist in his face," I ground out. Then, to the tune of Brett's attempt to cough over his laughter, I spun back to look at Parker. "Aren't you supposed to be working?"

He shrugged. "Technically, but since nobody has ordered food in over an hour, I closed the kitchen."

"And you didn't think to ask me if you could do that?"

"Contract says I can do that since I run it. Would you prefer I asked you for permission?"

"I'd prefer to be informed," I said sharply.

"All right." He stuffed his hands in his pockets. "Raven, it's been over an hour since anyone ordered food and it doesn't look like it's getting busier, so I closed the kitchen."

"It's a miracle you've made it this long without someone breaking your nose."

"It's a miracle nobody has suffocated you with a sock to shut you up."

"No wonder my brother is still single. His taste in the people he surrounds himself with is shit."

"At least his taste is the problem. Your personality is yours."

"Definitely sexual," Camille butted in. "No doubt about it. I'm starting to get jealous."

A breathy 'ugh' sound escaped me as I once again righted myself to look out to the water. "Give me a break."

"We tried," Lani reasoned quietly. "Then the testosterone arrived."

"I don't do well with walking cocks," I said, grabbing

my tumbler and putting my straw in my mouth. I knew there was a reason I'd been drinking this slowly.

All right, so part of it was because I'd have to go back to the bar to get another drink, but whatever.

"I have a question," Brett said after a moment of mutual silence from us all. "He's your brother's best friend, right?" He looked at me. "How have you not killed each other?"

"We're generally kept apart, so this new arrangement is very...testing," I answered. "The hatred is almost biological."

"It's the Karras blood," Parker added. "It's more prevalent in the women than it is in Ryan."

"So help me, Parker Hamilton, or I will unleash the full extent of that blood on you," I warned him.

Brett glanced at me. "You're Greek?"

"No, I'm from Russia."

"That explains the temper." He slowly nodded.

I wasn't going to dignify that with a response. It was quite simple. If you pissed me off, you saw my temper. The solution was to not piss me off. So, really, the fact that the I was sometimes...hot-headed...had nothing to do with it. *Other people* being idiots had *everything* to do with the fact I had a bit of a hot temper.

"I feel like so much of the past two years make sense now," Brett continued.

I pinned him with a hard stare.

"I'm gonna take him home before he keeps talking himself into his hole." Lani jumped up and brushed sand off her butt. "Will Sienna give me the key to grab my laptop?"

I nodded as Camille and Brett both stood. "Keep the tumblers. I have tons."

I wasn't going to attempt to move. Parker had come out here for more than just to tell me that he'd closed the kitchen. If that was it, he would have had Sienna call me or he'd have left by now.

I waved goodbye to my friends and stretched my legs

out right in front of me. I'd changed again before calling the girls, so I brushed some sand off the frayed edges of my denim shorts before leaning back onto my hands.

Parker sat down next to me and set his shoes on the sand next to him. "Do you ever think we should stop this childish fighting and be nice to each other?"

"All the time," I answered honestly. "Then you open your mouth and I forget why."

He peered sideways at me, a lopsided grin on his face. "Now it makes sense. The same thing happens when you talk."

I couldn't help but meet his slim gaze and smile back. I even laughed a little. It was the truth. I'd told myself so many times that we needed to be civil to each other since we worked together, at least while we were in work, but it was impossible.

It was a reflex. The childish banter and quick witted bullshit was nothing more than a reflex. It had been our relationship for so long, that despite the fact we hadn't seen each other for three years, it was all too easy to slip back into the status quo we'd maintained prior to him leaving.

It was just...easy. And, if I was honest, I didn't even know if I did hate him anymore. I didn't like him, but I respected him. Nobody would ever believe me, but I did. He was a phenomenal chef, and I respected his ability to master his craft. I respected his dedication and his passion, and despite the fact he pissed me off daily, I also respected the fact that, deep down, he was a good man.

No matter what I thought normally, it was the truth. Parker Hamilton was a good man who said slightly inappropriate, libido-licking things every now and then.

A gasp escaped my lips, and my entire body froze.

"What?" he looked at me. "Did a crab finally flick your clit or something?"

I spun and grabbed his arm. My fingers dug right into the solid muscle, and my heart jumped when I met his eyes. "New cocktail. I have to go back."

I let go of him as quickly as I'd grabbed him and scrambled up. The loose sand had me slipping once, but Parker somehow managed to catch my elbow and keep me on my feet. I had no idea how he'd gotten up so quick, but I wasn't going to question it. I don't even think I said thanks as I grabbed my cup and ballerina flats and ran to the edge of the beach.

We made it back to the bar in record time, only stopping to put on our shoes. The cocktail was screaming at me inside my head, and the only thing that silenced the sudden creative hit was the fact the bar was empty.

Sienna looked up as we walked in. "Boat show in Key West. Apparently that's where everyone is."

I glanced around. "Oh. Do you wanna go home? If there's nobody here, I'll close early and take the rest of the night off."

It was a rare occurrence, and one I wanted to take advantage of with this recipe in my head.

"Um, sure. Do you want me to finish cleaning up?"

"Hmm?" I paused before stepping behind the bar. "Oh no, no, you're good." I barely finished speaking before I turned back to the bar and perused the bottles.

Fruity.

It would be fruity.

Tropical. Fresh. The kind of one you could drink four of and it not be too sweet.

Coconut rum.

I grabbed the bottle and put it on the bar behind me. There was an exchange of voices somewhere nearby, but it was a blur.

Banana liqueur.

The bright yellow bottle clinked against the coconut rum one as I set it down.

Pineapple juice.

It was so simple.

"No tequila?" Parker asked with a smirk.

I paused. Tequila was always worth it. Reaching for a

shot measurer with one hand, I grabbed a mixer with the other. Parker removed the top of the mixer when I held it out to him and shook it. Measuring it out was the hardest part, so I shushed him when he started to say something.

Slowly, I went through the motions. Pour, taste, change. Pour, taste, change. I did it over and over until the balance felt almost right, and then I added a splash of orange juice.

One more sip, and it was perfect.

I pulled two highball glasses from the shelf and set them on the bar. Parker's gaze followed my every movement as I poured the cocktail into them both and slid one across the bar to him. "Try that."

He peered at me for a moment before picking up the glass. "What is it?"

"Just try it."

He did. Surprise raised his eyebrows as he looked from the glass to me. "That's really good."

I clapped my hands together once and actually bounced.

"Did you just pull that out of nowhere?"

"Kind of," I answered, picking up my glass. "It happens sometimes."

"What are you calling it?"

I grinned. "The Libido Licker."

"Is that a promise?"

"Drink enough and it should be."

He laughed. The sound was low and throaty, and it rumbled across my skin. An unwelcome shiver went rocketing through my body, and I focused on drinking so he wouldn't notice the fact my entire body just reacted to a goddamn laugh.

"I have an idea." He tapped two fingers against the bar and shoved his glass at me. "Hold on."

I blinked as he disappeared through the doors to the kitchen before I could say a word. The creative high had disappeared the moment I'd gotten the recipe right, so I slumped against the bar and stuck a straw in my drink.

By the time Parker re-emerged from the kitchen with a tray in his hand, I was on my second glass.

This Libido Licker was dangerous. It went down too easily. It would be so simple to get drunk and do stupid stuff.

Parker set the tray on the bar. Hummus and snacks covered it, and I frowned as I took it in.

"I just ate. Why did you bring food?"

"The hummus platter," he said, glancing at my glass. "Did you already finish one?"

"Maybe." I walked around the bar, keeping the glass firmly in my hand, and grabbed a strip of pita bread. "Why did you bring food?"

"Because I have a feeling this could go really well with the drink."

Frowning again, I dipped the pita into the regular hummus and took a bite. I followed it up with a sip of the cocktail—and he was right.

"Oh my god," I muttered, dipping the bread again. "This is so good. It's like a wine pairing but not."

"That's because it's not wine." Amusement threaded through his tone. "It's a cocktail pairing. Put it on the specials board or something."

"Do you think you could pair more cocktails with food?" I asked, wiping the corner of my mouth with a paper napkin.

He shrugged a shoulder. "We'd probably have to do it together, but it wouldn't be too difficult to get the drinks that complement the food."

"I never thought I'd say this, but you're a bit of a freaking genius."

His eyes met mine right as his lips tugged to one side.

Maybe it was the dark glint in his gaze.

Maybe it was the smooth curve of his lower lip as it spread into that half-smile, half-smirk.

Maybe it was the moment we found a middle ground, something we could agree on.

Maybe it was the—strong—alcohol.

Or maybe it was just insanity, because I placed my hand on his arm and pressed my lips to his. Soft, smooth, warm. It was the lightest of touches, and he didn't even move.

The ramifications of such a gentle touch were evident the moment I pulled away. With my eyes widening, I clamped my hand over my mouth and stepped back. My heart was thumping, and a horrified shiver tickled across my arms, making my hairs stand on end.

"Well," Parker said simply, "I guess we know the drink lives up to its name."

12
Parker

"I don't know why I did that." The words tumbled out of Raven's mouth, and she stepped back again. She'd barely removed her hand from in front of her face to speak and now it was back, stretched across the lower half of her face, covering her mouth completely. Her nostrils were flaring from the tiny gap she'd left herself to breathe between the top of her finger and her nose.

I didn't know why she'd done it either. The last thing I'd ever expected would be for her to kiss me. She was attracted to me—that was obvious from this morning with the pool table—but I assumed I'd be the one to break. Her control would never let her. Her pride would keep it contained.

But I hadn't broken.

I didn't know what the hell had happened, but I was pretty sure it was down to the mixture she'd put in the glass.

She'd been a little too liberal with the tequila the last time around.

She was looking at me, though, and she didn't look drunk in the slightest. Her gaze was focused, and sure, her cheeks were flushed, but that was more to do with the fact she'd kissed me than she'd been drinking.

And now, she wasn't moving except for blinking at me. I didn't know if she was shocked or horrified or both, but I knew one thing so clearly.

That kiss was nowhere fucking near enough.

My fingers twitched with the desire to grab her and kiss her properly. To make those damn blue eyes flutter shut. To make her red fingernails dig into my arms. To make her heart pound.

Every second I didn't do that was a personal victory. It was the ultimate exercise in restraint, because the ghost of her lips still lingered on mine, and the warmth of her palm on my skin felt like it was burning.

Temptation like nothing I'd ever felt before gripped hold of me. It tightened my muscles and pumped through my blood like adrenaline, making it harder and harder not to give in and fucking kiss her like I wanted to.

I wanted to curl my hand into her hair and tug her head back. Wanted to hear her gasp as the pull on her hair made her scalp sting. Wanted to feel her desperation as my lips hovered over hers before I finally kissed her.

This was Raven.

So, I couldn't.

I grabbed the tray with too much force and kicked open the kitchen door. It clattered against the wall, slamming slut after me, and I put the tray down on the side. The chrome top was cold against my palms as I gripped the edge and leaned forward, dropping my head.

My cock was fucking hard. Fucking hard at the thought I could walk out there and kiss her so damn thoroughly I'd wipe off all that red lipstick. That she'd be wet and would want me as much as I wanted her in this moment.

Raven.

She was Ryan's sister.

Off-limits.

Out of bounds.

So fucking *tempting*.

I couldn't do it to my best friend. One kiss from her could be brushed off as under the influence of alcohol and moved on from. The way I wanted to kiss her couldn't be brushed off as anything but selfish need from me. Selfish, greedy, inconsiderate need.

I didn't care.

I did. I did care. It was a lie. I'd never be able to look Ryan in the eye if I knew what it felt like to kiss her properly.

My respect for him outweighed my want for her.

The words rang like a lie even in the loudness of my mind.

Usually, yes. Yes, my respect for him outweighed anything else I could feel. But right now, it didn't.

Nothing did.

I had to get the fuck out of here before I did something I'd regret tomorrow. Before I did the one fucking thing that would destroy my friendship with him.

I left the tray on the side. I'd regret it tomorrow, but getting the hell out of Dirty was my priority. I'd forgive myself, I was sure.

I didn't even glance Raven's way as I headed for the door. I'd thrown my shit in my car before I'd gone to find her on the beach, and now I was glad for my hindsight. If I'd had better hindsight, I'd have made Sienna call her like she'd offered to.

"Parker?" Raven's voice was softer than usual, and she said my name at the exact moment I touched the door handle.

That was the only explanation for why I stopped and turned around. She was standing in front of the bar, almost directly across the room of me. She played with the damp cloth in her hands, winding it nervously around her fingers.

The apprehensive glimmer in her eyes hit me straight in the gut. It was so unlike her—a part of her rarely-seen softer side, the one she kept under wraps for everyone but a select few people.

She glanced away for a brief moment before saying, "Can we just...ignore that a moment ago?"

"Sure." I kept my gaze trained on her eyes. "It was the alcohol, right? Forget it."

She tugged the corner of her lower lip into her mouth with her teeth as she nodded. I took a deep breath when she looked down at the cloth in her hands. The only bright thing in her expression—her eyes—had gone, and I could almost feel the awkwardness rolling off of her.

Her eyelashes fanned long, spider-leg like shadows across her cheeks as she kept her attention downward. A deep breath made her shoulders rise and fall, and her lips pursed with the long, shaky exhale.

It wasn't awkwardness.

It was embarrassment.

It tinged her cheeks pink, shook her hands, and made each breath sharper.

She was embarrassed, and I fucking hated it, because she had absolutely no reason to feel that way.

I let go of the door handle and, in a few short strides, I closed the distance between us. Her lips parted just enough that I could see she'd scraped a fleck of lipstick off the bottom one where she'd bitten it moments ago. I lingered on that for a moment before hooking my finger under her chin, forcing her head up.

Raven swallowed, her tongue just teasing the inside of her lip. I expected her to say something, to push me away, but she didn't. She stood there, still not looking at me, but close enough that every short, sharp breath she took, no matter how quiet they actually were, seemed to scream at me.

"Raven." Her name was nothing more than a low hum on my tongue.

She snapped her gaze up to mine. The apprehensive

tone she'd spoken with peered back at me, mixing into a hurricane of emotions with her embarrassment and some frustration. Her cheeks got pinker the longer I looked at her, and when she opened her mouth to speak, I leaned in.

Placing my hands either side of her face, I took her mouth with mine.

Firmly.

Deliberately.

I wanted her to have no doubt that I absolutely meant to kiss her.

I slid my hands down her cheeks so I was cupping her jaw and my fingers curled around the sides of her neck. She shuddered when I pulled away only to go back and kiss her again, this time even harder. This time, she leaned into me, the cloth falling to the ground as she pressed her hands against my stomach. Her fingers curled with the dip in my abs, but all I could think about was the way her lips felt against mine.

Her lips were the softest I'd ever kissed. And I didn't want to stop.

She tasted like the fruitiness of the cocktail we'd both drunk. Like pineapple and coconut, like orange and...freshness.

Like everything I shouldn't be tasting, because I shouldn't have been kissing her.

As if she could read my mind, Raven pulled away with a gasp that sent a shiver down the back of my neck.

In the silence that followed, a phone rang from somewhere in the bar.

Of fucking course.

She pushed away from me and ran to the back without another word to me.

The phone stopped ringing.

Five minutes later, it was obvious she wasn't coming back.

I rubbed my hand across my face and did what I should have done when she asked if we could forget the fact

she'd kissed me.
    Left.

13

Raven

It had been twelve hours since Parker Hamilton's lips were on mine, and despite two showers, I could still feel the roughness of his teeth as they grazed across my lower lip.

It'd been twelve hours since he'd walked up to me and basically silently taken my mouth with his, and there was no ridding the sensation of his tongue as it teased the seam of my mouth.

It'd been twelve hours since I'd stood there and allowed him to kiss me, and I didn't know how to get rid of the guilt.

I'd kissed him first. I still didn't know why. Figuring it out seemed absolutely impossible. There was no rhyme or reason for why I'd stepped forward, laid my hand on his arm, and kissed him. I didn't remember wanting to. I didn't remember *even thinking* about doing it.

I just did it.

An impulse.

That was all it was.

Yet I couldn't shake the memory of the way lust filled his eyes—of the way he'd clamped his jaw shut before he'd stormed out.

Now, I knew I should've let him go when he came out of the kitchen. He was leaving, and stopping him was the stupidest thing I could have done. I could have texted him or even waited until today. Then, I could have apologized and we could have moved on. Forgotten it.

But, no.

I had to stop him.

I had to ask.

And he had to kiss me. Properly.

There was no reason for that one, either. He didn't need to kiss me, but he did. It served no purpose other than to give me a restless night's sleep where I, ridiculously, kept imagining my brother walking in on him kissing me.

On second thought, it wasn't so ridiculous when you considered it was his phone call that had made me push Parker away...and pushed me into hiding in my apartment until I knew his car had left the lot.

Talking to my brother with the taste of his best friend on my lips was the most awkward thing I've done in a while. It wasn't even just the taste of him. My lips tingled the entire phone call, and by the time I'd agreed to god only knew what so I could get off the damn thing, I'd realized one thing.

My lipstick was chapped and smudged in the corners, and while I knew me biting off loose skin was partly to blame, there was no denying that Parker was entirely responsibility for the smudging I'd struggled to get rid of.

All morning, I'd been trying to focus on one single emotion. I was confused and frustrated, torn and tired. I'd been dragging ass ever since I forced myself out of bed, and now, as I hid in the cellar under the guise of organizing it, I was still dragging my ass.

I had everything organized, it just happened to be on

the floor in front of me.

It was easier to keep shifting it around on the ground than to put everything up on the shelves and in storage where it belonged. If I did that, I'd ultimately be done soon, and then I faced the task of handling my emotions

I needed to get a hold on it. My grandmother wanted a lunch date to figure out what food I was putting on for the Karras family reunion. If I dared give her anything less than one hundred percent of my attention, I'd be hearing about it for the next five years.

Knowing that didn't make the task any easier.

Neither did the fact I knew that if I still felt as conflicted as I did when she showed up—*with Ryan*—that she'd sense it right away and not let up until I gave in and told her what was bugging me.

What I needed was a do-over. Of the entire weekend. Back to the point where I'd opened my big, fat wine-hole at the very least.

Failing the do-over, I'd take a memory wipe. Maybe even a concussion. That lead to short-term memory loss, right? I needed to forget every second of the kiss or it totally stood to destroy my entire day. Shit, my morning had been a bust, because here I was...sitting in the middle of the cellar floor, surrounded by bottles and crates and cans and boxes.

I didn't want to do a damn thing with any of it. I wanted to leave it where it was on the floor. Except...I couldn't. It all needed putting back. The rest of my family were due to arrive throughout this week, and I'd had to order in their favorite drinks especially. There was more in the cellar than usual, which had ultimately prompted my clean up.

I needed to be able to control *something*. I couldn't control this situation with Parker. I couldn't control my feelings over it, either.

Or him.

I couldn't control my feelings for him.

I didn't understand them. They'd come out of nowhere, the complete opposite to everything I'd ever felt for him before. Instead of wanting to be on the other side of the world to him, I wanted to be closer to him. And now he'd kissed me, I wanted to be even closer.

I wanted to know what would happen if we weren't interrupted. If, in the unlikely situation he ever kissed me again, I had questions.

Would he go further?

Would he kiss me deeper? Harder? Longer?

Would he push me against a wall and slip his hand beneath my shirt?

Would he wrap my legs around his waist the way he said before?

I had no right to ask these questions. I had no right to even be thinking about it. I knew that. This situation was wrong. It felt like the ultimate betrayal of my brother to be thinking about his best friend in such a way.

If Ryan ever knew Parker had kissed me, I didn't know what would happen to their friendship. Sure, Ryan and I bickered, but he was still my big brother. He was still the guy who, even from across the country, tracked down complete strangers whose name he'd heard from Mom to tell them that if they fucked with me, he'd fuck them up.

It didn't matter who they were. It just mattered that they could hurt me.

The u-turn in mine and Parker's relationship would not be welcome.

That much I was entirely certain of.

But it wasn't really a u-turn. It was a fluke, a one-time occurrence, something that I would make sure would never happen again.

Because it was that simple.

Maybe if I kept reminding myself of that, I'd be swallowed by guilt to the point I'd forget what it felt like to have Parker's hands in my hair and his lips against mine.

Maybe.

"Raven!" Yia-Yia snapped her fingers in front of my face. "You concentrate."

I blinked, pulling myself back to the conversation. "Sorry. I didn't sleep much last night."

"Why?" Ryan eyed me from over his cup of coffee.

"Can a girl just not have a bad night's sleep?" My question was honest, but my voice was a little too on edge to make it believable that was the reason. "I'm here alone tonight and I want a nap."

"No nap!" Yia-Yia rapped her knuckles against the table and glared at me with her intimidatingly dark eyes. "You help."

I propped my head up on my hand. "Why don't we just put all the food out? If we cut out half the menu, someone is just gonna complain. Cleo will get annoyed if there's no *tiganita*, Demetri will cry if there's no *bifteki*, Aunt Helena will moan all night if there's no *astakos,* and god forbid if there isn't enough *spanakopita* for Lia to stuff her face with."

Ryan wrinkled his face up. "Lia's coming?"

Yia-Yia tapped the side of his head with her pen. "*Né*," she said. *Yes.* "Why she not?"

Lia was a bone of contention for my brother. She wasn't technically family as her mom had married our cousin when she was six, and for as long as we could remember, she'd had a crush on Ryan.

I grinned. "Surprise."

He shot me a withering look. If our grandmother wasn't present, he would have told me to go and fuck myself for sure.

"What?" I asked, dropping the smile and taking on my most innocent, wide-eyed look. "I love Lia. It's not my fault if she has a crush on you."

Yia-Yia shook her head and tapped her ring finger.

"She's married?" Ryan asked hopefully.
She shook her head again, scribbling on the paper.
Oh, good. She wanted to play Charades.
"Engaged?" he tried again, a little less happy, but still quite brightly.
More head-shaking.
"Expected to be engaged?" was my guess.
Yia-Yia pointed a finger in my direction. "*Né.* He ask soon."
"She gonna say yes?" Ryan still looked hopeful.
"Until she sees how hunky you are." I grinned again. "Then she's gonna be asking for your phone number."
Another 'fuck yourself' look came my way.
"Child! Focus!" Yia-Yia turned the conversation back immediately to her menu.

Why she couldn't just use the regular menu, I'd never know. It wasn't like we didn't have enough time to order in a ton of stuff to make sure we had enough of everything for everybody. Parker could handle it—he'd worked in New York for years, for the love of god.

My grandmother was making a mountain out of a molehill. There was no need for all this screwing around, and I didn't even know why I was here except for the fact I'd been told to be. I was the drinks person in the family. This was a conversation for Ryan and Parker, not me.

I just wanted to know what drinks I needed to be mixing.

Whether or not those drinks would pair well with the food being served...That depended almost entirely on my ability to be able to work with Parker and his with me. The plan to do a pairing was great before The Kiss.

The Kiss*es?*

How was I meant to refer to it, except hopefully not at all?

"She doesn't know what she's doing, Yia-Yia," Ryan said, waving his hand in my direction. "Look at her. She has a point that everyone has their favorite, but she doesn't run the food here. When does Parker get here, Ray?"

I hit the Home button on my phone and checked the time. "Any minute."

Damn it.

"And I really have to go restock the shelves," I said, sliding my chair back from the table. "Alec is coming in to help him today, so he'll have time to help you do your menu."

Yia-Yia snorted, but she didn't say anything else.

Secretly, she was probably glad to be rid of me. I'd contributed absolutely nothing since I'd sat down. All I wanted to do was get the hell away before Parker showed up and an awkward situa—

The door swung open.

I saw his feet first. I didn't know why that was where I looked. Maybe it was because starting from the bottom and working my way up his body was easier to stomach than our eyes instantly meeting. Unfortunately, it also meant that I had to take in every inch of him as my gaze worked its way up over his light, ripped jeans, baby-blue polo shirt, and stubbled jaw.

He hadn't shaved.

"Finally!" Yia-Yia exclaimed, throwing her arms up. "Now we do proper."

"Err." Parker closed the door behind him. "What are we doing properly?"

I'm glad he could understand her broken English. It saved me having to translate.

"Menu." Ryan gave him a wry smile. "Raven was about as useful as a condom in a nunnery."

"Hey!" I turned to face him and set my hand on his hip. "I reminded everyone that we need all the food because our family is insanely picky."

"And that was very helpful," he drawled, not looking at me.

"Well, what did you expect?" Parker asked, walking right past me and sitting in the seat I'd just vacated. "Look at the menu she drew up for this place. It's only decent because I forced her into it. She'd serve chicken wings to a toddler if left alone with one for too long."

"Are we done with the bitching out Raven party?" My words snapped out of me.

"Raven!" Yia-Yia pointed a wrinkled finger at me. "Watch your mouth," she reprimanded me in Greek.

Sure. They can bitch at me but the second I use a marginally naughty word I'm in trouble?

That made perfect damn sense.

"I'm going to get some real work done," I huffed, turning away.

The only good thing that came from that was the fact I didn't have to look Parker in the eye.

I hummed along to the latest Ed Sheeran song as I finally finished putting the stock back on the shelves in the cellar. It'd taken the better part of two and a half hours to get it all back where it was supposed to be.

If this exercise had taught me anything, it was that I should never, ever do it again.

"Are you still in here?"

I turned at the sound of Ryan's voice. "Given the fact you're out there and I'm in here, it's pretty obvious."

"Jesus, Ray, what's up your ass?"

I waved him off. "I'm tired," I replied, only half-lying. "The summer rushes plus opening the kitchen plus this family reunion is making me tired."

"You don't look tired."

"Of course, I don't. I'm a woman. I have the capability to hide any emotions I want to."

"Except annoyance."

"Then don't piss me off." I grinned as I stood. "Is Yia-Yia still here?"

He shook his head and stepped back so I could leave the cellar. "She left half an hour ago. Something about needing lobster."

"Right. You didn't leave with her?"

"Are you kidding?" He followed me out to the bar. "If I left with her, I'd have to drive her home then come back."

"Why do you need to come back?" I spun and stopped right in front of him. "You're not staying here."

His eyes widened. "Uh, slip of the tongue." He side-stepped me.

I moved with him. "Ryan."

"I have a date tonight, all right?"

I grinned again. "Are you bringing her here?"

"So I can scare her off with my insane sister? Yeah, why not?" He snorted and physically moved me to his side so he could step past me. "I'm done here. Later."

I stuck my middle finger up after him.

He looks back and catches it. "By the way," he said slowly. "Did you do something to Parker? He's in a really shit mood."

"Why do you assume that's me?" Aside from the obvious.

"Because it's always you."

14

Parker

"It is not always me," Raven snaps. Something bangs from the other side of the door, and I'm guessing it was her fist against the bar.

"It's generally you," Ry replied.

"It's not me! If he has a cactus up his ass about something, go fucking ask him. I'm his boss, not his keeper." There was a pause. "I thought you were leaving."

Scuffles and mumbles followed, then the door slammed shut.

I didn't mean to listen, but they weren't exactly quiet. In fact, I could barely remember a time they were able to be quiet.

I picked up the dish that needed washing and took it back out to Alex. He didn't look at me as I dropped it on the side with a little too much force, and it was obvious he was avoiding making eye contact with me.

I couldn't blame him. I'd been in a foul fucking mood since I'd left here last night. I'd slept like complete shit. I'd even paid the extortionate fee to the gym in an attempt to break out of the shell of frustration I was wrapped in. It hugged every inch of my body, except I couldn't separate sexual frustration from plain ol' annoyed frustration.

Raven had ruined me. One accidental kiss had become one deliberate one, and nothing I did could shake the memory of that. Nothing shook away the memory of her body pressed against mine or her mouth yielding to the pressure of my own.

By kissing her, I'd thrown myself into some kind of fucked-up, self-made torture.

I wanted more.

I wanted her mouth on my neck.

My chest.

My stomach.

My cock.

And I wanted her to tell me how much she fucking hated me while she did it. Because then I'd have justification for the anger I felt. I'd have a lie to feed myself.

I didn't know when I'd stopped hating her, but it was recent. Somewhere between looking into her big, blue eyes and pinning her against the bar, I'd come to respect the woman she'd grown into. I'd come to respect her mind for business—her ruthlessness and accuracy in everything she did. Her creativity was second-to-none. I'd watched her create a cocktail out of absolute thin air.

Anyone who could pluck something so solid from nothing deserved respect.

More than that, I knew I respected her as a human being. I respected her strength and her vigor and her passion. Her snark and her stalwart approach to everything. I respected her control and her need for it.

I respected the woman she was, and that was something I never thought I'd do.

I wanted her, too, of course. Because of all those things. Because no matter how much she pissed me off, no matter how much the way she looked at me sometimes fucking grated on me, Raven Archer was one hell of a woman.

I wasn't surprised by it, not really. She'd been a force as a child. It only made sense that she'd defy physics as an adult.

"Can you make the hummus?" I asked Alex, grabbing the order folder.

"Sure thing, Chef."

I threw a thumbs up over my shoulder and, swallowing my feelings, stepped into the bar. Raven was standing behind it, her hair now pulled into a scruffy ponytail on top of her head, revealing the bright, white earphones that were in place in her ears. She hummed along to something that sounded suspiciously like Ed Sheeran.

Her hips swayed with it. She was wearing a plain, white tank with a floral skirt that moved with each flick of her hips. She'd changed from earlier, and I guessed she was ready for work, because the skirt had a thin, black belt that went around the waistband and it was a few inches shorter than should have been acceptable for working behind a bar.

Then again, I'd seen her work behind this thing, and she was the best damn tender I knew.

I put my finger and thumb in my mouth and let out a long, loud whistle.

Raven screamed, yanking the headphones from her ears and jumping back halfway across the bar. "What the fuck?" she shouted. "Are you stupid? I could have killed you."

"Yeah, your scream was terrifying," I said dryly, dropping the folder down on the bar. "I need you to check off this order and sign it before I can place it."

She exhaled slowly and walked to me. "You could have announced yourself."

"I did," I lied. "You were too busy playing Shakira to Ed Sheeran. Nice humming, by the way."

"Ugh." She actually said the word as she took the folder from me. Her bright red nails flashed as she skimmed the sheets until she found today's order. The tap of her nail against the paper as she placed it down was almost nails-down-a-chalkboard-sounding, but thankfully, she slid it down the list instead of tapping each item.

I leaned against the bar as she looked. The bar was due to open in a couple hours, and judging by the half-empty fridges, she wasn't ready for opening at all.

"All right." She grabbed a pen from the register and scrawled something that vaguely resembled 'RA' on the order sheet. "Go ahead and put that through."

"Thanks. Aren't you working today?"

Slowly, she dragged her eyes up my chest and face to meet my gaze. "Yes. I'm always working."

"Never mind." I held my hands up and stepped back. "Just, yeah. Never mind."

Her tone was perfectly steady when she said, "You're much safer in the kitchen, you know that?"

I barely glanced at her full, red lips before I grabbed the folder. "Yeah, I know."

If only she knew how much fucking safer it was in there.

I was ten seconds away from losing my shit.

It was the first time I'd worked with Alex without Wes around, and it was blatantly fucking clear that Wes was the superior of the two. Alex was barely holding on his composure, judging by the sweat that was constantly beading on his forehead.

Don't get me wrong—it was fucking hot in here. That was the nature of working in a kitchen. The amount of things that cooked at the same time was ridiculous, but it took a special person to handle the pressure. If I was honest, this felt like the vacation I'd intended to take when I'd come back to the Keys. Working in Dirty was so easy compared to working in New York.

Even the food was refreshing. Greek food was worlds away from the Steak and Seafood House I'd put on the map thanks to my skills. I'd given the restaurant the Michelin stars they'd long craved, but I wondered how long they'd keep that honor without me around.

For me, I'd always be Michelin-starred. Those three, shiny stars would always be mine. They were the legacy I'd worked so hard for, and that legacy didn't include stressed-out halfwits who fucked up at the glimpse of pressure.

It didn't include people like Alex.

"Where's the fucking tzatkizi, Alex?" I yelled over the whirring of the fans.

"Give me ten minutes!"

"I don't have ten fucking minutes. I need it five minutes ago."

"It's coming, Chef!"

"Defrost, now!" I snapped, draining vegetables and almost splashing myself with scalding hot water. "I don't have time for this shit!"

Something clanged. "On it!"

I was on the edge.

"This was supposed to be made this afternoon!" I reminded him as I filled veg dishes and put them under the hot light. "I said we were getting low!"

Everything had to be shouted over the extractor fans. It made me seem just as angry as I was.

"I know, Chef. I'm defrosting now!" he shouted back. "How do I thicken it from the water?"

I pressed my fingers into my temple. "You don't! You throw it the fuck out, Alex! Get me fucking fresh sauce four hours ago!"

Gordon Ramsay was my long lost uncle, if nobody guessed.

I was the first to admit that I wasn't the most delightful person to work with. The pressures of the kitchen brought out the worst in a man, but when I asked for something to be done, I expected it to be fucking done. When I asked. Not four hours ago.

"Ticket on!" Vicky called, walking into the kitchen and attaching a ticket to the board.

I spun and grabbed the one she'd left for me. "Vicky! Half hour wait," I told her. "We're running low on condiments. Tell them it's demand."

"Um, okay," she said, her hand on the door. "Do I need to tell Raven?"

"Does she take food orders?"

"Um, yes."

"Then yes, she needs to fucking know." I slapped my ticket onto the board on my side. "No more orders for ten minutes."

Vicky shuffled back to the door. "Okay."

It slammed after her.

"Tzatkizi, Alex!" I shouted, slamming my hand against the countertop. If the steel material of the hotplate were any weaker, it would have likely shattered with the harshness of my hit.

As it was, it was a good shock absorber for my annoyance.

Tzatkizi sauce appeared in front of me without a word from Alex. He literally dumped the bowl and then left. I didn't care—I just needed the sauce. I was almost certain he'd be fired tomorrow morning. I didn't expect to or need to wait as long as I had for the sauce he'd assured me he'd made a few hours ago.

I hit the buzzer for Vicky to come and grab some food. She came in with three more meal tickets.

It was Monday in Whiskey Key.

What the fuck was going on?

"Raven," I shouted across the kitchen before Vicky could leave. "I need her."

"Sure." Her voice carried over the noise and was followed by the slamming of the door.

I threw tomatoes into the frying pan and added

zucchini. I was working on a side dish now I had the tzatkizi I needed, and all I could do was hope that Alex had read the tickets and was working on the others I needed.

"Raven's busy," Vicky said loudly, coming in with dirty dishes. "She asked me what you need."

"I need her ass in here," I replied without turning around.

"I'm not sure she can do that."

"Make her."

I had no time for excuses. I needed her here to talk to me and that was the end of it.

Vicky came and went three times before Raven made her way into the kitchen. When she did, it was in a cloud of anger and a tongue spitting with insults.

"What?" she yelled over the noise of the fans.

"Stop food," I shouted back. "We're too slammed."

"There's less than Friday!"

I turned in time to see her examining the tickets.

"Fuck me sideways," she said. "You had twice the tickets last Friday. What's going on?"

"Stop food," I repeated, tugging down a ticket as I hit the buzzer for Vicky. She pulled the plates with towels and I said, "Table four. Five minutes ago."

Vicky nodded as she turned.

Raven's eyes narrowed. "Don't let your complexes out on her. She just runs your shit."

"Watch your mouth," I warned her, mixing a salad. With a metal spoon, I filled two salad bowls and passed them in Raven's direction with the dressing on the side. "Thanks."

She reached through the divide and hit the divide.

"Table eight," I told Vicky when she grabbed them.

Raven waited until the door shut. "Don't tell me what to do again." Her voice was like ice as it sliced through the air between us.

"You're in my kitchen, hotshot."

"I don't give a fuck. If you think I studied for years to mix drinks only to stand here and take your shit, you're mistaken."

I raised an eyebrow. "You insulting me?"

"No," she said, training her bright eyes on me. "I'm telling you to get the fuck on with it like I am."

"Getting on with it," I told her, pushing two plates under the lamp and hitting the buzzer. "But under more pressure than you."

Vicky appeared instantly. To her credit, Raven didn't say a word until she'd disappeared.

"You knew what you signed up to," she told me, her finger pointing at me. "You literally offered yourself to me for this job. If you're not up to it, get your ass the fuck out of here. Give me a damn good reason why I should tell people they have to wait forty-five minutes for their food per your latest order. Remember who I am, Parker."

The spoon I was holding fell to the counter with an air-slicing shatter. I gripped the edge of the counter and leaned down so that my eyes met hers beneath the shadow of the hot plate.

Parker.

I didn't give a fuck who she was.

In my kitchen, I wasn't Parker.

The door opened.

Vicky froze. Alex stood in the freezer entryway with meat in his hands.

My voice was low and heavy as I spoke, keeping my gaze on Raven's. "In my kitchen, you call me Chef."

Raven's eyes held mine with a devastating intensity. "And while your kitchen is in my building, you call me *boss*." She rammed the heel of her hand into the edge of the countertop. "Be in my office when you finish at nine-thirty, Mr. Hamilton. We have a few things to discuss."

She didn't even give me the decency of time to respond. She turned and left in a flash of dark hair and floral skirt. The door clicked shut to the swish of her leaving the space.

She did that. She occupied every space with ease,

filling it with her vibrant personality and take-no shit attitude.

I was over her attitude. Any awkwardness I'd felt walking in here and seeing her brother knowing I'd kissed her last night was gone. Any guilt had disappeared, too. It'd all been replaced by the stress of the evening's work and the annoyance at her.

Just days ago she'd told me never to undermine her, yet she'd done that to me in front of her staff. I didn't give a shit if she owned the entire town—she was in my kitchen. There was one boss in my kitchen and that was me.

Nine-thirty meeting in her office.

Raven Archer had one hell of a shock coming to her tonight.

15
Raven

I paced back and forth in my office. The anger that flowed through my veins was of another level. I was fuming—beyond anything I'd felt in a long time. It crawled over my skin with the vengeance of a pack of hungry leeches, and it sure as hell felt like it was sucking the life out of me.

The more I paced, the angrier I got. But I needed to pace. I needed to be angry. Being angry with Parker was easier than the alternative. If I was angry with him, there would be no chance of slipping up and kissing him again.

Slapping him, yes. Not kissing him.

I didn't know what I was supposed to do. I hadn't expected any of this to happen when I'd hired him. I hadn't expected to find respect for him or be as attracted to him as I was.

I couldn't even pin that as the root of my anger. The way I felt wasn't his fault, even if it was because of the way he was. I was the one who had little to no control over my feelings. I was the one who had a wild inability to stop myself wanting him whenever I glanced in his direction.

I didn't want to want him.

I wanted to forget that I'd ever had his lips on mine. I wanted to forget every time he'd ever touched me.

I wanted to go back to three weeks ago, before he'd come home, when he was still the barest whisper of a memory.

I preferred it when he was a memory instead of every living second.

Four knocks rattled my closed door. They jolted me out of my thoughts and back to the here and now.

Was it already nine-thirty? Impossible. I hadn't been in here much more than five minutes.

I picked up my phone from the desk and checked the time. Nine-fifty. I'd been in here for half an hour, and the bastard had the gall to show up late.

Twenty minutes late sure, but twenty minutes was twenty minutes. Did he get a kick out of pissing me off? There was no other reason for him to be here twenty minutes late when all he had to do was walk across the damn bar. He could have at least sent Vicky or Alec in to see me and let me know he was still busy.

Not that it was busy. It'd been two hours since he'd dragged me into the kitchen and been a dick to me.

Why the hell was I so damn annoyed still?

More knocks sounded at my door.

I knew it was him. That loud rap his knuckles made against the wood were so distinct to him. I didn't know how it was possible to tell who it was by something as simple as a knock, but I could and I did. It was one of those weird things, I guessed.

More knocks.

I was going to make him wait. It was petty, but I had a point to make. If he wanted to make me wait, I'd make him wait, too.

Never mind that I had no idea he was late until he'd knocked.

Parker knocked three more times. This time each one was louder and stronger than the previous, so I finally made my way to the door and opened it.

"Oh, sorry," I said, cutting him off before he could speak. "I didn't mean to keep you waiting."

"I was working," he shot back, following me inside my office. "You were just being fucking awkward."

"Watch your mouth."

He opened it. Then, he snapped it shut again. Whether he was actually doing as I said or was closing it to save the ranting for later, I didn't know.

"Sit down." I pointed to the chair on the other side of my desk. When he didn't move, I said more firmly, "Sit. Down."

He dragged it back and dropped onto it with the petulance of a child.

Now, I knew he was doing it to piss me off.

"Let's get something straight." I gripped the edge of my desk and leaned forward, hooking one of my feet behind the other. My gaze was trained steadily on his, and no matter how much ire his bright eyes glared at me, I wouldn't back down from him. "When you're at work, you will treat me with respect and you will understand that, even if you need me, I don't exist to pander to your every beck and call. If you need me, fine, but you wait. I'm doing my own job and that doesn't involve handling your shit."

He opened his mouth again and I held up one finger.

"And you do not ever demand that I call you something in front of other members of staff. I don't give a fuck what they did in New York. This is Whiskey fucking Key, not New York freakin' City. If you want to be called, then you use a little thing called respect and you ask. You don't blatantly call me on something in front of the people *I* pay."

"Then try to use a little respect of your own," he shot

back before I could make a motion to stop him. "Don't storm your ass into the kitchen, guns blazing, just because what I needed you for was important. You went in there with a problem. I didn't call you in there like that."

"When I told Vicky to tell you to wait, I wasn't being awkward. I was in the middle of a massive order, because the reason for the busyness we found out was there was a coach that had broken down on its way back from Key West to Atlanta. It was full of people who are all staying nearby and we were an obviously unscheduled stop."

"It would have been nice to be informed."

"I'm sorry," I said dryly, "I didn't realize you required all the info. Vicky was told to tell you. If she didn't, that wasn't my problem, but it still doesn't excuse your attitude. You don't ever embarrass me in front of my staff like that again, Parker. This might be a summer job for you, but I *live* here. This is my town and my reputation you're fucking with when you speak to me like that at work."

And that, I realized, was what it came down to. This was nothing more than a passing job for him. A bit of fun, even. But for me, this was my life. Dirty was my livelihood. It was my business, and more than that, it was my passion. I loved every second of my job and running my business, no matter how stressful it was.

I didn't care if he was Parker Hamilton, Michelin-starred chef and whatever other honors he'd earned in the past few years.

I did care that I was Raven Archer, mixologist and owner of Dirty.

I'd built my business up with a little help from my grandparents on my dad's side. They might have left the money, but I'd put in all the work. It was all me.

There was no way Parker would discredit what I'd done. Whether he realized it or not. It wasn't going to happen.

"You're right." He linked his fingers and stretched his arms out in front of him, cracking his knuckles. "Next time I wanna call you on your attitude, I'll drag you in here to do it."

"Yeah, you do that." I stopped. "Wait, what? No."

He smirked, leaning forward on his seat.

"You don't call me on shit, Parker. Not when your attitude is the reason for my shit."

"My attitude?" He raised his eyebrows and used the desk to push himself up to standing. "What about your attitude?"

I bristled. "What do you mean—what about my attitude?"

"Your attitude is the reason for *my* shit." His eyes darkened, flashing with something indiscernible. "In fact, it's you in general. Because even though I'm pretty sure I should be offended and really fucking annoyed with you right this second, I keep thinking that I didn't kiss you nearly hard enough yesterday if you're still talking."

What?

My mouth instantly went dry. I swallowed, but it wasn't enough, so I darted my tongue out and wet my lips. The relief didn't last nearly long enough, and before I could comprehend enough to string words together, he pushed off the desk and moved toward me.

My office was bright, illuminated by the highlights of the summer sun as it streamed through my back window. The golden rays bounced off his face, brightening his gaze as it stayed fixed on me.

His expression was intense—lips thinned, jaw set, eyebrows unmoving. It didn't change as he closed the distance between us, taking a giant loop around my body. Like I was chained to his gravity, I moved, spinning so I faced him the entire time.

I was between him and the desk.

It was too late.

My heart beat frantically, hammering against my ribs as Parker came so close there was barely a breath of space between us. I struggled to take in a deep breath. He was taller than me, wider too, so he took up every inch of my personal space he could without actually touching me.

I gripped the edge of my desk as my butt bumped into it. I was half-perched against the desktop, my attention wholly on the man in front of me.

Lust replaced anger.

I didn't want it to. I wanted to keep my anger.

But I also wanted him. Wanted him to kiss me. Wanted to know if it wasn't just a fluke.

Wanted to know if his words were more than hot air designed to build me up and leaving me hanging.

"You can't talk to me like that," I finally managed to get out, but it was barely more than a wheezing breath with a useless excuse for words mingled into it. "I'm your boss."

Like it mattered.

Parker placed his hands on the desk, his thumbs just brushing my wrists as his palms flattened against the solid surface. A shiver danced up my arms as a slow, easy smirk twisted up the side of his mouth as he leaned in. "That took you long enough to say, didn't it?"

"What's that meant to mean?"

"I don't think you really care," he said in a low voice. "Otherwise you'd be pushing me away from you right now."

I couldn't. I was frozen. Unless someone knocked on the door and interrupted us, breaking the moment, I couldn't do a damn thing.

I sucked in deep breath as he took another step into me, inching closer until his leg was just creeping between my knees. "You have to stop," I whispered.

"Why? Because I'm your employee or your brother's best friend?" he murmured back.

That was the million-dollar question, wasn't it? Why did he have to stop?

"Both. One kiss is an accident. Twice is a mistake."

"Now say it and mean it." He hadn't moved since he'd slipped his leg between mine, but my entire body burned with his closeness.

My chest was tight. I couldn't breathe. The words

were there, lying on the tip of my tongue, ready to fall, ready to scream their way toward him.

Stop. It's wrong. All of this is wrong.

But, they didn't come. They were stuck, because I didn't want to say them.

It was all semantics. His closeness with my brother, the fact I employed him—they didn't matter in this moment. All that mattered was the way my skin still tingled where his thumbs had brushed my wrists and how quickly my heart was beating.

What was this?

What was happening?

I had no clue. I just knew I didn't want it to stop.

"I can't," I whispered, gripping harder onto the desk. My gaze dropped to where his shirt stretched over his shoulders. The fabric hugged his muscles like it was made for him—and to distract me.

Parker's hands slipped over my legs and under my skirt. Slowly, his thumbs probed my skin on my inner thighs, almost as if he were testing how far he could go before I'd make him stop.

Goosebumps came to life and prickled over my legs. From my hips to my ankles, I felt them come up in a wave with a shiver, and this one, I couldn't contain. It wracked my body in a quick hit that made my lips part with its intensity.

Parker smiled. One hand escaped from beneath my skirt and crept up my body. He ghosted his fingertips across my collarbone and along the side of my neck until he'd taken my jaw in his hand. His touch was feather-light, just gentle enough to be teasing, yet strong enough that I could feel every inch of his fingers as they rested against my skin.

"Still a mistake." Once again, the words fell from me as a whisper. It was too light and breathy—I'd intended the words to be firm and steady, but the way my body was reacting to him had let me down.

Again.

"Still doesn't sound like you mean it," he murmured,

dipping his face close to mine. "Stop talking, Raven."

"No."

"I'll make you."

I knew exactly what I was doing when I said, "So make me."

He did.

He closed the distance between our lips and kissed me. It wasn't like before. There was nothing gentle about the way he pressed his mouth to mine and moved his hand so it slipped into my hair. There was nothing soft or tentative about the way he pushed his body between my legs and flicked his tongue between my lips to meet mine.

But, it was just as easy. Just as right. Just as perfect as it'd been before.

Maybe more, because as I grasped at his shirt to pull him closer, desperation tinged the air. It swirled around us with each kiss, each touch, each breath we gasped for between those very kisses and touches.

I couldn't pull him close enough. I couldn't bring his body close enough to mine to satisfy the heat that pumped through my veins. He'd put the heat there and now it seemed like there was nothing he could do as he gripped my hair in his strong hand and pressed his hips against mine.

His cock, hard and thick, pressed against my lower stomach. My clit throbbed, and a wave of need washed over me.

I didn't want this to stop at a kiss.

I wanted *everything*.

Maybe it wouldn't change how badly he annoyed me. Maybe it would be dangerous, the ultimate risk right now, but I didn't care. All I cared about was the fact he was kissing me and he wanted me—and I was kissing him, and I wanted him right back.

I slid my hands up his body as he pushed me back on the desk. Something fell to the ground to the sound of pens scattering across the floor, but neither of us stopped to pick up the mess.

Parker parted my legs and flattened his hand on the desk right by my hip. As he pulled away, I could barely catch my breath, and the dark glint that flashed in his eyes made me shiver. There was something wild about the way he looked at me, about the way he wanted me.

His hand was still firmly buried in my hair, still gripping tightly, when he brought his mouth to my ear. "Tell me not to kiss you again," he whispered. "Tell me not to fuck you...*Boss*."

He was being cocky, and I knew I should. Stop was the only word that should have been able to leave my mouth, but instead of doing what he said, I whispered right back, "No. I won't."

He inhaled sharply and, running his nose across my cheek, brought himself back to meet my gaze. Eye-to-eye, neither of us moved, and neither of us said another word. Controlling my breathing was a struggle, and the deep, bassy beat of the music creeping in from the bar didn't help me with regulating it at all.

"Have you thought this through?" Parker asked me quietly.

"Have you?" I fired back.

"Yes, and it's a damn bad idea."

"So, why not just leave?"

"Because I've never wanted anyone who infuriates me as much as you do." His voice stayed strong. "And I have the unnerving urge to make you lose control."

I ran my tongue out over my lips. "Yet, here you are. Still talking. Don't you have a better use for that mouth?"

"Yes. You're about to come in it." He'd barely finished speaking before his mouth was back on mine.

This kiss was even harder than before. More desperate. Devouring. Relentless. By the time he was dragging his lips down the curve of my neck, mine felt chapped and sore, but the tingles that vibrated over my skin overpowered it.

I dropped my head back when he grazed his teeth

across my neck, nipping my skin lightly. My clit was throbbing, and the wetness between my legs would have been uncomfortable if he hadn't already made his intentions perfectly clear.

He tugged at my shirt to free it from the waistband of my skirt. He'd barely pulled it free when he had my arms above my head and the tank free of my body. I was about to complain, but he released me to pull his own shirt over his head.

I didn't get a chance to admire his body as he gripped my hips and, with a step back, kissed his way down my body. I dropped my head back again, when all I wanted to do was throw myself down to lie flat on the desk. My wrists hurt with the pressure of keeping me supported. An ache that sharpened when Parker yanked on my skirt, sliding it right down without lifting my ass off the desk.

His mouth found mine as he brushed his finger over my thong. He could feel my wetness, if the smile he kissed me through was anything to go by. He didn't say anything. He just laughed quietly, especially when I tried to squirm away from his touch.

He didn't allow me to. He pulled my hips back to the edge of the desk and dropped to his knees.

This time, I reached behind me to clear anything from the desk, knocking a folder to the floor, and lay back. Right as my head hit the desk, Parker slipped two fingers beneath my underwear and pushed it to the side. I held back a gasp as he ran his fingers through my wetness, finding my clit in seconds.

He replaced his fingers with his mouth. His tongue deftly moved across the tender wetness of my pussy, circling my clit with its tip. I threw my arm over my eyes to block him from my view as he explored the most intimate part of me with his mouth.

His lips, his tongue, his teeth—gentle, hard, hesitant. He used every trick in his arsenal. It didn't matter if it was his mouth or his hands. He played me with them both, owning my body to the absolute brink of desire. He played me until I had to lower my arm from my eyes to my mouth to muffle the sound of my orgasm when it came.

Parker slid his tongue up my pussy. I lay back on the desk, my face covered, my cheeks heated with a mixture of pleasure and embarrassment. I couldn't believe what'd just happened, yet at the same time, I wasn't surprised in the slightest.

He kissed his way up my stomach. My body still trembled from the orgasm, but if he noticed, he didn't let on. He trailed his mouth up my bare stomach and over my breasts until he was standing between my legs and his cock pressed against my pussy.

His pants were still on.

I took offense to that. There was no way I was lying there, wet and freshly orgasmed, without him being as naked as possible.

I gripped hold of him and pulled myself up. At least, I think he did. He moved up at the same time I did, so I assumed he pulled me with him.

My hands slipped down his muscular arms to his waist. I dropped them further as he pressed his lips to mine. My legs ached to wrap around his waist as my fingers found the waistband of his pants.

His tongue found mine.

My fingers flicked the button open.

His hands pulled my hips against his own.

I tugged on his pants, freeing his cock.

His cock, hard and firm, almost fell into my palm. I wrapped my hands around it as my body pulled him closer. My hand wasn't enough. I wanted so much more than was being offered to me.

Come here," Parker murmured, one hand around the back of my neck as he kissed it. He pulled me up to my feet then, with smooth, easy movements, spun me around and bent me over the desk.

My hands broke my fall. I was on my tiptoes as he

fumbled behind me, but I was still shaken from my orgasm, so I didn't look back over my shoulder. Plus, there was something strangely sexy about being in the position I was.

Sure, I was exposed to him, but he'd just had his tongue between my legs.

You didn't get much more exposed than your clitoris in someone's mouth.

The sound of something ripping traveled through the air to my ears, and I bit the inside of my cheek. I knew that sound, and I knew what was happening next.

Seconds passed before I felt Parker's hands glide across my ass. His thumbs dragged along until he'd pulled my underwear clear of my pussy. He'd barely let me go before his cock was pushing against my wetness. I held completely still, my heart going wild, as he slowly pushed himself inside me.

Keeping control of my breathing with his almost hesitant movements was the hardest thing. I felt every inch of him as he buried his cock inside me right to the hilt, and a part of me wanted to moan. I was still tender, still sensitive, and that meant I was hyper-aware of everything.

Of his hand on my ass.

Of the fingertips digging into my hip.

Of his own restraint as he held his cock deep in my pussy.

"Are you just gonna stand there?" The words escaped me before I could stop them.

Parker leaned forward, somehow moving deeper into me, and wound my hair around my hand. One sharp tug brought my head back, and he kissed the side of my neck. "Just deciding how hard I have to hate-fuck you."

I swallowed, the lump in my throat thick and unmoving despite my best efforts. "That depends how much you hate me right now."

"You have no idea," he said right into my ear before pulling back.

Judging by the way he pulled out and slammed back into me so hard our skin slapped as it came together, he hated me a whole lot.

That was okay, because I hated that I'd lost control. I hated that I'd gone this far.

I hated that I wanted to go this far.

I hated everything he was and everything we were doing, but not because it was happening. I hated it because it didn't feel wrong like it should have.

No. Being fucked by Parker Hamilton felt perfectly right. Even if I was bent over my desk with a bar full of people on the other side of the door.

Every movement he made punctuated our mutual feelings for the other. Years of hate and our more recent attraction mingled into a desperate desire that fueled his thrusts. There was nothing kind or careful about the way he fucked me. It was hard and dirty and unforgiving.

I bit my cheek to keep in the sounds of my pleasure. The stinging of my scalp where he still had a tight grip on my hair combined with the wild way he pounded his cock into me mixed up into a mounting ball of pleasure that pulsed dangerously close to the edge of oblivion.

I opened my mouth, and three knocks at the door shattered the moan that rested on the tip of my tongue.

I reached back, but Parker stilled inside me and relaxed his hold on my hair.

"Raven?" Sienna called. "Is everything okay?"

"Yes!"

Parker slowly eased out of me.

"Okay, well, it's getting busy again."

"I'll be right there!" I clenched my fist as I brought it down to the desk.

Parker slammed back into me. A sound somewhere between a squeal and a moan left my mouth, and I had to clap my hand over it, but it was too late.

"Are you all right?" Sienna shouted.

"Yes!" I froze. "I...stubbed my toe getting up."

Parker fell forward, pressing his face between my shoulder blades. His whole body shook with his silent laughter, and I had to bite my tongue to stop myself laughing, too.

"Okay..." Sienna paused. "Then I'll see you in a minute?"

"Yep. That works."

"Okay."

Neither of us moved until we were sure she'd gone.

"Stubbed your toe?" Parker asked, his lips moving across my skin. "Really?"

"I had to think quickly!"

His hand wound back around my hair, and again, he kissed my neck. "You better come quickly, too, because you aren't leaving until you have."

Before I had a chance to respond, he straightened and resumed his rhythm from before we were interrupted. He didn't miss a beat as he continued fucking me with the same unforgiving thrusts. It didn't take long for my body to respond the way it was before, and I closed my eyes as the first wave of pleasure rolled through me.

He let go of my hair.

Grabbed my hips.

Held me still.

And fucked me even harder.

My arms collapsed under me, and I buried my face in them as I crumpled to the desk. Despite that, he still didn't relent.

Seconds. It took no more than a handful of seconds for my orgasm to hit, and it hit me hard. My entire body clenched and trembled. Sweat beaded on my skin. My lungs burned. And none of that mattered to him as he dug his fingers harder into my skin.

He groaned. The second it left his mouth, he slowed until he stilled. He held himself inside me for a good minute. The only sounds were both our breathing as we tried to regulate it, tried to get back to normal.

But I knew one thing.

We would never be normal again.

16
Parker

*F*uck.
Fuck. Fuck. Fuck. Fuck.
I loosened my grip on Raven's hips, gently bringing my hands down to her fucking perfect ass. Slowly, I pulled my now semi-hard cock out of her wet pussy. She pushed herself up onto her elbows, and her whisper of "Shit," wasn't nearly quiet enough if she was trying to keep it from me.

It wasn't out of place, it just wasn't quiet enough.

I rolled the condom off and threw it into the trash. My entire body was tense, and not because I'd just come harder than I had in a long time, but because of this situation.

It was a good idea when she was coming in my mouth.

Now, with it all said and done, neither of us could have ever made a worse choice than this.

There was no longer a line. We'd crossed it. We'd spit

on it and rubbed it out. We'd completely removed any trace of any kind of line with what we'd just done.

I backed away as Raven moved herself to standing. This was so fucking awkward, and it didn't get any less awkward as she grabbed a few tissues from the box on the other side of her desk and wiped between her legs.

Neither of us said a word until we were fully-clothed again. She grabbed a brush from a drawer and tugged it through her messy, dark hair, looking somewhere over my shoulder. "In the interest of not fueling any workplace gossip, you should probably leave out the back."

She was right, but... "You're not gonna talk about what just happened?"

She uncapped a lipstick and looked in the mirror. Ignoring me, she brushed the wand over her lips, leaving them parted to dry. She put on another coat, followed by some gloss, then rubbed her lips together.

"Raven."

"No!" She ran her fingers through her hair and finally looked at me properly. "Because I need to process what the hell we just did, try not to throw up with guilt, and do my job, okay? So, no. I'm not gonna talk about what happened right this second."

Yeah. The guilt. It was creeping into my bloodstream. It was vicious, and it was accompanied by the hint of self-loathing.

"I'm not working tomorrow," I said, stopping by the door.

She nodded. "I know. That's probably for the best."

Was it?

It didn't matter. She had her mind made up, and it would take an act of God to change it. She didn't want to talk about it right now, and maybe that was the best choice. I sure as fuck didn't know what to say to her.

I left and turned to the back without another word. Nothing I could say would make what we'd just done any better. It wouldn't change the fact that I didn't regret it, either. It would just worsen this already screwed up situation.

I leaned against the wall as soon as I stepped outside. Then, it really hit me. I'd just fucked Raven. I'd just bent her over a goddamn desk and had sex with her. She'd cried my name as I groaned hers. She'd come all over my cock as I had inside her.

I'd just done the one goddamn thing I shouldn't have.

I had no idea what would happen next.

But none of this would ever be the same again. That much was obvious.

I rested my feet on the table on the back porch. It was almost completely silent in the back yard at my parents' house, and I welcomed the peace. I hadn't had any peace from my own mind since I'd left Raven, and I was wholly to blame for that.

I'd been able to think of nothing but her. Of nothing but what we'd done and how it'd felt. Of how I should regret it, but I couldn't.

That was the worst part. I didn't regret it at all. I couldn't.

I'd wanted to fuck her. She'd wanted it, too, no matter what she said from this point on. It'd been mutual—more than mutual. She'd responded just as enthusiastically as I'd been, and there was no denying it.

It still didn't stop the guilt, and no matter what she said, we had to talk about it. She couldn't avoid me forever. Sooner or later, we ran the risk of telling Ryan what had happened. The risk of one of us slipping up was too great.

Plus, we needed to talk about work. No doubt it would be really awkward now. The key was not letting on to anyone else that something had happened.

Work.

Home.

Family.
Friends.
We were fucked. We'd fucked ourselves by fucking each other.

And the worst part? I didn't know how I felt about her now, but I sure as hell no longer hated her. I no longer just respected her, either.

There was something...more. Some intangible feeling I couldn't put into words. I couldn't hold onto it long enough to form enough of a sentence to describe the way I felt whenever she looked into my eyes or opened that sassy mouth of hers.

It was foreign. Scary. Unwelcome.

I wanted her in ways I couldn't bring myself to admit to.

"Good morning." Mom slid the door shut behind her. "Please take your feet off my table."

I quietly laughed as I lowered my feet to the chair closest to me. "Morning."

She glanced at the chair with pursed lips before sitting next to me. "I suppose that's better."

"Life is about compromise, Mom."

"Hmm. How are you feeling this morning? You didn't seem yourself last night."

"Stressful day." That was the vaguest, truest answer I could give. "I didn't sleep well, so I'm glad I'm not working today."

She sipped from her coffee mug and set it on the table. "Are you and Raven getting along well?"

I meant to say "Better than before," but what came out was a heavy sigh.

Mom looked at me. Her dark eyes flitted across my face before she finally smiled, looking away.

I turned to her. "Why are you smiling like that?"

"You like her."

"I'm not entering into a discussion fit for teenage girls, Mother."

"I'm not attempting to do that at all. But, clearly, you're feeling conflicted over something, and this is the only possible thing it could be. I have to admit, I wondered if the two of you had some hidden feelings beneath all that fighting."

"No hidden feelings," I said. "Ever. The hate was...is...real."

"Except you don't look like someone who hates her."

"She doesn't have to be object of my hate for it to be directed toward her."

"Do you have feelings for her?"

Another sigh escaped me. I was getting a headache with this line of questioning. It was bad enough I had it inside my own mind. I didn't need my mom's interrogation, too.

"She's a smart, beautiful woman," I said. "But she's also Ryan's sister, so anything I may or may not feel about her is irrelevant."

Something I should have reminded myself before I stuck my cock eight inches inside her.

"Hardly irrelevant." Mom picked her mug back up and tucked her ankles beneath her chair. She wasn't looking at me, she was staring out at the flowers lining the side of the yard. "I'm sure Ryan wants nothing more than the both of you to be happy, regardless of how that happens."

"Just drop it, Mom. I'm trying to reconcile these unwanted emotions with my friendship with him and this isn't helping."

"Yet you still fall into my traps." She turned her face toward me and smiled serenely.

"Great. Thanks." Keeping the annoyance out of my voice was harder than I thought I'd be. "Don't you dare do anything with the information you just weaseled out of me."

"Wouldn't dream of it, darling," she said breezily, standing up. "I always fancied Raven as a daughter-in-law."

I gaped at her as she crossed the porch and disappeared back inside. The sliding door squeaked behind her as it bounced off the frame and stayed a few inches open.

Fan-fucking-tastic.

I should have excused myself the moment she walked outside, because there was no way in hell she wasn't going to take that information and run with it.

The idea of my mother knowing I had *feelings* for Raven was more than a little alarming to me. Given that her best friend was Raven's mom, the thing I hadn't meant to say was probably making its way around the Karras family right now. I hoped like hell it wasn't, because that meant Ryan would find out from someone other than me.

The entire situation was my fault. I knew that. If I'd only kept my selfish wants in check, none of this would be happening, and I wouldn't be worried that Mom would be spilling my secret.

The secret I barely understood myself. I couldn't wrap my head around the things I was feeling. It was so new and unexpected. This was supposed to be easy—one summer, a few days, only necessary interaction with Raven.

But, it hasn't worked out like that. We'd spent more time together than was necessary, and we still had to pair the cocktails with the meals. There were things that needed to happen, and I needed to not let these developing feelings get in the way of that.

First and foremost, we had a business relationship. That needed to be the primary focus here. The personal one was what it was.

We'd always been fucked up.

Now, we were maybe beyond that. All I could hope was that she didn't have the same dumb feelings I was developing for her. Then, we'd be able to move on.

I needed us to be able to move on.

That was exactly how I ended up outside Dirty after lunch...On my day off.

There was no doubt in my mind that Raven was here. She always was. I didn't know if it was because she lived above the bar or because she was really that much of a control freak, but if I walked through those doors, I'd find her.

Getting through the doors was my problem.

She seemed grateful that I wouldn't be working today. Like she wanted the space. Honestly, I did, too. I wanted space from her, but the more space I took, the more confused I found myself. Clearing this situation up was my ultimate priority.

I was twenty-eight. Bantering with her like a child was one thing—leaving something like this hanging was something else all together.

I had neither the desire nor the patience to ignore this for longer than necessary.

I wouldn't lie and say that catching her off-guard wasn't something else I was hoping for. She was most outspoken when she was caught unawares, and that was the thing I wanted. I didn't want her to have prepared an entire speech or whatever for me. While I had no doubt that I could see right through whatever bullshit she'd attempt to feed me if that were the case, I still didn't want to waste my time listening to her spewing it.

Because, she would. This was Raven. This was controlled, stoic, steady Raven. This was the side of her she exercised to the letter. This was the front she gave out to the world, because losing control involved emotion, and neither losing control or emotion were things Raven was particularly good at expressing.

I'd seen her do both.

That was how her ex-boyfriend got his windshield smashed.

I had no desire to put my car in the shop because her temper got the better of her.

Besides, she still owed me breakfast.

My phone buzzed from its hole in the car door. The

sound was almost violent against the plastic, and the 'ding' that accompanied it was far too loud. I grabbed it and hesitated when I saw her name on the screen, but my curiosity won over and I opened her text.

    Raven: *Is it fun sitting in the parking lot?*
    Me: *Are you gonna shout at me?*

Of course, she'd seen me. I'd been sitting here like a tool forever.

    Raven: *If you're coming here to talk, get on with it. I'm tired of wondering if you're going to finally get out of that damn car.*
    Me: *You didn't answer my q.*
    Raven: *Of course I didn't. That would mean I'd incriminate myself when I ultimately lose my temper at you.*
    Me: *It takes two to tango, hotshot.*
    Raven: *Yeah, well, it only takes one to punch you in the balls, which I should have done yesterday.*

Ouch.

I got out of the car and stuffed my phone into my pocket. If her text was any indication of how this conversation was going to go, I had no right walking into that bar. The smart thing would have been to stay into my car, drive away, and tell her I'd see her tomorrow.

I wasn't a smart guy.

I was apparently a guy with a death wish that needed to be fulfilled by a crazy hot, half-Greek spitfire I couldn't get the fuck out of my mind.

The lights were all blaring when I stepped on. The radio was nothing but a quiet burr in the background, and the noise coming from the kitchen had me itching to go in there. It was my first day off since she'd hired me and only because she'd made me take it.

"Go in there." Raven's voice came from somewhere behind the bar. "I know you're dying to."

I walked to the bar and leaned over it. She was sitting cross-legged on the floor in front of a fridge, two beer bottles in her hand.

"How did you know?" I asked her.

"Psychic." The bottles clinked as she put them in. "I think Wes was going to call you. Alex isn't happy Wes is in charge."

"Then Alex should learn how to do his job."

"I did mention that." She moved, swinging her legs beneath her so she was kneeling instead. "That didn't go down too well. Apparently, he forgot who pays his wages."

I was glad I wasn't Alex.

"So, I told him to sit his ass down outside like a child and come back when he had some respect."

"He's still out there, isn't he?"

"I don't know. I don't give enough shits to check the kitchen." She said all that without looking at me. She crawled to the other fridge and opened the door. "So, feel free to go out there before you chew my ass out."

"Why do you think I'd—never mind. Hold that thought." I shook my head as I headed for the kitchen.

I pushed the door open to the view of Wes working his ass off. That guy wasn't being paid enough, I was sure. When—if—I left Whiskey Key, he needed my job. He was good enough and he was a quick learner.

"Hey, Wes. Raven said Alex was outside. Wanna explain?"

"Chef. Hey." He glanced over his shoulder. "He used attitude on Raven and she didn't exactly like it."

That told me everything I needed to know.

I sighed. "He's definitely still outside?"

"As far as I know."

I put two fingers up in thanks and headed for the back door that lead to the back seating area. Two steps outside told me that Alex wasn't here. The fact his jacket was on the table was further confirmation of the thing I'd suspected—he'd quit. He wasn't cut out for this job. I'd known it the first time we'd worked together alone, and this wasn't surprising to me at the least.

I was equal parts pissed and happy. Pissed because this was my day off and now I'd have to work, but happy because it meant I didn't have to deal with a mediocre member of staff any longer.

I grabbed his jacket from the table. The material silently crumpled in my hand. I didn't know what annoyed me more—the fact I'd hired someone who was apparently useless, or that he didn't have the balls to say he was quitting. That was all I expected. A note, a text, whatever. Just the information straight from the horse's mouth.

I slammed his jacket onto the side in the kitchen and pulled my phone from my pocket. Wes startled at my hard slam, but he said nothing as I lifted the phone to my ear.

"Shit the—" Raven poked her head inside one of the kitchen doors. She trailed off when she took sight of me with the phone. The call ticked over to voicemail after ringing several times, and that was the thing that pushed me over the edge.

"Alex, if you're quitting, at least have the decency to say so instead of leaving your jacket in the garden seating area. If you can't take the heat, I'm glad you've gotten the fuck out of my kitchen. In case you didn't understand, in the absence of your resignation, you're fired." I hung up and stuffed the phone back into my pocket.

Wes caught the jacket when I threw it at him. "Wash it, Chef?"

I nodded once, sharply.

Raven cleared her throat.

I turned to her. She was standing half in the kitchen, half out, and she was hugging the edge of the door. Her bright, red fingernails stood out against the light wood. "Can I help you?" I asked, much calmer than I felt.

"I came to see if you're okay, but now I'd like to talk to you. Privately."

Wes froze.

Raven smiled at him, one that reached her eyes and made them sparkle. "Don't worry. I promise, this is personal. My brother just called."

That last part was a lie. Her right eyebrow twitched, and I knew that was her tell. It was definitely personal what she wanted to talk about, but while Ryan probably had something to do with it, he wasn't the reason for it.

"Are you good to continue prep for a while?" I turned to Wes. "I shouldn't be long."

"All good, Chef," he answered, heading for the back door that lead to the small washer-dryer area Raven had for our chef's stuff. "Take all the time you need."

That wasn't the answer I wanted.

Raven nodded toward the door. I followed her through the back part of the restaurant and out to the hall that lead to her office, cellar, and apartment. She stuffed a key into the one door I'd never been inside and twisted.

One door separated her apartment and bar. How did I feel about that? I wasn't sure. That didn't seem like a lot of space at all...Never mind the deadbolt on the other side of the door that I noticed as I closed it.

"Throw the bolt through," Raven threw over her shoulder. "It'll stop anyone interrupting us. They can call me on extension one if they need me."

I clicked the bolt through and walked up the solid wood stairs. "I didn't know anyone could call you."

She held the vodka bottle tight in her grip in her kitchen area. "I never told you my extension."

"Your management skills need some work."

She rolled her eyes as she added whiskey to both glasses.

"Vodka and whiskey? What are you making this time?"

"Winging it." She pulled pineapple juice from her fridge and poured some into both glasses.

"Whiskey and pineapple juice?"

"White wine." She grabbed a green-tinged bottle and

poured a splash into each glass. "I told you, I'm winging it. And I feel like alcohol is needed here."

She wasn't wrong.

"I trust you," I said. "I think."

I left her in the kitchen and walked through the hall to the front room. It wasn't big by any means, and she had all kinds of girlie clutter all over the place. Magazines and books littered the wooden coffee table that sat perfectly in front of the L-shaped sofa. Something that looked a lot like an e-reader was balanced on the arm of the brown, suede sofa, and a pair of—hopefully—clean socks lay on the top of a cushion.

Fresh flowers brightened the room, and the lone, wide windowsill was full of photos in frames. Drawn to it, I walked there and bent forward to see the photos. There were some I recognized—one was from her twenty-first birthday, another from her senior prom. Some were family pictures, and the others were more recent. Camille and Lani were in a couple, and one was a selfie gone wrong judging by the fact I could only see half of all their heads.

"Here."

I turned at the sound of Raven's voice. She held a glass out in front of her, and I stared at it as I took it. "I'm thinking it might be early for this."

She shrugged and sat down. "My great aunt Maria arrived this morning and immediately came to question me about my sex life. I need both our drinks to be able to function today."

"Yet you still managed to put on your lipstick."

"My lipstick is like a bra. It's a good support system, and the only person who's able to take it off is me."

I begged to differ, but still. "You wanted to talk?" I sipped the drink. It was crazy strong so, with a nudge to a stack of magazines, set it down on the table.

She nodded and tucked her hair behind her ear. She copied what I'd just done by setting her glass on the table, too. Her breasts rose as she took in a deep breath, and she punctuated the exhale by falling back on the sofa and diving her hand into her hair.

Clearly, whatever she had inside her head was staying there. Still, I waited. Never mind that I'd come here to talk to her. If she wanted to talk right this second, I had to wait for her.

She was out of control. Only someone who knew her as well as I did would be able to tell it. She was in a situation she couldn't control, and she was struggling. Her jaw was tight and her fist was clenched, and her gaze flitted back and forth, focusing anywhere in the room but on me.

Her avoidance was so obvious it was almost laughable. Still, I waited some more. I didn't know what to say to her. I sure as hell couldn't tell her about the feelings I was developing, and I couldn't tell her we could ignore what happened yesterday.

There was no ignoring that.

There was only damage control.

The problem was I didn't know if I wanted to do damage control.

And looking at her sitting there in front of me with her thick, dark hair, captivating blue eyes, and fire truck-red lips did nothing but convince me that damage control was the wrong choice. Watching as a lock of hair fell from behind her ear so she could replace it again did nothing but endear her to me.

It didn't matter if she was giving you a look so sharp it could slice steel or telling you exactly what she thought of you, she did it all with an air of self-confidence. It was rapidly becoming clear to me that she marched to the beat of her own drum, one so many people didn't know existed. She didn't care what anyone thought of her, and as far as she was concerned, those opinions didn't exist in her world.

She was confident and strong, ruthless yet gentle.

She was beautiful, always.

But right now, doing absolutely nothing, Raven Archer was breath-taking.

Me?
I was fucked.

17

Raven

The way he looked at me was unnerving. His gaze was unwavering, intense, almost soul-piercing. I didn't know what it was about his eyes, about the way they looked at you so steadily it felt as though he could see right through you.

That was how it felt knowing he was looking at me despite the fact my own gaze was trained on the wall in front of me. It felt as though Parker could see right through my silence and into the deepest part of me where the words were stuck. Where they couldn't break through the thick silence I was suffocating in.

How was I supposed to tell him how I felt when I didn't even know? Was I supposed to tell him that I'd spent half my night struggling against my inability to regret what we'd done? Was I supposed to tell him that no matter how hard I tried, the guilt was never more than a whisper? Was I supposed to tell him that I'd looked in the mirror and told myself that having sex with him was wrong but I couldn't bring myself to believe it?

Was I supposed to lie? To tell him all the things I knew I should have felt but didn't? Hell, I was guiltier that I didn't feel guilty. It was the most screwed up situation.

It wasn't supposed to be like this. I wasn't supposed to feel the things I did for Parker Hamilton. I was supposed to be able to exercise the same control over my emotions the way I did the rest of my life and my business, but he shot all that to shit.

He wasn't the same guy I once knew.

I knew that, but I had no idea how right I was when he walked onto my parents' back porch. He'd never been tempting or dangerous to me, yet now, he was the catalyst for everything that could go wrong in my life. I wanted him but I didn't want to. I wanted to feel his lips against mine one more time.

His hand in my hair. His body against mine.

I wanted more than just the memory of those things. I wanted the reality of them, and that was why I couldn't speak. The words were stuck on my tongue, whatever they were. I had no idea what I wanted to say. This entire situation needed to be cleaned up, but I didn't know how to do that. I didn't think some lemon spray and a wet cloth would cover this.

Hell, a bottle full of bleach wasn't anywhere near enough for what we needed.

"I have to say that you excel at talking." Parker spoke after several silent, awkward minutes. "I agree with everything you've said."

My gaze flicked to him, and I glared. "I know asshole is your default mode, but there's no need to throw yourself into it so enthusiastically."

His quiet chuckle danced across my skin. "I know, but I want you to start talking before you bore me to death."

"I'll kill you myself if I have to."

"There's the Raven I know so well."

"You're such a monumental cockend."

"That's the nicest thing you've ever said to me. Except when you moaned my name, of course."

I bristled. "I did not moan such a thing."

He quirked an eyebrow. "I heard you loud and clear, hotshot. It was practically a fucking prayer."

"Then I need to get to church and pray for my soul."

"I'll join you. Your soul needs more than one prayer."

"You're making this impossible!" I grabbed my drink and swallowed a mouthful. A shiver ran through me at the cocktail's potency. That was what happened when my brain overtook my common sense.

Hell reigned free.

"Then talk." Parker's words were clear and concise.

This was all I had. If I didn't talk soon, he would, then I'd be screwed.

"What the hell do we do?" My words spilled from my mouth before I could do a thing about them. "How do we take what we did and move forward? Are we meant to pretend it didn't happen?"

"Yeah." He said the word so simply, I didn't think he'd bothered to think about it at all. "That's exactly what we have to do. Never discussing it again is the only way Ryan will never find out."

"Right. Of course. So simple." I sipped from my glass again. It burned as I swallowed.

"Actually, doing that is another thing," Parker continued. "Because from my own personal experience, when I think about something too much, I tend to voice it. Which means I'm pretty fucked, because I can't stop thinking about fucking *you*."

I set my glass down and avoided eye contact. "I can see how that would be a problem for you."

"I see how this is going. I'm talking and you're avoiding. In more ways than one."

"It's pretty cocky of you to assume I've done nothing but think about having sex with you." Cocky, not incorrect. If only he were wrong.

"Cocky, confident...Are they really that different?"

"Parker, you're a fully-grown man. Stop talking to me like you're a dumb teenager, because if that's the way this conversation is going to go, I'm not interested." I swung my gaze up to meet his and found him scooting across the sofa to me.

His eyes were dark and hooded as he got closer, and his attention dropped to my lips for the barest fraction of a section before his gaze settled comfortably on mine. He was right next to me now, within touching distance, and that was exactly what he did.

He touched my hair, teasing several strands between his finger and thumb. A shiver tickled across my arms, and he leaned in, bringing his lips too close to mine. "You want to have a conversation like an adult, Raven? Then stop hiding stuff. Be honest with me about how you're feeling right now. That works two ways, hotshot. You can't have me be honest with you only to keep your own feelings inside."

"Actually, that sounds like the perfect way for this conversation to—"

He cut me off by pressing his thumb against my lips. His eyes still focused on mine, he said, "My biggest problem with you right now isn't that I can't stop thinking about what we did. It's not even that there isn't a part of me that doesn't want to lie you back right now and fuck you all over again. My biggest problem with you is that I'm trying to hate you the way I have done for years, and I can't."

Uh-oh.

"I want you more than I hate you, and that screws with me. Because no matter how many smart comments you make at me or how you try to hide how you're feeling, I can't deny the fact that a part of me wants more than just your body."

Oh no.

Now we were in trouble.

I didn't know what to say back to that. He wanted me to be honest? Fine, but it wasn't as easy as he thought it was.

Putting the way I felt right now into words was impossible, because I had no idea how I felt.

"It doesn't...You can't..." I let go of a long, deep breath. "You know that can't happen. What happened yesterday shouldn't have happened. The point of this conversation is to discuss what happened and make sure what what happened never happens again, and that doesn't involve what you or I or Mother freakin' Nature wants to happen because absolutely one hundred percent none of that can happen."

Parker paused. "I don't know if I'm more impressed you said that without taking a breath or the amount of times you used the word 'happen' or 'happened' without getting tongue-tied."

A frustrated groan escaped my lips, and I pushed up to standing. "You know nothing else can happen, so don't tell me how you think you feel, because that just fucks up this entire situation."

"As opposed to its already non-complicated standpoint."

"Can you stop being so annoyingly logical?"

A lopsided grin stretched across his face. "Now I understand why you're such a smartass. It's kinda fun."

I wasn't going to smile.

Nuh-uh.

No way.

Not a—

Shit, I was smiling. Of course, I was.

I rubbed my hands down my face and shook my head. I might have smiled, but I wasn't going to laugh. "I'm an accidental smartass."

"Just like I'm accidentally really good in bed." That grin was still in place.

"You're not bad on a desk, but I have no comment about the bed."

"I can make that happen."

"That is not happening." I pointed a finger at him.

"That doesn't solve this problem."

"True," he said slowly. "But it would remove a great deal of stress from it. At least for the short term."

This was ridiculous. This conversation was going around in circles. There was no way in hell I was going to get anything decent out of this conversation.

"Clearly, you're not in the right frame of mind to discuss this today." I ran my hands through my hair. "Let's try again tomorrow."

"Raven." Parker saying my name made me stop and turn back to him.

He got up from the sofa and came toward me. My heart beat a little faster every time he took a step and came closer to me. By the time he reached my, my heartbeat was too wild to control, and my entire body was buzzing with his nearness.

He hesitated before bringing a hand to my face. His palm was soft against my cheek, and I stared at him as he slid his hand through into my hair. I knew what was coming. Stopping it should have been my ultimate goal, but the closer his mouth came to mine, the more I wanted him to kiss me.

One kiss. That was all it was. One firm yet soft kiss that sent sparks across my skin.

One kiss that made me believe in the words he'd just said to me.

One kiss that stirred the feelings I'd shoved away into the wilderness of my mind.

"We're not going to talk about this again." His voice was low, his nose brushing mine as he slowly pulled back. "Because the outcome isn't going to change. I'm still not going to hate you, Ray, and you're not gonna hate me either. I'm still going to want to kiss you. Still going to want to fuck you. All talking about how wrong this is does is make me want you more."

I opened my mouth, but he slid his hand back to my cheek and pressed his thumb to my lower lip.

"Now, if you tell me right now that I'm wrong and

Mixed Up

you don't want me, that I'm a delusional idiot who needs punching in the face, then fine. No more conversations and no more of this. I'll just be the guy who works in your kitchen you've known your whole life. But if you tell me I'm right and that I'm not the only one torn between want and loyalty, then we're both terrible people, so we might as well be terrible in private, in our own time."

"On a desk?"

"Desk, bed, wall, pool table—I'm not fussy. I have ideas for all four places."

My lips curled up to one side, but I sighed. "You make it all sound so simple."

"Good, because I don't think it is at all." He ran his thumb across the curve of my lower lip. "I just need to know if I'm justified feeling the way I do."

The thumping of my heart was becoming almost aching—like a warning that I was walking into a situation that would shatter it.

"You're leaving at the end of the summer, so on one hand, it's not a big deal. On the other...The fact I find myself struggling to despise you is."

Parker smirked. "Maybe I am leaving, maybe I'm not. Would if I have a job if stay?"

"Only if you have a reason to be here."

"Maybe I will." He leaned in again. "Help me find one."

So, I said the only word I could, given the circumstances.

I said, "Okay."

***

If I had to give my past self any advice, it would be: Don't, under any circumstances, give your family cocktail making lessons. You will regret it.

That advice would have been good at eight a.m. when I agreed, and forty-five minutes ago when my grandmother, great-aunt, and cousin walked into my bar.

See, what I should have done was told them I was sorry, but I couldn't do it today. Especially since Aunt Alexa had yet to arrive and there had already been one smashed glass thanks to Great-Aunt Maria's overzealous pouring.

"Too much!" I yelled, waving my hands around. I took the tequila bottle out of Maria's hands and put it a good two arms-lengths away from her. "One shot. The Pussy Pounder only needs one shot."

"Are you mixing drinks or filming a porno?" Parker's voice made me turn to him. He stepped into the bar wielding a large, silver tray that had the hummus platter and more on.

Yia-Yia's nose twitched. "I smell food. Is it good?"

"I sure hope so. And if it's not, I didn't cook it." He winked at me as he carefully put the tray on the bar surface.

"And if good?" Yia-Yia demanded.

"Then obviously, I cooked it."

She smiled slyly at him.

"Thanks," I said to him, ignoring the way my cousin, Athena, was staring at him. "How are you doing, Theney?"

All right, maybe not. But I had some kind of claim on him now, right?

Probably not, given the fact nobody could know we were apparently getting physical.

"I think I have it." She blushed and pushed the drink to me. "What do you think?"

I grabbed a fresh straw and put it in the drink. "Not bad, but just a little more lemonade."

"Mmm, good." Yia-Yia hummed, half a ring of calamari in her hand.

Parker grinned. "I made that."

"No, you didn't. Wes makes the batter." I ran the cocktail shaker Athena had just used under the tap beneath the bar.

"I fried it."

"You said you made it. You didn't." I shrugged and shut off the tap. "Just pointing that out."

Great-Aunt Maria snickered from her stool. She flung her hand out in Parker's direction and opened her mouth. Her fingers collided with the side of a full glass of Blue Balls, and it was only Parker's lightning-fast reflexes that saved a second glass from destruction at her hands—quite literally.

I grabbed the glass from him and slid it away.

Great-Aunt Maria looked at the glass as though she'd done something to offend it.

Parker put his hands on the bar and leaned over to speak quietly. "Maybe you should relocate this to your mom's kitchen so she breaks her glasses instead."

I sighed. "This whole thing is a bad idea," I said back just as quietly. I glanced at my family. Great-Aunt Maria had slid her glass back in front of her and turned to the food, but Yia-Yia had moved the glass just far away that it was safe.

I slid out from behind the bar and motioned for him to join me in the corner. "This is a disaster. In the past forty-five minutes they've been here, I've lost a glass, dented a cocktail shaker, and had to throw out an entire pot of raspberries because in case you didn't notice, Great-Aunt Maria has butterfingers."

"On the bright side," Parker replied, shoving his hands in his pockets. "It's only one glass, I can probably bash out that dent, and there are plenty of raspberries in the freezer."

I fought my smile. "That doesn't help the fact my cousin makes doe-eyes at you every time you walk past. Or the fact Yia-Yia has inquired as to the state of my uterus no less than five times, like I've just gone through immaculate conception right here in my bar."

"Your cousin is making doe-eyes at me? I didn't notice." His own eyes belied that with their sparkle.

I smacked his chest. "I don't care, I was just pointing it out."

"I would have believed that a lot more two days ago," he muttered, the words no more than a low buzz.

"Whatever. You have to help me get rid of them."

His eyebrows shot up. "How exactly do you expect me to do that?"

"I don't know. If I knew how to get rid of them, don't you think I'd be doing it myself?" I whispered, glancing in their direction. Thankfully only Athena was looking at us, so I offered her a reassuring smile. It was apparently enough, because she smiled back and returned to the conversation.

Parker peered at my family for a moment. "So, why do I get stuck with this?"

"Because you have ideas, and if you want them to become reality..." I whispered again, this time trailing off and leaving it for him to finish.

"That's playing dirty, Raven,"

With the flash of a grin, I spun on the balls of my feet and headed back over to the bar.

I was playing dirty—but so did he every time he kissed me.

18
Parker

One phone call to my mom had cleared the issue of the Karras' temporary invasion of Dirty. Sure, Mom had made some suggestions I flatly denied—like I was doing this to make Raven happy—and handled it.

I wasn't doing it to make Raven happy, per se. I was doing it because I wasn't stupid, and the happier she was, the happier I was likely to be.

If our relationship was maintained by us either fighting or fucking, I was going to choose fucking.

Our conversation this morning hadn't exactly gone as I'd intended. Of course, it going as I'd intended implied I'd had a plan, and I'd been winging it like hell. I didn't know what I wanted to say to her until I finally had the chance to say it. It was new, it was scary, and it felt as though we were balancing on a tight rope, just waiting for the other shoe to fall and it to come crashing down.

It had been nine hours since that conversation.

There was always the chance I was looking too much into it. I didn't know if we were truly in the same place, and I was getting to the point where, inside my own head, I was debating whether or not it was a better idea to walk up to Ryan and ask him if he cared that Raven and I apparently had feelings for each other.

On one hand, I'd seen him go after the guys who broke her heart or fucked with her.

On the other hand, his reaction to me doing this behind his back would surpass that. It wouldn't even be the act itself, it would be the secrecy. Her entire family would act the same way. I wasn't oblivious to the fact that her mom had tried to set us up when she was seventeen. She'd dropped it pretty quick after Raven had *accidentally* dropped a match on one of her bushes, but there was no doubt that at the first whiff of any kind of niceties between us, everyone would hone in on it and start asking questions.

Much the way my mother currently was, except there were a lot more Karras' and Archers, and they were a hell of a lot crazier than the Hamiltons.

Plus—I was still leaving in a few weeks. A potential job was lined up in Washington state, and the money notwithstanding, the challenge would be fun. I hadn't lied to Raven earlier when I'd told her I might not leave. The problem was, I needed security, despite the fact I liked to travel.

If I was going to stay in Whiskey Key, I needed a reason.

And I wanted her to be my reason.

I shut off the lights in the kitchen and poked my head into the bar. "Is Raven here?" I asked Sienna.

She set a glass on the shelf and looked over at me. "She's in her apartment. She told me to tell you to go up."

"Thanks." I smiled and took a step back.

"Parker?"

I leaned out of the doorway again and met her eyes.

"Yeah?"

Pausing, she bit the inside of her lower lip. "Is something...going on with you and Raven?"

I stared blankly at her for all of a second. "Why would you ask that?"

Instantly, she blushed. "Nobody except her closest friends go up to her apartment. I've only ever seen Brett and Ryan go up there. You guys have been getting along all day, and I guess I jumped to conclusions. Sorry."

We needed to be meaner to each other.

With a snort, I said, "Don't worry. We're just working on something for the bar. Her family is less likely to need her at ten at night than they are at ten in the morning."

She smiled and threw me a thumb up. "Gotcha."

"Thanks, Sienna." I winked and headed back into the kitchen. The second the door shut, I shuddered. That girl had been too in my space ever since I'd started working here, and if Raven really knew that she'd attempted to kiss me the night she asked me out—something I'd blocked from my mind—then I doubted the working environment here would be as enjoyable as it was.

Never mind that I had to interview someone for the kitchen to replace Alex, and the guy who was coming in was the guy who'd tried to hit on Raven.

I knocked on the door to Raven's apartment and tried the handle. It clicked, opening the door, and I stepped in. The sound of Ed Sheeran traveled down the staircase to me. The woman had a real obsession with Ed Sheeran, it seemed. If she wasn't humming to his music in her headphones, she was listening to him, and maybe even—

Singing him. She was singing him.

Shape of You got louder the closer to the top of the stairs I got. So did her voice. And god, she could mix cocktails like a beast, but an alleyway full of cats would get a higher score than her in a singing contest.

"Is something dying up here?" I asked the second I opened the door at the top of the stairs.

Raven jolted, holding a glass of white wine in her hand.

I raised an eyebrow. "Isn't that against the rules for a mixologist?"

She slid her finger across her phone screen, and the music quietened. "No. It's pretty much common knowledge that we don't mix drinks unless we have to. That, and this is really good wine, so I'm making excuses for it."

I laughed, closing the door behind me. "As long as you aren't singing anymore, you can drink whatever you want."

"You're only saying that to get into my pants."

"Trust me, even if I didn't want in your pants, I'd be saying it."

"Are you saying I'm a bad singer?"

"Actually, I'm trying not to say that."

She sighed and perched on the arm of the sofa. "I'm lucky I'm pretty."

"And oh-so-modest, may I say?"

Her blue eyes found mine, and her lips curved to one side. She raised her glass to her lips, but the act of drinking wasn't enough to hide that tiny smile of hers. "I try."

I laughed and sat on the sofa. My keys dug into my thigh, so I pulled them, my wallet, and my phone out of my pockets. Dumping them on the coffee table in front of me, I turned my attention to the dark-haired beauty a few feet away from me. "All right. Cocktails and meals. Shall we get started?"

"We can, but I was hoping for a few minutes silence before that."

"That works. I just had to convince Sienna there's nothing happening between us."

"Technically, you were lying. There is nothing happening right now." She slid down off the arm onto the cushion. "It's all semantics and specifics."

"That's how you got away with being grounded so much as a teen, isn't it?"

She rolled her eyes. "Look, if my parents left loopholes, I exploited them. That's normal teen behavior."

"That's politician behavior. You're in the wrong career, hotshot."

"Mom dropped me at the gas station and said 'be back at ten.' I was back there at ten. She didn't specify there or home."

The chuckle escaped before I could stop it. "How did such a hellion become so put together?"

Raven turned in the seat, swinging her feet up on the cushion between us. "I got it all out in my teen years. By the time I did mixology, I had no rebellion left in me."

"Lies. You have rebellion left in you. Someone as wild as you were doesn't lose that."

"I wasn't wild." She paused, hugging her glass to her chest. "Maybe I feel a little rebellious sometimes, but for the rest of it...I have a business to run, and my promise to my grandparents means I can't fail. And if I fail, it means all I did in school was for nothing. It's like you training for years to be a chef and then putting sandwiches together in Wal-Mart or something. Not that a job isn't a job, but it's a waste of your skills."

"Now remember the time you put a brick through your ex-boyfriend's windshield and tell me you weren't wild."

"That was a one-off."

I raised an eyebrow. "How about the time you ran into the football team's change room and stole all their pants? Underpants and otherwise?"

"That was a dare," she said slowly.

"When you broke into the head's office and stole your school report because you knew you'd bombed that semester?"

"That was an unfortunate incident."

"That was captured on tape."

"That's what I'm referring to." She paused. "So, I wasn't a model team. We weren't all quarterback and dating the head cheerleader's sister."

So stereotypical. "I can honestly tell you I never once dated Amelia Cross or her sister." I shook my head. "I'd have rather cut off my hand than dated her. She was a bitch of the highest level. I'm waiting for the day she steps into the promo of those Real Housewives shows."

Raven swilled the wine in her glass. "She hated me. Probably because I put hair removal cream into her shampoo and she slowly started to lose her hair."

"I can't help but feel that's a valid reason to hate you."

"I didn't say it wasn't. But, in my defense, she shouldn't have stolen my bra during gym class and hung it from the streetlight."

The memory of our high school flashed in my mind. "How did she get it up there?"

"Physics," she answered simply. "Something she quickly learned about when everyone looked at my boobs instead of hers."

"I feel like this conversation has veered highly off topic," I said. "Not only because I'm now looking at your tits, but because I feel like I just stepped into one of those dumb TV shows about revenge."

Raven put her glass on the coffee table and picked up the polka dot folder. "Well, focus, because I'm ready to work."

"When are you not?"

"Exactly. Are we pairing these cocktails with dishes or not? My mom texted earlier and booked a table for fifteen. I need this done by then so I can give them a set menu."

"I can cater for them."

"I know you can. I just don't want to." She grinned. "I like to be awkward."

"I never noticed."

"Don't be a dick."

"Wouldn't dream of it." I flashed her grin right back at her and grabbed the menu. "All right, talk me through your cocktails."

Raven tucked her hair behind her ear and opened her folder. She went through several pages before settling on one. "I want to start with the appetizers."

So, start with them we did. We talked through each flavor and taste until her glass was empty. When that happened, she poured herself another glass of wine and brought me a bottle of beer. We moved slowly through her menu and mine until we had a decent amount of main dishes to cocktails. Double and triple checks happened, along with a heavy dose of doubts, but eventually, we made a menu that was marginally acceptable to Her Royal Highness, Duchess of Cocktailville.

"That was harder than I thought," I said, putting the menu down.

"Than *you* thought?" Raven raised an eyebrow. "I'm the one who had to create a whole new drink."

"And I'm sure the Cock Blocker is going to be a huge seller." I paused. "Maybe not for straight men or women. Or gay men."

She tapped her pen against her bright-red lips. "It's the ultimate wingman or best friend drink."

"If my wingman ever cock blocked me, I'd give him a black eye."

"Is that how my brother got a black eye on your twenty-first birthday?"

I stopped. "No, that was the chick he hit on. He forgot she had a glass in her hand, and she had a better aim than most baseball pitchers."

"Seems reasonable." She dropped her pen to her knee. "I'm sticking with Cock Blocker. It's that or Spank Bank."

"Spank Bank will sell better."

"Even if it doesn't come with item for said spank bank?"

Again, she made me pause. "Maybe go with Cock Blocker and put Spank Bank in the, er...notes section on your phone."

Her grin was so wide and infectious. Her eyes glittered with her silent laughter even as she delicately covered her mouth with her hand. There was just something about the way happiness spread across her features and lit up her face that was so enamoring. I could watch her laugh all day, without sounding like a weirdo.

Something about her being happy made me stupid happy.

I didn't like it at all.

"Good idea." She tapped out something on her phone, giggling. "Thanks. I feel like tonight was really productive."

"It was...in a roundabout way."

"Did the Cock Blocker cock block you?"

"You didn't make it, so no."

Raven jumped up off the sofa and darted around to the kitchen.

"That wasn't an invitation to make it!" I threw myself over the arm of the chair after her.

She grabbed a bottle of vodka from the bottle rack on the side. Hurrying my feet, I reached her just as she set the bottle on the side. The second her grip loosened, I swept her back and away from the alcohol.

In my experience, her cocktails lived up to their filthy names. I didn't need this one working against me.

I pulled her into my body. Her ass tucked against my pelvis, and she laughed wildly, wrapping her little hands around my wrists. I had almost a head of height on her when she was barefoot like she was right now, but there was something laughable about the way she fought me.

My arms had her locked into me, yet she wriggled and writhed like her life was dependent on it. My cock hardened with every time she moved her ass against it, and it didn't take her long to notice it, because she quickly stopped, almost sagging back against me.

I splayed my fingers across her stomach. The yoga pants she wore didn't give much resistance against my hand where her skin was concerned. I could feel the way her heart was beating where she was pressed so firmly against me and my left thumb crept up just high enough to feel that beat. It was the barest vibration against the side of my thumb, yet it was still harsh enough that I could feel every boom-boom as it rocked against her ribs.

She took a deep breath in. It was sharp and harsh, pushing her chest back into mine. A shiver spread across my skin as hers touched mine. The warm brush was more than enough to make me shiver and swallow back the heat of her touch.

"No Cock Blockers," I said into the softness of her hair. "Unless you want me cock blocked."

"That wouldn't be useful to me at all."

I laughed and spun her around so she was facing me. Looking down into her eyes, I pushed a loose strand of hair from where it was caught in her eyelashes and tucked it behind her ear. "Is that all I am to you? A cook and a cock?"

"That sounds like the title of a strangely hot porn movie." She paused. "But you could be worse things to me. Like a potential murder victim."

"Pretty sure I've spent twenty years being your potential murder victim." I grinned and wrapped my arms around her shoulders.

She slid hers around my waist and tilted her head back to meet my eyes. "Probably closer to twenty-two that I can remember, but close enough."

I dipped my head and brushed my lips over hers. "The more you talk, the less certain I am this is a good idea."

"Sex is always a good idea."

"I meant you and me."

"I know, but we've already established that this is a bad idea, so I chose to focus on the sex."

"I change my mind. You might be a good idea after all."

Raven threw her head back and laughed. The only way she stayed standing was because she was holding onto me, but the way her laugh bounced off the walls had me smiling down at her.

There was something about her when she laughed. It was so free and loud, so bright and warm. I could listen to it all day—as long as I was the person making her laugh. She needed to do it more. And by more, I meant all the time.

Her laugh tapered off into a gentle giggle before she went fully silent. A wide smile was still on her face as she brought her eyes back to mine. "I don't know why that was so funny, but it was."

"It really wasn't," I said. "I was just being honest."

"Maybe that's why it was funny. Because it wasn't actually funny at all."

"Raven? You talk a lot."

"I know, but I hear kissing shuts a girl up."

"Are you asking me to kiss you?"

She shook her head. "Merely planting the idea in your head."

It was my turn to laugh as I briefly rested my forehead against hers. She bent her fingers, grazing her nails across my back, and blinked up at me. The way her eyes glittered with her silent amusement pulled me in.

Raven Archer had her own gravitational pull, and I was afraid there was no breaking free.

I pushed my lips against hers. It was just a kiss, one measly little touch, but the warmth of her lips spread across my skin, teasing me into wanting more.

And want more, I did.

My hand snaked into her thick hair, and I swept my tongue across the seam of her lips. She shuddered as she parted them, allowing me to kiss her properly. The fabric of my t-shirt stretched as she pulled on it. It was simple but desperate.

My heart pumped fast, sending blood right down to my cock. She was right against me, and the exact moment she felt my growing erection was obvious in her tiny gasp, and in the way she leaned in to me.

Mixed Up

It was amazing that we'd gone from hatred to this the way we had. It almost didn't seem real, but I wasn't going to risk it. I was going to take the chances I had, because she was becoming more and more addicting every day.

Raven pulled away. Entangling her body from mine, she grabbed my hand and tugged. Without a word, she lead me across her apartment and through a door at the opposite end of the living room. Opening it revealed it as her bedroom, and she really didn't need any words after that.

She pulled me through the door, kicked it shut, and leaned up to kiss me. Her fingers fumbled with my shirt, and mine with hers as we moved back toward the giant bed in the center of the room. Both our shirts had been discarded and lay on the floor by the time her legs bumped against the edge of the mattress.

Raven fell back naturally. The momentary loss of her hands on my body sent a chill across my skin. I leaned over her on the bed and grazed my teeth over her lower lip as her hands found my sides once more. Her back arched, pressing her body into mine, and she wrapped her legs around my waist to hold me against her.

Unlike before, that was all me, this was all her. She was pulling me in, guiding me where she wanted, telling me what she needed from me. And I let her, because the second we were no longer separated by clothes, she wouldn't have a say.

I think she knew that.

She knew that the moment I was inside her, she'd no longer have any control, so she was exercising it now.

I let her.

I let her run her hands over me, pull my cock against her, undo my jeans with her nimble fingers. Let her pull them down, let her slip her hands inside my boxers, let her tease my hard cock.

She controlled the pace as I kissed her. Every movement and every touch was orchestrated entirely by her until she brought my hands to the waistband of her pants.

Then, I took over. The yoga pants peeled easily down her long legs, and the moment she was free of them, I parted her legs and lay over her.

My cock pressed against her pussy. My hands slid across her skin. My fingers probed her thighs and ass. My tongue flicked against hers.

She gripped my back, whimpering as I ground my hips against hers. My grip on her ass was tight, and my fingers just brushed against the rough, lace band of her thong. I wanted to rip it off her, to sink inside her until she screamed again. My cock throbbed as if it were reminding me just how badly I wanted her in that second—just how easy it would be for me to free it from my boxers fully, push her thong to the side, and slip inside her.

I pulled back from her and reached for my discarded jeans. Neither my pockets nor my wallet showed up a condom, but judging by the sound of a drawer opening and closing, I didn't need one.

Raven shoved one into my hand, kneeling on the edge of the bed. I stared into her eyes as I opened the packet and rolled the rubber on. Her cheeks were flushed bright red, and that only added to the sparkle of her eyes.

Pushing her back down on the bed, I slipped between her legs. She curled herself around me, locking her ankles at the base of my back, and reached between us. Jolts of pleasure ran through me when she wrapped her fingers around my cock and guided it toward her. With one flick of her thumb, she'd moved her thong to the side, and now, she had my cock at her wet pussy.

Slowly, I thrust my hips forward, and I eased inside her. She gasped when I paused, her pussy hugging the entire length of my cock. I waited for her to look me in the eye before I moved.

Then, I fucked her.

I fucked her until her body went rigid and she cried out.

I fucked her until my body was tense and I groaned

Mixed Up

into her mouth.
    I fucked her until neither of us could move anymore.

19

Raven

The sound of my phone buzzing on the nightstand was loud, jarring, and very, very annoying.

It wasn't the most pleasant sound in the world to wake up to.

Groaning, I rolled over and batted my hand around on the top of the nightstand. Then, I realized the bed was vibrating. It was a mammoth effort to open my eyes, but somehow, I managed it so I could look down the gap between the cupboard and my bed. Just like I assumed it was, my phone was wedged between the leg of the bed and the wooden side of my nightstand.

I fished it out with my finger. The moment it was free, it stopped ringing.

Of course, it did.

I picked it up and looked at the screen. Ryan. I frowned—it was early for him to be calling...wait, no it wasn't. It was seven-thirty. I'd overslept.

No sooner had I finished the thought than my phone buzzed again. It was Ryan.

"What do you want?" I demanded, answering the phone.

"Did you oversleep?" came his response.

"Maybe. I was tired. What do you want?"

He laughed. "Have you seen Parker?"

"You just woke me up. Do you think I've seen Parker?"

"Shall I call back when you've had coffee?"

"Can you get to the point of this irritating conversation?" I shoved the covers to the side and swung my legs out of the bed. I hadn't bothered to throw any clothes on before I'd fallen asleep last night.

Ryan sighed. "Ilsa said Parker didn't go home last night. She came over this morning when his car wasn't in the drive and asked me if I knew where he was. I don't, and you're the last person I know who would've seen him, so I'm calling you."

I jerked around and looked at the other side of the bed. Messy and unkept, but no Parker.

"No idea." I swallowed and glanced at the floor. His clothes were gone, too. Only mine remained. "Hold on." I put my phone down and checked the notification bar. There were no messages from him, so if he wasn't here and hadn't gone home, maybe he was downstairs?

I threw an oversized shirt on over my head and quickly pulled some panties up my legs before grabbing my phone again.

"I don't have any messages from him," I said, opening my bedroom door. "I can't hel—" I finished on a scream, because the missing man was standing shirtless in my kitchen.

"Raven?" Ryan said into my ear right as Parker glanced over his shoulder at me. "Are you all right?"

"Ssshhh—shit!" I held my finger in front of my

mouth. "Spider!" I said to Ryan. "I walked into the bathroom and there's a big spider in my tub."

Parker rubbed his hand down his face and shook his head.

"You're screaming at a spider?" Ryan's amusement was evident in his restrained tone.

"It's a big one. It scared me." I slammed my bedroom door behind me. "I just locked it in there."

"It's a spider."

"You're not helping." This was the worst lie ever. "I need to get rid of it, so I have to go. If I haven't heard from you by the time Parker starts work, I'll tell him to call his mom. Bye!" I hung up and threw my phone on the sofa like it was on fire.

"What the hell was that about?" Parker asked, spatula-flipper thingy in hand.

"You're still here!" It came out as more of a squeak than anything.

He stared at me for a moment. "Yeah, but I'm kind of stuck on the fact I've been both a stubbed toe and a spider this week."

I sunk my fingers into my hair. It was messy, and my fingers got caught on some small knots as they threaded through the locks. "Ryan called and woke me up." I summarized the phone call. "And I panicked when I saw you, because I didn't know you were still here."

"Why wouldn't I be here?"

"I fell asleep and thought you left!"

He shook his head, turning back to my cooker. "I fell asleep, too. I didn't wake up until your alarm went off this morning."

"Why didn't you wake me up? I'm late and I have to put orders through today."

"You didn't move," he said. "So I shut it off, took a shower, and came to make breakfast."

Now that he'd mentioned it, I could see his dark hair was wet. "Okay, well, you need to call your mom and tell her you aren't dead or anything."

"I'll text her soon. I can't do it right after Ryan's called you, can I? That won't look suspicious at all."

"Half an hour. Say I left you a voicemail to see if you were coming into work because you were MIA and you realized you forgot to tell her you weren't coming home."

"The fact I have to tell her I'm not coming home is, in itself, ridiculous."

"And that's why I live alone." I smiled and pulled a bottle of water out of the fridge. "What are you making?"

"Omelets. Yia-Yia left me omelet seasoning so I thought I'd try it."

I peered over his arm at the pan. "Where did you get the ingredients?" I knew for a fact I didn't have eggs in my fridge.

"Downstairs." He glanced at me as if the answer was obvious. Which it was, honestly. "Your fridge is both impressively empty and sadly understocked."

I shrugged and leaned against the counter. "I don't eat breakfast unless I'm forced to."

Parker slid the omelet out of the pan and onto a plate in one smooth movement. Then, he picked up the plate, and held it out to me. "Well, I'm forcing you to eat."

I might not have been a big breakfast eater, but I wasn't going to turn down food.

"I can deal with that." I smiled and reached for the plate, but before I could take it, he swung his arm out wide where I couldn't reach it. "Hey!"

He grabbed the front of my shirt, yanking me toward him. I'd barely righted my footing when he dropped his mouth to mine and planted a slow, easy kiss on my lips. Releasing me like he'd done nothing out of the ordinary, he put the plate back between us and also handed me a knife and fork. "Morning."

I snatched the plate and cutlery before he could take it away again. "Thanks. I think?"

He laughed as I sat at the table. "Your good morning

was screaming at me. The least you could do was kiss me."

I rolled my eyes and stabbed my fork into the cheesy, melty, eggy goodness. "You should have announced yourself. Left your pants on the floor or something."

"I'll remember that for next time."

"Next time? This is going to happen again?" I was teasing him, because let's be honest. There were worse things in life than having sex with a hot guy, then waking up to find said hot guy making you breakfast while half-naked.

"Yep. I'll just remember to call my mom first."

I laughed, then moaned as I finally put the first forkful of breakfast into my mouth.

Parker side-eyed me. "If you want to finish your breakfast in peace, don't do that again."

I flipped him the bird. His other option was to just ignore me, but that would be too easy, of course. So, I deliberately moaned with my next mouthful. And the next. And the next.

All the while, I watched Parker. He kept glancing over his shoulder at me, his lips twitching up to one side. He knew what I was doing, and that was kind of annoying. It was less fun when it didn't bug him.

"You're annoyed that isn't annoying me, aren't you?" he asked, dumping cheese into the pan.

"Kind of." I picked up my water bottle. "I can't help but feel like my intentions were grand, but the execution of it was really not."

"I would argue that your intentions were dumb."

"I think you're supposed to compliment a woman whose bed you stole."

"I didn't steal your bed." He put down the spatula and turned. I swear to god, his abs winked at me. "I borrowed half of it. Stealing it would imply you had to sleep on the floor."

"Maybe I did. I was very asleep. You could have put me on the rug and I wouldn't have noticed." I picked up my empty plate and carried it over to the sink. "For all I know, you had the entire bed."

He grabbed me wrists and pulled me into his body. "Raven, you're the biggest starfisher I've ever met. If anybody stole the bed, it was you."

"It is my bed." I blinked up at him. "And I've had it to myself for a long time."

"That's because you talk in your sleep." He kissed the end of my nose. It was almost too tender, but I couldn't deny the fizz of delight I felt.

"I do not talk in my sleep." I prodded his chest.

"You totally talk in your sleep. You were asking someone to take the dog out at three a.m., and you don't even have a dog." His eyes crinkled as he smiled. "I asked you who the dog was, and you told me it was Satan's hellhound."

"Um."

"Apparently, Satan's hound was hungry."

"Um..." Crap.

"So, I'm starting to wonder what goes on in that pretty little head of yours." He pulled me even closer to him, dipping his head. "And if I should be scared you might kill me in my sleep."

"Look," I said, raising my eyebrows. "If I haven't killed you after twenty-something years of you pissing me off, I'm not gonna off you now that you're giving me orgasms."

"If I knew that was all it took to make you like me, I would have done it years ago. It would have been worth the risk."

"Is it worth the risk now?"

"I need another night in bed with you. Your dreaming about Satan's hellhound has given me doubts."

I pursed my lips, and he took that as an invitation to kiss me again. I didn't mind. He tasted like fresh coffee and smelled like sunshine. Whatever the fuck sunshine smelled like.

"Parker?" I murmured against his mouth. "Your omelet is burning."

He let go of me so fast I staggered back. True as hell, when he pulled the omelet off the heat and put it on a plate, the underside was a little...black.

"This is pure gold," I said, walking back toward my room, giggling a little too much. "The three-starred Michelin chef just burned an omelet."

His dark eyes locked onto me. "I'm going to leave this for Satan's hellhound. Just in case he's hungry tonight, too."

I stuck my middle finger up at him and headed into the bathroom. "If he is, and he comes, I hope he shits on your head!"

His laughter was the last thing I heard before I locked the door and started the shower.

Why did that feel all too natural?

Satan's hellhound.

I'd spent the entire morning figuring out how I could have possibly talked in my sleep. As far as I knew, I was a snorer, not a talker. Not that snoring was any better, but at least there was no chance of saying anything really dumb like I apparently had.

Where did that even come from? What the hell was going on in my subconscious mind?

Was the hellhound code for my brother? Or my crazy family?

Both were viable options.

It was why I was at my parents' house in Key West and not at work. Never mind that I still had an order to place. According to my mother, that could be done anywhere as long as I had my laptop and phone with me, but the seating plan for dinner at the reunion couldn't be done anywhere else or even brought to me. Nope, it had to be done on my mother's kitchen table with ten Karras' in the general vicinity.

I didn't expect it to go well.

In fact, I knew without a doubt it was going to go the way my dream apparently did last night—Hell. It was going to go to Hell, and it probably wouldn't even take the handbasket.

"Did anyone find Parker?" Mom asked, putting a mug of coffee in front of me.

"Find him? What is he? A lost puppy?" I rolled my eyes. "He was never lost, he was just...somewhere else and out of touch."

"Where was he last night?"

I shrugged and clicked my pen. "I don't know. He walked into the bar and I told him he needed to call his mom before a big, fat Greek search party got unleashed on the Florida Keys. He grumbled something about being almost thirty and not needing to check in with his mom every day, and I told him he should move out or quit bitching."

It was a close enough summary. So what if the first part was a big, fat lie?

"Did you get rid of your spider?" Mom took the seat next to me.

"My spider?" I blinked at her.

She slowly raised an eyebrow.

"Oh, Henry. He's trapped under a glass." I sipped my coffee. "I figure he'll either run out of oxygen or I can make someone get rid of it for me."

"Why didn't you ask Parker when he showed up?"

"Because he'd probably throw it at my head for his own amusement." If the spider were real, that would be a possibility.

"Was he wearing the same clothes when he came in this morning?"

"Mom." I held my hands out and gaped at her. "I don't know. I didn't even look at him. I was working—like I should be right now."

"I still think it's strange that you were the last and first person to see him. Don't you?"

"Given that nobody saw him between him finishing and starting work, I don't find it weird at all, actually." I opened my laptop. "Someone else obviously saw him during those hours. We just don't know who."

"I'd love to know who. Wouldn't you?"

"What the hell is up with all these questions?" I finally looked her in the eye. "I'm already here against my will and better judgment given the noise from the living room. Must you continue to torture me further?"

Mom grimaced. "Sorry, Ray. I just find the entire situation strange. Ilsa said something about a conversation they had and, I don't know. I think I jumped to conclusions."

I slammed the pen down and glared at her. "Mother. Are you suggesting that he and I spent the night together?"

"Who spend night together?" Yia-Yia shuffled into the kitchen, today's dress a vibrant yellow that actually compliment her dark, olive skin. "Raven. You answer."

"Parker," Mom jumped in before I could. "But I was wrong. Apparently."

"Apparently? There's no apparently about it." Yes, there was. "If he and I ever spent the night together, it'd be because I'd be figuring out what to do with his dead body. Just because we're actually nice to one another now doesn't mean we're sleeping together."

Yia-Yia sniffed the orange juice carton before nodding. "He want you."

Both me and Mom turned to her. "What?" I asked her.

"That boy, he want you." She poured the juice into a glass without looking at us. "I see in his eyes."

"Who want who?" Great Aunt Maria stepped into the kitchen, her accent almost thicker than Yia-Yia's. "We have mimosa?"

"We don't have mimosas, Aunt Maria." How Mom was keeping a blank expression, I didn't know.

"What's the use of having Raven if we don't have mimosas?" Great Aunt Maria switched to Greek.

Mixed Up

I knew this would be a shitshow. More surprising was my mom's stream of questions. I didn't know what Parker's conversation with his mom had been about, but I knew it couldn't be good.

I left my family to the discussion about mimosas—I could barely understand their Greek now anyway—and picked up my phone to text Parker.

Me: *Important. Are you there?*
Parker: *What happened? Did someone burn down the house?*
Me: *Mom asked me a lot of uncomfortable questions. Did you talk to your mom about me?*

Nothing.

Me: *PARKER.*
Parker: *She might have weaseled out of me that I have some confusing feelings for you.*
Parker: *Wait.*
Parker: *She promised me she wouldn't tell your mom.*
Me: *YOU'RE AN IDIOT*
Me: *THEY TELL EACH OTHER EVERYTHING THEY'RE LIKE CHILDREN*
Me: *THIS IS A DISASTER*
Me: *YOU FOOLISH DICKNUGGET*
Parker: *Is your caps stuck or are you shouting at me?*
Me: *Calling you a dicknugget didn't clue you in?*
Me: *I'm going to Google lucid dreaming so I can make Satan's hellhound eat you in my dreams tonight.*
Parker: *I don't know what to say to that, so*

I'm going to say OK, I might deserve it.
Me: *Ugh.*

He was going to kill me. I knew I should have killed him years ago.

Me: *And there is nothing remotely confusing about the way you feel when you want to insert your penis into my vagina!*
Parker: *That's the least sexy thing I've ever heard.*
Me: *GOOD. Now you won't be so confused.*
Parker: *Actually, I'm more confused, because, as you put it, I still enjoy the idea of inserting my penis into your vagina.*
Me: *I can't believe we're semi-sexting and my family are arguing about the lack of mimosas. In Greek.*
Parker: *Did you start that seating plan yet? Why do you even need one? I talked your grandma into a buffet. Buffets don't need seating plans.*

And that was a very good point.

"Aren't we doing a buffet?" I asked the moment there was a break in the conversation. "Parker just reminded me. We don't need a seating plan for a buffet because everyone just grabs food. Not to mention it's a reunion and not a goddamn wedding."

Yia-Yia grinned. "I still smash plates."

Obviously. "I haven't been at a party with you where you haven't. But, I'm just pointing it out. Nobody is going to stick to the plan. Everybody will complain, and then move, so, it's all a—"

"I'm not sitting next to her!" Demetri snapped, storming into the room. My fourteen-year-old cousin, Alexa the Second as we affectionately called her, was hot on his heels. "If you put me with her, we'll have a reunion and a funeral!"

"Your funeral!" Alexa the Second shouted at him. "And I'll spit on your grave!"

I slumped forward on the table.

"I'll spit on you right now!"

"Where are the mimosas?"

"*Mamá!*"

"Ay, children!"

"You started this!"

"And I'm finishing it!" Mom hollered, slamming her hand on the table, making it jump.

I sat up and looked around. Total silence had descended on the kitchen. Between Great Aunt Maria's misgivings about the lack of mimosas, Yia-Yia's frustration at fighting, and the actual fighting, it had been pandemonium. Now, the only sound that remained was the ticking of the clock on the wall and the blaring of the television in the other room where Great Uncle Alex was watching some game show.

"There will be no seating plan," Mom said after a moment. "But you two will be firmly separated, and Aunt Maria will be by the bar."

"Awesome," I said, closing my laptop. "It's always a thrill to drive forty-five minutes to get nothing more than a headache. I could have called if I wanted that."

"Sit." Mom ordered me. "Everyone else out."

The teenagers ran out of the kitchen, but Yia-Yia and Great Aunt Maria hovered as if they were undecided about whether or not to let my mom dictate anything to them. After one sharp look from Mom—that I think made Yia-Yia snicker—they left.

"Since when did you and Parker text?" Mom asked me in a low voice.

I stared at her flatly. "Since when did it matter who I'm texting?"

"I'm your mother. I can ask you whatever I want."

"Yeah, well, if the police give me the right to remain silent upon arrest, I'm pretty sure I have the right to remain silent here, too." I stuffed my laptop into my purse and grabbed my phone.

Mom laughed into her coffee mug. "You're smarter than he is."

I paused in the door. "I wasn't aware that had ever been up for debate, but you're right. I am. Maybe you should interrogate him instead."

Her smile was wry. "Maybe I will."

Of course, my silence had given her everything she needed to know, but that was beside the point.

I didn't know what the point was, but I knew it wasn't that.

I hoped it wasn't that.

20
Parker

"Where were you last night?" Ryan leaned against the wall, his arms folded across his chest. His eyes, a shade or two darker than Raven's were focused on me as he asked his question.

I slammed my fist into the bread I was kneading. Lying to him wasn't something I assumed I would have to do. It was stupid of me, but I thought he'd be the last person to ask me where I was. "I stayed with a friend here."

"Who?"

"You don't know them. We met last week." Kneading the bread was satisfying in this conversation. It was keeping my mild annoyance in check.

Not that I had a right to be annoyed. I was the one hiding something from him, after all. He was just asking me a reasonable question. One I couldn't answer honestly.

Well, I could, but telling him I'd been sleeping with

his sister whilst in a kitchen wasn't the greatest idea in the world.

"All right." Ryan frowned, but he didn't move. "I gotta say, I didn't enjoy getting woken up by your mom so early."

"Sorry, man. By the time I'd left here, it was too late to message her." I dumped the bread into the plastic bowl to my right and covered it.

"Why were you here so late?"

"Working. Your sister wanted to do a cocktail pairing and last night was the only chance we had."

"When did you leave?"

"Late. I don't know." I pushed the bowl to the side and turned to the side. I twisted the tap, washed my hands, and then reached for my bottle of water to drink. "Maybe like eleven? Eleven-thirty?"

"Why couldn't you do that this morning?"

"Is she here right now?"

"True." He relaxed his frown. "Just seems weird."

The door to the bar swung open with a flash of dark hair and bright, red fabric. Raven's fitted dress matched her lips, and there was no way that was by accident. "Jesus, Ry, give it a rest." She bumped the door closed with her hip and squeezed past him with a crate in her hands. "All I've heard for the last few minutes is you bitching in here."

"When did you get back? And I don't bitch."

"Twenty minutes ago. I finally escaped the clutches of Lucifer and the ridiculous waste of time that was that trip." She dumped the crate on the side.

"Did you bring lunch?" I turned to face her.

With a sigh, she rested her forearm on the side of the crate and looked up at me through long, dark lashes. "Why would I have brought lunch? Do I look like your personal assistant?"

"Because it's lunchtime," Ryan answered. "And we're hungry."

"What are you even doing here? You know I'm

paying him to have his time wasted by you, right?" Raven pointed one finger in my direction, but her attention was focused completely on her brother. "Don't you have a job to do?"

"Day off."

"Wanna get this side of the kitchen and be useful?"

"Are you gonna pay me?"

"I promise not to pull out baby pictures next time you take a girl home to the parents. I won't even get out the home video of you playing with your penis like a helicopter."

I choked on thin air. I'd seen that video, and it wasn't pretty. It was Raven's go-to revenge tool whenever he pissed her off. One week or one year into a relationship, every single one of his girlfriends had seen the video of him sitting on the coffee table and spinning his penis like a helicopter propeller.

Ryan shrugged. "If you ain't paying, I ain't working."

"Great." A smile spread across her face, and I didn't know if it was genuine or vengeful. "Then get out, let him work, and I solemnly swear to save the propeller video for your wedding."

"That's fine...I'll save the video of you sobbing over the N-SYNC break up for yours."

"Go ahead. I don't care. That was a traumatizing day."

"I have a headache." I rubbed my hand across my forehead and headed for the fridge for a new bottle of water. "Is there any kind of painkiller that will make you two be quiet?"

"Yeah. It's called chloroform, but it goes over Raven's mouth," Ryan answered.

The plastic salt mill she launched at his head missed by millimeters, but only because he moved.

"I'll call you later!" he shouted over his shoulder, running for the door.

"Asshole!" Raven's voice was louder than his, unsurprisingly, and the rattle as she slammed her fist into the shelf beneath the heater lamps made me cringe.

Several seconds of silence passed before I said, "I guess your morning went well."

She spun her face toward mine. "Well? No, it did not go well. Not only was my drive out there completely pointless because everyone forgot about the buffet, as you well know, I was subjected to my aunt's displeasure about the lack of mimosas, my grandmother's insistence "the boy want" me, my teenaged cousins threatening to spit on each other's graves, and my mother's question time with the fucking president based on how many things she wanted me to answer. Oh, and at least three-quarters of this bullshit happened in Greek, so it took me way too long to unravel the quick-fired complains before someone else had started. Then, I get back here and save your ass from the same awkwardness I dealt with this morning, so you're welcome!"

Well, shit.

"And yes, I did bring lunch, but I couldn't tell my brother that!" She pulled a sandwich out from the paper bag inside the crate and dumped it on the side next to the plastic box.

I didn't quite know how to deal with this situation. She wasn't even angry, she just looked...stressed. Like she'd already had enough and it was barely even midday. The bar wouldn't open for another four hours, but she'd lost two and a half this morning where she had to go to Key West. Whatever clusterfuck she'd been involved in at home—I'd barely understood what she was saying—had obviously taken its toll on her.

Raven pulled things out of the crate and slammed them down onto the side. They were all various sauces and seasonings that I'd put on my list, and they'd obviously been delivered separately to yesterday's order.

"These are yours," she said, putting one last bottle down with a little too much vigor. All the others bounced with the force of that one hitting the metal top.

With Ryan gone, I knew we were alone. I walked up behind her, stopped, and wrapped my arms around her shoulders. She stilled for a fleeting second before she slumped, relaxing back into me, and brought her hands up to my wrists.

"Sorry," she murmured, the word barely audible. "Karras overload."

I smiled into her hair. "That's a real thing. You should get a doctor's note."

"Will you write one for me?"

"I'm not a doctor." I laughed the words into her hair before I kissed the side of her neck and released her. We might have been alone when I hugged her, but Wes was due in any minute, and given the questions he'd asked about why she and I hated one another so much, it would have led to even more questions.

Questions I didn't want to answer, because I didn't *have* the answers.

"Is this the stuff they didn't deliver yesterday?" I picked up the tub of black pepper.

"Yep." She smacked her lips together and leaned against the edge of the side, then she folded her arms. Luckily for my concentration, the dress wasn't too low-cut, but I still lingered there a little longer than I really needed to. "The guy is an idiot. I don't like him, and as soon as I can find another supplier for this stuff that doesn't charge me my firstborn, I'm going to switch."

"I can look," I said, grabbing a couple things to put away.

"Can't you just take the deliveries? Last week, he asked me if my skirt was meant to be so short or if it'd ridden up because I'm so hot." She rolled her eyes, handing me a bottle.

"Valid question. I've seen the things you wear."

Her look went from indifferent to exasperation. "I barely had a chance to change and come back down when he was at the door. He asked me if I'd put the dress on especially for him."

I ran my gaze across her body. "Did you put it on for

me?"

She slapped my arm. "I put it on for the poor suckers who keep coming back to the bar just to see me bend over."

I frowned. "I've seen you bend over behind that bar. I'm not exactly sure how I feel about that."

"Morning. Fuck, it's afternoon. Afternoon, shit." Wes stepped through the door and stopped dead when he saw Raven in the kitchen. The door he'd come through was the heavier one, and it swung back, hitting him in the back and making him jump forward at the impact. True to form, he grabbed the side table where we kept all the keys and knocked that bowl onto the floor. The plastic rattled and the keys screeched as they all skidded across the floor.

Raven pursed her lips, fighting a smile. "Hey, Wes. How was your morning?"

He opened and closed his mouth like a desperate fish before his cheeks heated. "Good. It was good. Thanks. Sorry about the…you know. The language."

"Don't worry about it." She grabbed the empty crate and swept it off the side before heading for the door back to the bar. "Fuck is my favorite…f-word." She shot me a sly glance before disappearing out into the bar.

Wes stared at her leaving. "Is it me," he said slowly, "Or is she in a better mood than normal?"

"Careful." I put the last bottle on the shelf and looked at him. "She's got the hearing ability of a supernatural creature."

"Noted." He finally dragged his attention to me. "What do you need doing, Chef?"

I rattled off a list of things he could do—giving him a little more freedom by the end of the list—and headed out for the bar. Pushing the door open, I stepped into the bar and picked up a packet of napkins that had fallen onto the floor.

Raven glanced at me. "Oh, thanks."

"Stop being so happy. You're scaring my staff."

That glance became a lingering stare with a wide grin. "Yeah, yeah. I was just being nice."

"That's why he's scared."

"I've always been perfectly nice to Wes." She snatched up the napkins I just put on the bar.

"But you were nice to me."

"I'm sorry, I'll be a raging bitch to you next time." She smirked, but it came off too amused to have the affect she obviously intended. "Can you get back to work now?"

"In a minute." I paused. Irrational nerves twisted my stomach, making me feel almost sick. I knew what I wanted to do, and asking someone on a date wasn't exactly something that made me uncomfortable on a regular basis, but something about this woman just threw me.

Raven narrowed her eyes. "What?"

"What are you working tomorrow? Are you closing?"

Slowly, she shook her head. "Sienna and Rosanne are covering closing. Why?"

I leaned on the edge of the bar. "I kinda wanna stay with you tonight," I said under my breath. "But I can't. So, let me take you out tomorrow."

"Aren't you working?"

"The new guy is coming in in two hours. He has more experience than Alex is. Let them handle it for a night. Besides, we won't be too far away."

She peeled off the opening of the napkin packet, peering down at it. The plastic crinkled and rippled beneath her touch, and as much as I wanted to reach out and stop that damn noise, I knew I couldn't.

"You think that's a good idea?" her voice was quiet and hesitant.

I wasn't alone in my nerves.

She had them, too.

"No, but we've already covered that a thousand times. Let's stop beating a dead horse and get on with it." I paused. "I fucking hated lying to Ryan earlier. I wanted to be honest with him and tell him where I really was last night, but I can't do that yet."

"We can't have this conversation here." Her hands

shook as she put the napkins down and crumpled up the packet. "Sienna will be here—"

"I'm not telling him a thing unless this is for real." She froze. "I mean it, Raven. Either go out with me, away from here, or we quit this shit right now."

Her bright red lips thinned before coming together. Uncertainty flashed across her features, creasing the corners of her eyes, before she finally relaxed and let a sigh escape those colorful lips. "You promise nobody will know?"

"No. I'm not unrealistic."

"At least you're honest." Her lips pulled to the side. "All right, you got it. Four sound good?"

"Four on the outskirts of town. Do you think Lani would let you park at the newspaper?"

"Definitely."

I pulled into my parents' driveway and killed the engine. The hushing noise that accompanied the end of it and the interior lights going off was strangely satisfying.

A part of me didn't want to go inside. I knew all about the chat Raven had with her mom earlier, and she was right when she'd texted me that our moms told each other everything. There was no doubt that they'd taken Raven's chat with Alexandra and run with it. They'd have created every possible outcome and all of those likely ended up in marriage and babies, if I knew them, and I did.

I'd driven around the Keys for as long as I could before finally accepting that I needed to get on the road and get home. I'd texted my mom that I'd be late before I'd taken off, but despite my best efforts, the hazy, yellow light coming through the closed curtains in the living room window told me that someone was awake.

I'd bet a hundred bucks it was my mom.

I dragged myself out of the car, hating the way my childhood home looked as the moon reflected off the gray, slate tiles on the roof. I didn't want to think about what it said about me that I'd have rather been in Whiskey Key with Raven. That I'd have rather been in her kitchen, watching her mix drinks. On her sofa, watching her doodle on a pad the way she did when she didn't think anyone was paying her any attention. In her bed, breathing in the fruity smell of her shampoo as her hair spread across the pillow.

I was falling for her.

Too hard. Too fast. Too deep.

Too dangerously.

I'd spent my entire life hating her, yet now, here I was, falling in love with her.

Doing something that I knew, deep down, I had no place doing.

Somehow, I'd managed to break through that hard exterior she threw out to the rest of the world, and I was slowly uncovering the heart that lay beneath it. The only problem was, I didn't want to stop looking. I wanted to keep tearing away the layers of her until I knew every inch of who she was, because despite knowing her our entire lives, I didn't really know her that much at all.

I knew she hated me. I knew she had no time for fools, and that she ran on sparkles and sarcasm. But I didn't know what her favorite food or color or drink was. I didn't know what her biggest fear was or where she imagined her life in ten years. I didn't know if she preferred books or movies and whether she was a cat or a dog person.

It amazed me that I knew her so well without knowing anything about her.

The beep of my car locking was thunderous in the silence of the street, and the flashing lights lit the houses up in orange for a few seconds. I forced myself to walk to the door and let myself in. The TV was a quiet buzz in the background, and I paused after locking the front door.

My gut twitched with the knowledge that someone

knew where I really was last night, and I couldn't deny the relief that flooded through me when I caught sight of the back of my father's head. His graying hair was barely visible in the low light from the lamp in the corner of the room.

He hit a button on the remote control and stood up. The remote clattered as it bounced off the table, and he turned to me, a small smile on his face. "You should know," he said, slowly considering each word he spoke, "that your mother and Alexandra have ideas and are on the warpath. Something about you having feelings for Raven and going missing. I don't think they've put two and two together yet."

With that, he winked and walked past me to the stairs.

That was good to know.

I couldn't even thank him for the warning, because by the time I'd really grasped what he was saying, he was gone.

21

Raven

"I don't know what I'm supposed to do." I ran my fingers through my hair and looked at my two best friends. "I have to meet him in thirty minutes and I can't help but feel like my family knows."

Lani bit the inside of her cheek. "It's just, like, a date, right? Why don't you just tell them?"

Camille flapped her hand at her. "You know why she doesn't can't tell him. How well would your sister respond to the idea of you bumping uglies with her best friend?"

"I don't really care," Lani said flatly.

This wasn't helping.

"I want to tell my family, but it's not that simple. I really don't want to hurt my brother." I dropped onto the sofa.

"So, stop fucking his best friend. Really, this entire situation could have been avoided if you'd kept your legs shut." Camille snorted.

That was her. Right to the point as always.

"Thanks for that stunning insight, Cam. It was life-changing. I'd not considered that myself." I picked a loose thread on the hem of my dress. "My mom has been texting me all day asking what I'm doing tonight because isn't it my night off? Did I want to go for dinner or drinks?"

"Let me guess." Lani smiled. "We're covering for you."

"No. I ignored her." I smacked my fingers against my chin. "All day long. So, she texted me more. And I ignored her more."

"That's the dumbest idea I've ever heard."

"And you're dating *my* brother." Camille reminded her.

Which brought me to a new point.

"Cam! Your best friend is dating your brother!" I bounced, spinning around.

"Uh...yes?"

"How did you feel when you found out?"

"Betrayed. I felt like my entire world was shattering beneath me. I was so angry for so long." She paused. "No, wait. That's how I felt after the last episode of *The Walking Dead*."

I had no idea how I tolerated her.

"It's an unfair comparison." Lani shifted. "Brett and I were best friends and had feelings for each other long before we fought and I ever came home. She was more on the side of us getting together than not."

"Yeah," Camille said. "But, if you'd gotten together behind my back, I probably would have been pretty pissed off. Like, I'm your best friend and you can't be honest with me over something kinda important?"

"So, the secret part would be what would piss you off?" I asked.

"I think so. You should trust your best friend to accept whatever you have to tell them, whether they like it or not. That's the point of friendship. Trust and respect. The second you do something that will affect them and you don't tell them, that respect no longer exists."

I groaned and leaned against the back of the sofa. "What have I done?"

"Do you want me to start from the top, or...?"

"You're no longer helping me, Camille."

"Of course, I'm not. Why are you surprised?"

"Cancel your date," Lani said, crossing her legs and tucking her feet beneath her thighs. "That's all you can do right now. I mean, it's a date, but it's not like you haven't already fucked the guy. And, by the way? I totally called that you wanted him."

"We both did," Camille muttered.

They really, really weren't helping.

"I don't think I can do this," I said softly. "I have these feelings for him—real feelings. An accidental fuck is one thing, but this is something else. I can't keep doing this without my brother knowing."

Lani tucked her hair behind her ear. "Then make a choice, Raven. You either cancel right now, or you kinda have to go. Or...just change your date."

"Change it?"

"I can get Brett down here in a few minutes...Call your brother...See how he reacts to you getting along."

"That's not a bad idea," I admitted.

"That's a terrible idea." Camille shook her head. "It sounds good in theory, but what if one of you slip up? You've hated each other so fiercely for so long that one wrong move, and it'll be obvious."

It was a terrible idea.

Everything was a terrible idea.

My life was going to shit and it was all my fault.

Actually, that wasn't true. I had a great life. I'd just made some poor decisions recently, and I needed to fix them. I wasn't this kind of person. I wasn't really secretive. Private, yes, but not secretive. None of what I was doing right now was me.

My friends were right, though. I had to cancel the date. If only so that I could sit here and figure out what I wanted to do about the whole situation. I'd been immature about the decisions I'd made, and now I needed to be the adult I was.

My brother wasn't a bad person. He might be angry at first, but surely he'd understand eventually. I didn't ask to feel this way about Parker. I didn't want to imagine him as the person lying next to me when I couldn't sleep at three in the morning. I didn't want to consider that the arrogant shit I'd grown up with could be the person to give me butterflies with no more than a smile.

I didn't ask for it and I didn't plan it, but that didn't mean keeping it a secret was okay.

I picked up my phone and brought up our messages.

Me: *I have to cancel.*

God, that was harsh. I didn't even say hi. What was wrong with me?

Me: *That came out harsher than I planned. I didn't mean it.*
Me: *I meant it. I have to cancel. But I didn't mean it in a mean way.*
Me: *Shit, this is a disaster.*

I shook my head. "I made a clusterfuck of that."

"As opposed to your perfect handling of the situation as a whole."

"Shut up, Camille." My phone buzzed, drawing my attention back to it.

Parker: *I know. I figured.*
Parker: *I'm in the parking lot. Can I come up?*

I jumped up and ran to the window. His car was sitting in the back corner in one of the slots marked as 'staff,' but I couldn't actually see him.

Me: *Come in through the back and Lani will let you in. The door's locked.*

"Can you let Parker up?" I asked Lani.

She rolled her eyes, but her tiny smile gave her away. So did the fact she stood up and ran for the door.

Camille watched her go. The moment the door shut, she swung her head around to look at me so fast her hair whipped her in the face. "Don't you find it a little freaky he was in the parking lot when you texted him?"

Shaking my head, I said, "He probably knew I'd flake and, at the very least, need some persuasion. He's also kinda weird like that." My lips twitched.

Camille blinked at me. "You love him."

"I don't talk love at the dinner table." My heart thumped.

"You're not sitting at the dinner table."

I scrambled up and reseated myself at the table. "I am now."

"He's your person!" she hissed, following me and grabbing the chair opposite me.

"Dinner table!"

"I don't care! You're grinning like a fool. He's so your person."

I mimed zipping my lips right as Lani lead Parker into the room. The second I laid my eyes on him, my entire body went into some kind of freaky overdrive. He was perfection, from the comfortably fitting pale blue shirt that ended with rolled sleeves just below his elbows to the dark, ripped-at-the-knees jeans he was rocking so well.

It was unfair, the way he made my heart beat so fast. Life was a marathon, but he made me feel as though parts of it needed to be sprinted.

Like right now. I had the urge to walk across the room and fold myself into his arms. I'd only been there a few times, yet I knew how it would feel. I knew his chest made the perfect pillow, and his heartbeat was the perfect rhythm. I knew it felt like a safe place, like nothing could ever touch me there.

I didn't need a safe place, but I'd found one. And he was six-foot-three and deadly handsome.

He wasn't just my safe place—he was my happy place, too.

That thought was startling. He'd always been my own personal hell, so if I could feel this way about him after really not so long at all... Granted, we'd spent an awful lot of the past couple of weeks together because of work, but still.

"What are you talking about?" Lani asked, drawing my attention away from Parker. "And why are you sitting at the table now?"

"Some conversations can't be had at the dinner table." I folded my arms at sat back.

"In other words," Camille said, standing up, "She's avoiding my questions."

I grinned.

So, did Parker.

"I also know when I'm not wanted," she said, scooting toward the door.

"But not when to shut up," I pointed out, still grinning.

"You owe me a drink for that."

"You owe me about ten for the last fifteen minutes."

She paused in the doorway. "Let's call it quits. Have fun!" Then, she ran.

"I need a new friend," Lani muttered, going to the sofa to grab her purse before she followed Camille out. She hesitated right behind Parker, put her hand to the side of her face in a phone motion, and mouthed, "Call me!" before she disappeared just as quickly as Camille had.

Mixed Up

With them gone and the sound of the lower door echoing through my apartment, Parker shut my front door and threw the bolt across to lock it. The silence was thick and uncomfortable, the awkwardness of unsaid words lingering heavily between us.

I swallowed. I didn't want to be the one to break the silence, and judging by the way he stood and stared at me as if he was waiting for me to speak first, he didn't either.

Still, somehow had to.

So, I said the one thing I was trained to say in awkward situations.

"I think we need a drink." I got up and walked into the kitchen. "Remember that drink I told you about that hardly anyone knows about? It works here."

"You mean the one you won't name." Laughter followed his words.

"I'll name it. It has a name. It's just offensive to some people."

"I don't get offended very easily. What is it?"

I grabbed a bottle. "Three shots of tequila. Two of pineapple vodka. One of coconut rum. Lime. Blackcurrant." I poured approximately three shots' worth of tequila into my glass.

"Is that for—wait, never mind. I see that's per person." He paused as he drew level with me. Slowly, he turned his face and looked at me. "One glass of that will put someone over the limit."

I put the tequila down and met his eyes. "It's okay. I have a comfy sofa."

His lips pulled up on one side.

I couldn't help but smile back before turning back to my alcohol stash. "You're right, though," I said, picking up the pineapple vodka. "It is kinda lethal. I'm not sure anyone should actually drink it, because it's basically the world's largest shot that you sip."

"Yet, you still won't tell me the name."

I finished adding the spirits and reached for the lime

cordial. The light, green juice mixed with the clearness of the spirits. As it swirled and curled around the liquid, I grabbed the blackcurrant and unscrewed it. One dash of that in each had a weird-looking battle between green and purple happening in the glass. Neither juice really settled, even after the distribution of it had settled, so it took a few stirs with straws to get it fully mixed.

I picked up one glass and handed it to Parker. "Here is your Wet Cunt."

He stared into the glass, saying nothing. Then, his shoulders trembled. His hand shook. Right at the moment he put his glass down, a laugh bubbled out of him, and he gripped the edge of the counter. "You called a cocktail a Wet Cunt?"

"No, it's *The* Wet Cunt, but saying enjoy The Wet Cunt is sometimes too suggestive. Especially after a Wet Cunt."

"Does this live up to its name like your others somehow do?"

"Does The Wet Cunt give you a wet cunt? I don't know. Stop making me say that word. There's a reason I don't say it often and it's this. It's all or nothing."

"Sorry, but it rolls off your tongue really well."

"That word rolls of nobody's tongue well." I handed him back his drink since he'd stopped laughing—not that my overuse of that controversial c-word had helped his amusement any. "Try it."

"I would be more likely to try this if you'd labeled it arsenic." He was looking at it again. "I just saw how much liquor compared to not is in this thing."

I shrugged and brought my glass to my lips. "Everyone needs one in their life."

"Now, I get the cocktail names. The innuendos are fun."

"It's taken you this long?"

"No, but I don't think I fully understood the extent of it until now. All right, here goes." He took a mouthful of the drink and swallowed. Eyes bugging, he coughed, slamming the glass down.

I grinned.

He watched me make it. More fool him.

"Jesus, woman, are you tryna kill me?" he rasped, hand on his throat.

"My track record points to yes," I answered. "But I'm kinda fond of you now, so no. But maybe I should have made you this before."

"Are you sure there's no arsenic in there?"

"Positive." I slid the glass back from the edge of the counter with mine and grabbed two, taller glasses. "I also might have made them slightly stronger than necessary."

He straightened and fixed those dark eyes on me. "Why? Why would you do that?"

"Seemed like a good idea at the time." I poured the strong drinks into each glass and pulled the lemonade from the bottle rack. "And it was...For my own amusement." I flashed him a grin and uncapped the lemonade.

He grabbed me. The lemonade bottle went sliding across the counter and tipped awkwardly into the sink, but I didn't have time to protest the spray of fizz that went across my kitchen and up the side of my fridge.

Parker had his hands wrapped around mine and pinned the base of my back. My body was flush against his, and heat swept through me when he dipped his head so his lips were close to mine. "I didn't realize how good you were at avoidance until just now."

"Yeah, well. A girl has to keep some secrets."

"We need to talk."

"We need to talk about why you were in my parking lot."

He stilled. Obviously, that thought had just occurred to him. "Coincidence?"

"Parker..."

He sighed and released me. He leaned back on the little kitchen island and folded his arms across his chest. "I got in last night and my dad warned me that our moms are on the warpath. I left to come here, and my mom followed me."

"She followed you?" I raised my eyebrows. "How did you know?"

"Because she has the stealth of a rhino, and her giant Range Rover isn't really inconspicuous. Your mom taking photos of my car from the passenger seat made it pretty obvious, too."

"She was just taking photos of you driving? Does nobody have limits around here?"

He gave me a look that said, "Stupid question."

I shook my head. "That's ridiculous."

"Right. So, when I got here, I pulled into the bar, hoping she'd think I was coming into work. I came in and waited. Vicky kept an eye out for me, and right as I got your text, she left."

"You weren't outside at all."

"Technically, I was standing outside the front door, so I was in the parking lot."

"Semantics." I pushed everything away from behind me and pulled myself up to sit on the counter. "That's the craziest thing I've ever heard. Do our moms not have limits or boundaries? She's been texting me all day as it is about my plans for tonight, so I'm not sure I'm entirely surprised at what they were doing."

Parker shook his head. "I'm not surprised at all. They're crazy. It's like their kids are adults and now they've reverted back. I'm finally understanding why you were such a crazy bitch as a teenager."

"You assume I'm not anymore? Aw, that's so nice of you."

"Thanks for the warning. Note to self: never break Raven's heart if you like your windshield."

"One time." I slapped my hand against the top of the counter. "You break a guy's windshield one time!"

"I sure as hell hope it was only one time. And I still maintain that you're lucky you didn't get arrested."

Mixed Up

"I still maintain you're lucky you've made it twenty-eight years without me doing something to you."

Parker grinned. It lit up his entire face, from his lips to his eyes. Hell, even his cheeks got a little pinker. "It took twenty-eight years for you to do something to me, and I happen to like the things you do to me."

Straight face. Straight face. Straight face.

I had to keep a straight face.

"I thought we were going to have a sensible conversation here." Of course, 'sensible' got thrown out the window the moment he brought up the fact our moms were stalking him.

"I don't think we can." He walked to me and bent forward, resting his arms on my legs. Dark lashes obscured a little of his eyes as he looked up and met my gaze. "Why did you bail on me?"

I found the thread on the hem of my dress and rolled it between my finger and thumb. "Because it doesn't feel right. The more I think about what we're doing and about how I'm starting to feel, the more I realize I can't do this unless Ryan knows. It feels too dishonest, and now our moms are on the case…It's even worse."

Parker ran his thumb over his lower lip. "I agree with you."

"You do? You said yesterday—"

"That I wanted to know if this was real before telling him? Yeah, I did, and I do, but not at the expense of your feelings, Raven. If telling him makes you feel like we have the freedom to explore this thing we have between us, then I'll tell him."

"You'll tell him? Shouldn't I?"

The shake of his head was almost solemn. "I'm the one overstepping the line. You're his sister. He doesn't need reassurances from you that this is more than just a boredom thing."

I pursed my lips.

"Think of it this way." He stood, but he kept his

hands on my thighs. "If, in six months, you call it quits, he's not gonna come to you and give you a hard time. He'll come to me and ask me what the hell I did for you to make that choice. You're his sister, and our friendship isn't gonna change that. You come first to him and you don't even realize it." He reached up and pushed hair from my face, his touch so gentle. "I'm sorry I ever thought that you'd be okay with not telling him."

"It wasn't just you." I took his hand with mine and looked down. My hand was more tanned than his, but so much tinier. His fingers swallowed mine as they curled. "We both decided not to say anything. Maybe if we had, this would have been sorted out and we'd know what we want."

"Knowing what I want isn't dependent on anything other than you and me. I want you. Against all the crazy, nonsensical odds."

"What if this hurts your friendship? What if this doesn't work out and there's a chink in your relationship you'll never be able to fix?" I look up into his eyes. Confusion and uncertainty mix with determination, all warring with each other. "Nothing is worth your friendship. Not me and not anyone else."

"You'd give up the chance to make this work just to make sure my friendship with him doesn't change?"

"Of course, I would."

22
Parker

I searched her face. "Why?"

"Because." She trailed off, pulling her hand away from mine. "You've literally been best friends your entire lives. I still don't even know if I like you as a person. I like you enough to want to fuck you on a regular basis, but otherwise..."

I laughed and squeezed her thighs. "The feelings mutual, hotshot. The jury is still out over here too."

The slightest smile flickered across her lips. "What we've already done is risky and crazy. I think he'll be hurt by that, but I don't want to lie to him anymore. I don't want it to go so far that the end of summer comes and you decide to stay and then we have to tell him everything."

"He'll be fine. Listen to me." I cupped her face, brushing my thumbs across her cheekbones. "He'll be angry we didn't come clean sooner, even though it's only been a week. He'll feel betrayed and he'll be pissed, and I'll take the brunt of that because I can and because I should. But when it comes down to it, you said it yourself. It's gonna take more than this to destroy our friendship."

"Are you sure?"

"I'm sure."

I hoped.

I hoped like fucking hell I was right, because I wasn't sure at all. Teasing Raven about her temper might have been one of my favorite things to do, but it was a trait she shared with her brother.

Still, I knew she was right.

I knew it yesterday when I had to flat-out lie to him to his face. In hindsight, I wished I'd just been honest. I wished I'd followed my gut and I'd told him the truth, but it seemed too blunt. I wanted him to know that I had feelings for her before the rest came out, because that was all that really mattered in my eyes.

All that mattered was that I cared about her more than I should have.

"Camille and Lani were right," she muttered, dropped her eyes. "I should have thought it through before I opened my legs."

It was so unexpected that I burst out laughing and let my hands fall from her face. It was, actually, a hard point to argue, so I agreed with her. "I should have thought it through before I got between your legs."

"It sounds better when you put it like that."

I tapped my finger against her lips, smiling, and then ran my fingertip along the curve of her mouth. "I might be taking the shit for this, but you're still taking half the blame."

"Fine." She rolled her eyes. "But as to the immediate issue, I'm hungry."

I knew where this was going. "I vote take-out."

"There are words I never thought I'd hear you say."

Holding up my hands, I walked backward. "I can appreciate a good take-out pizza as well as anyone else, hotshot. Plus, if I buy it, I'm kinda cooking for you."

"No, you're not. You're really, really not."

"Then you can buy your own pizza."

She pouted, but it was the mischief in her eyes that had me grinning.

"All right, all right. Is there a Domino's around here?"

Raven opened the drawer next to her and whipped out a take-out leaflet emblazoned with the pizza chain's logo. "Yes, and we're quite well acquainted."

I left Raven's apartment early. I had to be back in a few hours, so as pointless as this trip was, it had to be done. I needed to shower, change, and talk to Ryan before anything went any further. We'd agreed, somewhat selfishly, that since I was already at her place last night, there was no point in leaving.

Now, I was regretting it. Even though I'd texted my mom, I now had to admit to my best friend that I'd spent two nights with his sister.

Any ounce of surety I'd expressed to Raven yesterday deteriorated the closer I got to my house. It didn't help that our parents were neighbors—the chance of running into him before I'd even pulled up into the drive was high. Higher still during the walk from my car to the house.

I had no idea what to say to him. How the fuck was I supposed to start it? I wished that I'd been honest before. That when he'd asked me a few days ago, I hadn't let Raven interrupt him, and had told him the truth. I wished a whole fucking damn lot, but no matter how hard I tried, I couldn't wish that I'd never come back.

At first, I did. I wished I'd never returned to my hometown and collided with Raven Archer. Now, today, I was glad I had. It was still unexpected and uncertain, but that didn't mean it was wrong. I couldn't believe that it was wrong.

There was no way it was wrong to want someone as badly as I wanted her—uncontrollably.

The fear was still there. The fear that with one choice, I could wreck the best and longest friendship I'd ever had. Not to mention the only truly real one. With success came struggles, and true friendships were one of those struggles.

Love was another.

The idea that I might have to sacrifice one for the other was too frustrating to consider. I wasn't in love with Raven, but I knew I was falling fast. There was something about her beyond the snark that was all too endearing.

I turned onto the street. It was still early enough that the sky still held a faintly residual glow of the sunrise, and the orange hue tickled the horizon as I pulled into the driveway.

My car door opened at the moment the neighbor's front door did. Stepping out of my car, I turned in the direction of the Archer house and laid eyes on my best friend.

His eyes were hard. Lips thinned. Jaw set.

The knowledge snaked through me with the guilt of a hundred men.

He knew.

Ryan crossed the yard to where I was standing. He stopped on the other side of my car, his expression unchanged, and said, "I think we need to talk."

23

Raven

Thirty minutes before.

The sound of Parker's car leaving the lot reverberated through the open window. The sun was rising, lighting the sky up in the most beautiful, colorful way, yet I couldn't appreciate its beauty.

I couldn't appreciate the radiant orange as it colored my kitchen. Couldn't enjoy the golden hue of the rays as they danced off the mirror by the door and bounced around the room as the sun rose.

All I could think of was the way my stomach swirled with the worst uncertainty. Did I really want Parker to shoulder all the blame for him? I was as complicit as he was. I was as much involved as he was. He'd insisted on being the one to have the conversation with Ryan, but that didn't mean I had to sit here and do nothing.

The longer I knew I was sitting here doing nothing while he went to the most awkward conversation of his life, the more I knew I had to do something.

I tugged sweats up over my ass and headed for the door. I'd promised Parker I'd say nothing. I swore I'd sit pretty until I was told to run or that a tornado was headed my way. I wanted to stick with that as much as I wanted to be the person who would tell my brother the truth.

The battle waged inside me as I headed for the bar. I locked my apartment door behind me, pocketing the keys. My phone burned a hole in my pocket, bumping against my thigh with every step I took. It was my focus as I bent down in front of the first fridge with my notepad and clicked my pen.

I needed six Budweisers. Four Coors. Six and nine light beers respectively.

Was Parker in Key West yet?
Did my brother know?
Could I cope with this?

I shook my head. I scooted across to the next fridge. Orange. Apple. Cranberry. I needed all the juice.

I couldn't let Parker take the rap for this. I had to step forward and take responsibility for this.

Standing, I grabbed my phone from the bar. My brother's name stared back at me from the screen, his dreadful Facebook profile photo filling the little square.

Parker's dark eyes flashed in my mind.

The need to be the one to tell Ryan nudged at me yet again. Was I a bad person if I didn't? He was my brother. If the situation was switched I'd be annoyed.

I had to tell him.
I grabbed my phone.
Selected *Messages*.
Tapped *Ryan*.
Hit the bar.

Me: Are you awake?
Ryan: Early start. Sup?

I was going to be sick.

Me: *I'm seeing Parker.*

It flashed up on the screen. Stayed put like the asshole it was. I stared at the screen until the other bubble popped up.

Ryan: *Outside of work?*

Shit.
I swallowed.

Me: *Yes.*

Five minutes passed as I stared at my phone.
He didn't reply.
I hoped like hell I'd done the right thing.

24

Right now.

"You're right. We do need to." I stuffed my hands in my pocket.

It was obvious that Raven had beaten me to it. I think I knew she would. She simply didn't have the capability inside her to lie to her brother the way our relationship required her to. It was pretty obvious that the moment I'd left this morning she'd texted Ryan.

"The back?" Ryan nodded his head to the alley that separated our back yards.

I followed him through. He took the left turn into his yard, and I didn't blame him at all. If I were in his situation, I'd be taking his side, too. The fact he'd picked his yard said volumes to me.

Ryan sat in the chair in the corner of the porch. He pulled one knee toward him and looked out at the backyard.

I did the same. Except my seat was on the opposite

side of the porch to his.

"Raven texted me this morning." His voice was flat. "Told me she was seeing you."

I swallowed.

"I thought she was messing with me, and then I put it together. You working together. Your night away. Not fighting. I didn't put it together until thirty minutes ago, mind you, but I did. In the end."

I rubbed my hand across my chin. Did he want me to answer?

"Last night." He paused. "Were you with her last night?"

"Yeah." I said it slowly. "I was."

He nodded. "How long?"

"Not long. No more than two weeks."

Ryan scrubbed his hands through his hair and, clasping them at the back of his neck, spoke to the ground. "I don't understand."

"Neither do I," I said honestly, looking out at the end of the yard. "I don't know this happened, Ry. But it did. And I couldn't fight it."

"You hated each other forever. What the fuck?"

"Yeah, I know. I don't get it either."

"So, why'd she tell me and not you?"

I couldn't help the smile, no matter how I tried to hide it with my hand. "I told her that I'd tell you and take it all, but she's stubborn as fuck, and I guess she needed to beat me to it."

Ryan laughed. "That sounds like her."

I leaned forward, my hands falling between my knees. I focused on the end of the yard, on the barely-flowering bushes that lined the perimeter. Neither of us spoke, and I was thankful. I was thankful that he didn't seem to be mad, simply confused, and that he was" apparently willing to hear my side.

That was all I needed.

"I'm not gonna pretend that I know what I feel about

her," I started. "But I'm confused. I'm conflicted. And I'm afraid that I can't be without her. There's something about her that pulls me in. I don't care what happened before—I care what happens now. And, man, I know, you're not gonna like it, but I care about her more than anything. I don't fucking know why or how, and I'm gonna kick her ass for telling you first, but I can't change the way I feel about her."

Ryan nodded. Slowly, like he was taking it all in. Like he was processing the shit I'd just thrown at him.

Silence.

Then... "What if," he said, his voice low, his eyes fixed out onto the grass. "What if I told you that you had to choose? That it was me or her? That it was our friendship or her?"

I knew the answer. He might not like it, but I knew it.

"I won't break her heart for you." I'd never been surer of words I'd spoken. "Ry, you're my best friend, but I won't hurt her because of something you feel. I'm sorry. I wouldn't do that to her, no matter the cost. She doesn't deserve that."

And that was true.

No matter what the future held for us, Raven didn't deserve that kind of heartbreak. Not that I was saying I would break her heart, but the risk wasn't work it.

That was when I knew—I was right. I wouldn't. I wouldn't hurt her for him. If he'd asked about anyone else, it would have been easy. But not her. Not Raven.

"Good." He still didn't look at me. "Because I won't ask you to. Just don't kiss in her front of me, yeah? I'm so used to you fighting that it might make my head explode."

I laughed quietly. "You're taking this better than I thought you would."

Shrugging, he finally glanced at me. "I don't know how I feel about it yet. It's weird. But, you haven't been seeing each other for that long, and I completely believe it happened by chance. There's no way you deliberately sought one another out. If that happened, I'd be getting ready for one of your murder trials."

He wasn't wrong.

"Parker?" He looked at me properly. "Thank you for telling me."

"I didn't. She did." I smirked.

"Are you sure you know what you're getting yourself into with her?"

"Yes...And that makes it even more confusing."

He laughed. "All right, I gotta go see her and pretend I'm pissed off. Payment for telling me by text. She's a big, fat chicken."

"She is," I said, getting up when he did. "But I gotta admit, I'm glad I didn't have to say it."

"I would be, too."

EPILOGUE

Two weeks later.

"This is a mess!" I slammed the cloth down on the bar. "How do they expect me to handle all these damn requests? Like, sure, I can find high chairs at a three-hour notice. Oh, and you want the pita bread cooked to a certain color? Sure! Don't worry, I won't sit you anywhere near each other despite having no control over it at all, and no, it's not a big deal that I've closed my whole freaking bar for the day!"

Parker blinked at me. "Do you need a Xanax?"

"I need to run away," I muttered, snatching the cloth back up. "This is ridiculous. How are we expected to do this?"

"With a great deal of stress and craziness."

"So, like every other day, then."

He laughed. "Pretty much. But, you've got this handled. Food is cooking. Cocktail jugs are almost done. I think you're just getting a little wild over it all."

I glared at him. "Look at my phone. Look how many messages there will be."

He picked up my phone. His eyes briefly widened. "Sixteen messages?"

"That's been my phone all day. Great Aunt Maria has asked me no less than sixty times if I will be making jugs of the Pussy Pounder. Yia-Yia wants to know if you've got enough gyros meat and has called me three times to ask. Dad wants to know how much whiskey I have in stock and wants his name written on one bottle so everyone leaves him alone. Aunt Alexa wants to know if my grandpa will be there. And that's just the start."

"Is your grandpa coming?"

"Yes. That's the scary thing." I sighed. "I don't think my heart will hold up to this reunion."

"Your heart?" Parker sputtered the words out. "How old are you? Ninety-five?"

I threw the cloth at him, but he caught it. "Stop it. I'm having a meltdown over here."

"I know. I'm watching you. It's a little scary."

"It's what you're signed up for."

"Is it too late to back out of this relationship thing?"

I wiggled my finger at him. "Don't think I've forgotten how you and Ryan came in here after he found out about us. You don't get to tease me about being a little crazy when he dragged you in here by the scruff of the neck for absolutely no reason at all."

"Yeah, well, that wasn't my idea."

"That absolutely was your idea and you know it."

"Mighta been."

I shot another glare his way. "Don't you have a shit ton of stuff to be doing instead of annoying me?"

"No. It's what you're signed up for." He grinned.

"Ugh." I grabbed the cloth from his hands and shoved my way past him. Tablecloths still needed throwing down on the long tables I'd had to rent. At least I didn't have to pay for those—after Parker and I 'came out,' my grandmother started passing me her credit card because I needed my money for my upcoming wedding.

I didn't know who was planning this wedding or when it was, but I smiled and went along with it because I didn't have to pay, and she'd be gone in three days.

I would miss her, but my god, I was looking forward to the peace that my family's absence would bring.

"Have you told your mom you're staying yet?" I glanced over at him, picking up the tablecloth.

Parker shook his head and came to help me. "I think she's probably figured it out, but I need to figure out my living situation first. Living with my parents wasn't in my ten-year plan."

"You've barely been there in the last few days!" I whipped the sheet over the table, and he grabbed the other side of it. "You've spent most of your time here. You hardly have a living situation to figure out, do you?"

He raised an eyebrow. "Are you telling me to live here?"

"I'm telling you that you practically do. I washed your socks this morning, for the love of god."

"Can you do my red t-shirt, too?"

"If I had something to throw at you, I'd be doing it." I smoothed out the top of the cloth and moved to the next table. "But thank you for proving my point."

He grinned, unfolding the cloth. "You're welcome. If you want me to live with you, all you have to do is ask."

"Let me start this by saying I don't particularly <u>want</u> you to live with me." I took the corners form him. "I'm merely stating that you practically already do. I think doing someone else's laundry is one of the criteria. Asking someone else to do it for you definitely is."

I was going to put that red shirt in with one of his white ones to teach him a lesson.

"I should bring the rest of my stuff here," Parker mused. "It would lessen my commute."

"Commute? You haven't commuted for three days,

you tool."

His grin widened. "Exactly, and I'm finding that I like it."

I side-eyed him as I moved to the third and final table. "If you want to live here, all you have to do is ask."

"I dunno—have Satan's hellhounds made anymore appearances in your dreams?"

"They probably will tonight. With any luck, they'll be chasing you."

He laughed as he came up behind me and wrapped his arms around my waist. After brushing a kiss over my bare shoulder, he said, "I did find an apartment."

"Great. Go pay rent for you to decide you want to finish work and not leave." I rolled my eyes and escaped from his clutches to finish straightening the cloth.

"You're right. It really is a lot easier to just live with you."

"I wouldn't say it's easier."

"I didn't mean in general. Work-wise, it's easier. Otherwise, I'm probably slowly torturing myself." He grabbed me back and kissed me. "You're just lucky I love you."

My heart jumped. He'd never said it before. "Lucky is stretching it a bit."

"Say it back or I just made a complete tool of myself."

"You always make a tool of yourself."

"Raven. You're giving me a complex."

I laughed and, gripping his shirt, reached up onto my tiptoes and kissed him firmly. "Next time you decide to visit your parents," I said, trying not to laugh again, "Bring the rest of your stuff back. I guess I won't set my dream hellhounds on you, because you really are pretty lucky I love you."

Parker grinned, squeezing me against him. "Now, I hate to break up this lovefest we have going on, but I'm going to burn food if I don't put you down."

"Are you making gyros?"

"Yes."

I wriggled away from him and shoved him in the direction of the kitchen. "Go. And bring me a taste test."

"A taste test, huh?" The grin didn't leave his face as he opened the door. "Fine, but you owe me a blow job."

My lips twitched. "Hellhounds, Parker. Hellhounds."

His laugh echoed, even after the door shut.

I couldn't stop my smile. I expected a lot of things at the start of this summer. Hiring Parker wasn't one of them—and falling in love with him definitely wasn't. I was the mixologist, but there was no doubt at all that he'd come home and mixed up my world.

Four weeks ago, I would have minded.

Now, I didn't mind at all.

In fact, I was glad.

Because, somehow, as little sense as it made to me, there was no doubt about it.

Parker Hamilton was my person.

Cocktail Recipes

The Pussy Pounder

(serves two)

Two shots: Red Berry Vodka
Two shots: Strawberry Curaco
One shot: Cherry Sours
One shot: Tequila
Top with: Lemonade

Add ice, garnish with orange, and enjoy!
(Make it a Dirty Pussy Pounder by adding more tequila.
Three shots should do it.)

The Slutwhisperer

(serves two)

Three shots: Tequila
One glass: Champagne
Add some: Pink Lemonade
Blend with: Frozen Raspberries

Add ice, more raspberries, and serve!
(Make it a Sexy Slutwhisperer by adding some berry vodka.
Two shots should do it.)

The Blue Balls

(serves two)

Two shots: Blue Curaco
Three shots: Coconut Rum
One shot: Blue Raspberry Sours
Top with: Lemonade

Add ice, pop in some cherries, and serve!
(Make it Hard Blue Balls by adding more rum. Five shots is your friend.)

The Libido Licker

(serves two)

Two shots: Coconut Rum
Two shots: Banana Liqueur
Add some: Pineapple Juice
Top with: Orange Juice

Add ice, an orange slice, and serve!
(Make it a Wet Libido Licker by adding tequila. Four shots should do it.)

Dirty Screw

(serves two)

Three shots: Vodka
Two shots: Tequila
Top with: Orange Juice

Add ice, an orange slice, and serve!
(Make it a Sexy Dirty Screw by adding more tequila. Two more shots are good.)

Filthy Hooker

(serves one)

One shot: Jack Daniels
One shot: Tequila
Splash of: Coke
Dash of: Lemon Juice

Down in one.
(Make it a Wet Filthy Hooker by doubling the JD and tequila.)

The Wet Cunt

(serves one)

Three shots: Tequila
Two shots: Pineapple Vodka
One shot: Coconut Rum
Add some: Blackcurrant cordial
Top with: Lime cordial

Pour in short glass and enjoy. As quickly as possible.
(Caution: Not for the faint of heart.)

About the Author

Emma Hart is the New York Times and USA Today bestselling author of over twenty novels and has been translated into several different languages. She first put fingers to keys at the age of eighteen after her husband told her she read too much and should write her own.
Four years later, she's still figuring out what he meant when he said she 'read too much.'

She prides herself on writing smart smut that's filled with dry wit, snappy, sarcastic comebacks, but lots of heart... And sex. Sometimes, she kills people. (Disclaimer: In books. But if you bug her, she'll use your name for the victims.)

You can find her online at:
www.emmahart.org
www.facebook.com/emmahartbooks
www.instagram.com/EmmaHartAuthor
www.pinterest.com/authoremmhart

Alternatively, you can join her reader group at http://bit.ly/EmmaHartsHartbreakers.

You can also get all things Emma to your email inbox by signing up for Emma Alerts*. http://bit.ly/EmmaAlerts

*Emails sent for sales, new releases, pre-order availability, and cover reveals. Each cover reveal contains an exclusive excerpt.

Books by Emma Hart

Stripped series:
Stripped Bare
Stripped Down

The Burke Brothers:
Dirty Secret
Dirty Past
Dirty Lies
Dirty Tricks
Dirty Little Rendezvous

The Holly Woods Files:
Twisted Bond
Tangled Bond
Tethered Bond
Tied Bond
Twirled Bond
Burning Bond
Twined Bond

By His Game series:
Blindsided
Sidelined
Intercepted

Call series:
Late Call
Final Call
His Call

Wild series:
Wild Attraction
Wild Temptation
Wild Addiction
Wild: The Complete Series

The Game series:
The Love Game
Playing for Keeps
The Right Moves
Worth the Risk

Memories series:
Never Forget
Always Remember

Standalones:
Blind Date
Being Brooke
Catching Carly
Casanova
Mixed Up

Printed in Great Britain
by Amazon